Keeping it Casual

THE MATCHMAKING MOTOR COACH

BOOK THREE

BARBARA BARRETT

The first book in this trilogy, The Sleepover Clause, *is dedicated to my hometown of Burlington, Iowa. The second,* Seduction on Wheels, *covers a cross-country trip from Iowa to California, retracing a trip I took as far as Arizona a few years back. This third book is a love letter to the rest of the state of Iowa beyond the southeast corner.*

Alex and Geoff, on their way to audition a young singer in the northwestern corner of the state, stop for treats at one of my favorite spots in the state, Pella, where they feast on Dutch pastries.

They head west through Des Moines and then on toward Council Bluffs, turning north before they reach the state line and drive along I-29 with the Loess Hills on their right. My husband and I have taken this route many times as we've driven north to his hometown of Sioux Center, Iowa.

Though I'm only a part-time resident of the state these days, it has given me great pleasure to relive my travel experiences in Iowa as I've revised this trilogy.

One

Alexandra Appleby slumped behind the steering wheel of her rental car. For several minutes she'd knocked, to no avail, on the locked front door of the converted firehouse that was now the headquarters of McKenna Custom Coaches. As a last-ditch effort to rouse someone, she'd driven to the back of the building, hoping to find signs of life. No one. Sure, it was earlier than most businesses opened for the day, but if people lived here as well, where were they?

She checked her watch for what must be the tenth time in as many minutes. Noted the finger tapping of her right hand on the steering wheel and forced herself to stop. Blew out a breath.

She'd arrived in the southeastern Iowa town of Burlington the night before and had gone immediately to her motel, figuring she could begin her quest this morning after a good night's sleep. But with no one apparently around, she'd have to postpone her plan. She had limited time to accomplish her goal. What would she do if this didn't work?

Fortunately, before she had to devise a backup tactic, another sedan pulled up and parked several feet away. After what seemed like an interminable wait but was really a matter of seconds, the driver's

door opened and a man of about thirty-five made his way to the building. His face and sweats were caked in mud and other debris, and his
hair was disheveled. Despite the grime, though, he was a world-class
hunk, about six feet tall, light brown hair, and a remarkable physique
the dirt couldn't hide.

Was this Graham McKenna? It had been almost a year since she'd
last seen him. And then only briefly. She remembered the man being
slightly taller and thinner.

His gait was slow, strained. He almost stumbled once, even
stopped about ten feet from the door on which she'd pounded a few
minutes prior. When he bent, gripped his thighs, she shot from
her car.

"Are you okay?"

He didn't seem to hear at first, until she realized he was trying to
catch his breath.

"Who're you?" Voice slurred, he attempted another few steps, only
to pull up again.

"Let me help you to the door."

He hesitated briefly, then almost fell into her. Something jabbed
her. Keys. He couldn't be an intruder if he had keys; he had to be one
of the McKennas. No time to debate whether she could trust him
enough to go inside with him. The man needed help. "Okay if I unlock
the door?" He nodded.

He leaned heavily on her as they made their way into the building.
Her white slacks would take a beating, but she didn't have a choice.
He seemed out of it, as if he'd been drugged.

He indicated a light switch tucked away on the back wall. She
flipped it, illuminating the cavern of a garage. A blue-and-black motor
coach occupied the center of the room, although she barely noticed it
as he veered off to the right. They came to an interior wall with three
doors.

"Other key." He headed to the door closest to the front of the
building.

She unlocked this inner door and helped him into the room, then
located another light switch inside.

"Thanks," he got out before he collapsed on the couch.

"You need a blanket." By the time she'd retrieved an afghan from the back of the sofa, he was asleep. She covered him, then stepped away to study the man.

A real pretty boy. That type abounded in Los Angeles, her home territory. A long time ago, she'd learned the hard way to avoid the category. Too much into themselves.

She should probably take off and return later, because this wasn't Graham McKenna. She was no shrinking violet where men were concerned, but she was also savvy enough to realize lone women should not put themselves at risk around men they didn't know. But he was so out of it, should she leave him on his own?

She tried to recall some of her nurses' training from years ago. People with concussions weren't supposed to be left alone or allowed to sleep. He didn't appear to have been in an accident or to have met foul play. His clothes were dirty but not torn, and he wasn't bleeding or bruised. Most likely, no concussion. Instead, he was sick. How sick, she couldn't tell. But guys, especially incredible specimens like this one, didn't nearly collapse in strange women's arms or allow them into their personal spaces unless they felt so horrible they didn't have a choice.

She'd stick around. At least for a little while. Until she got a better idea about his condition. This garage was her intended destination anyhow, and her no-personality motel room was the only other place she had to go.

But she was also a woman of action. Sitting around with nothing to do except watch a man sleep wasn't easy. She flipped through two magazines she found in the room—one featured male athletes, and the other focused on sports medicine. When that effort ended within ten minutes, she sought another way to occupy herself.

Although a flat-screen television took up a large space on the facing wall, turning it on might wake him, and he really seemed to need his sleep.

The place appeared to be a studio apartment, the area in which he now slept serving as living room with a tiny kitchenette off to the side.

Over on the other side, a couple of pieces of exercise equipment had been stacked against a wall. One of the room's two doors probably led to his bedroom. She peeked in. Yep, that's what it was, all right. A hastily made bed, but aside from that, fairly neat. She took a step forward, backed up. It was one thing to watch the guy as he slept to make sure he was okay. But to roam around his private space was creepy, despite her curiosity.

She could use a drink of water, and the small kitchen area was more public. Water glasses were in the second cabinet she opened. After filling one with tap water, she remained in the small dining area, taking in her surroundings. The fridge presented a mystery. It was packed with fresh vegetables and fruits, various juices, and a freezer full of neatly marked, foil-covered containers. Not typical bachelor fare —like aging pizza slices and beer—although a thin layer of freezer ice covered several items.

How long was he going to sleep? Had he eaten recently? Maybe he needed food.

First things first. She hadn't finished her tour. The second door led to his office. Here was another surprise, because the space lacked nothing in the way of comfort. Large desk, surface almost clear with the exception of a business-card holder. Plush visitor chairs. Several colorful brochures, each featuring a different style of motor coach, covered one wall.

She examined one of the business cards. "McKenna Custom Coaches, Geoffrey McKenna, Customer Relations." So he was related to Graham. Most likely his brother. Perhaps Geoffrey was the one she should be talking to instead of Graham. At least get on his good side. She'd already begun that campaign by getting him to his couch, albeit unknowingly.

She snapped her fingers. Couldn't hurt to take it one step further. She marched to the kitchenette. Might not be able to fix a chef-worthy meal, but she could still make coffee, pour juice, scramble eggs and toast bread. Nothing like a hot breakfast to revive a person.

For the next fifteen minutes, she went domestic. As the aroma of fresh coffee and toast wafted its way toward McKenna's nostrils, he began to stir.

"What do you think you're doing?" a high-pitched woman's voice demanded from the outside door.

Alex twisted around to discover a tall blonde in pigtails and mud-covered sweats about to charge her. Although she'd found no signs of a woman inhabiting the apartment, this one certainly thought she belonged here. "Staying with Geoffrey to make sure he's okay. Thought he'd like some breakfast when he woke."

"*Making sure he's okay?* He didn't have an episode, did he?"

"Episode? Not sure what you mean. I stopped by looking for Graham McKenna and ran into Geoffrey instead. He was ready to pass out, so I got him in here before he hit the floor."

"What, what happened?" Geoffrey asked from the couch as he flung the throw to the side.

"You seem to have passed out." The other woman shuttled over and plopped down beside him, then kissed him briefly. "Was it your" —she stopped and glanced at Alex—"you know?" Geoffrey jerked up. "Good grief, no. I'm fine. Just tired from all that sandbagging."

The woman checked her watch. "It's nine fifteen. Didn't you come back early for a meeting at nine? Is this woman your appointment?"

Alex, the nonappointment, cocked her head and smiled.

"Who're you?" he asked, rubbing his chin, his question reminiscent of the scene at the back door.

"You were having difficulty walking when you came home, so I helped you to your couch, where you promptly fell asleep. Thought I'd better stick around in case whatever got to you was more than the need for a few winks."

"Oh, right. Thanks."

"So?" The other woman probed. "How are you?"

"I'm fine, Eileen. Just tired. My, uh, appointment cancelled at the last minute, so I was on my way to bed when I, uh, ran into her."

Although the other woman—Eileen, he'd called her—seemed to have claimed her territory, Alex wasn't ready to turn her *ward* over quite so fast. "Are you hungry? I scrambled some eggs and made toast. They're getting cold."

Geoffrey studied her as if her words hadn't registered. "Breakfast?"

"The name's Alexandra. Alex." Rather than wait for him to ask, she dished up the eggs and poured the juice and coffee. "Here you go."

He slipped off the couch and came over to her. "Call me Geoff, like everyone else."

Before he had a chance to pick up the fork, Eileen slipped between them and commandeered the plate.

"I'll take this. He can't have eggs."

"Oh," was all Alex said

"C'mon, Eileen. She went to a lot of trouble, and everything smells great." He made to take the plate from her, but she held back.

"You don't have to eat this meal to avoid hurting her feelings." The woman turned to Alex. "I'm sure you meant well, but if he eats these eggs, he is going to feel worse than he already does." So there'd be no more debate, she slipped over to the small sink, scraped off the contents and ran the disposal.

Finished, she grabbed a notepad and pencil from the counter and offered them to Alex. "Graham probably won't be back for hours. If you want to leave your name and number, we'll see he gets the information." She smiled without smiling, a dismissal Alex recognized from her dealings with Hollywood decision makers.

"Never mind." Alex brushed by Eileen's outstretched hand on her way to the door. "Take care, Geoff." She left without acknowledging the other woman.

Could the woman have been more obvious? No one, at least another woman, was supposed to have anything to do with her man. Had she ever acted like that? No, because there'd never been a man in her life long enough to become that possessive.

Even though she still hadn't run into Graham McKenna, she'd met his brother, the one who wasn't seeing one of her stepsisters. She'd actually befriended him, at least taken care of him briefly until his personal general marched in.

Maybe she should've thought this through more. Paved the way with a phone call or email. No, she hadn't wanted to give Jenna, one of her two stepsisters, any reason to refuse seeing her. Alex had years of ignoring her siblings to make up for and needed to do this right.

As she emerged from the firehouse, a pickup pulled up, and a male and female poured out. At least that's who they appeared to be under all the mud caking their clothes. The woman's sagging auburn ponytail caught Alex's attention. "Aubrey?"

The woman gazed her way. "Yes? Should I know you?"

Alex stuck out a hand. "I'm Alex. Alexandra Appleby, your stepsister."

Aubrey waved off the handshake. "Sorry, my hands are too grimy to touch anyone else." She turned to the male behind her. "Mitch, quick. Stop the truck."

The guy, a dark-haired hunk also covered in all that filth, turned and thumped on the truck bed. The vehicle jerked to a stop, and the passenger window came down.

A blonde stuck out her head. "What'd you forget?"

"Look, Jenna. It's our stepsister, Alex."

The door opened, and leggy Jenna DiFranco emerged to join them. "It is you. What are you doing in Burlington, Alexandra?"

A tall, athletic-looking male jumped out of the driver's side and came around. At last, the object of her visit. "Hi. Graham, isn't it?" she said.

"Hi, yourself. We met briefly last year at Jenna's mother's."

"And my dad's. Right."

"I'm Mitch McKenna, Gray's younger brother," the other guy said.

This one, whose hair was darker than his brothers', had penetrating blue eyes, the kind that could entrap a woman if she didn't turn away. Alex blinked instead. As far as good looks went, her stepsisters had hit the jackpot in the male-companion sweepstakes. And her mother thought nothing good came from Iris Appleby.

Mitch offered his hand, then quickly retrieved it. "Sorry. I'd shake, but my hands have been hauling and setting sandbags for hours. No telling what they've touched."

"Sandbags?" This was the second time she'd heard the word in the last few minutes. Apparently, one didn't participate without emerging in muck.

Jenna edged her way in front of her man. "Haven't you heard? The river has risen beyond its banks due to the heavy snowmelt from this past winter. That's why we all look and smell so bad. We've been sandbagging all night to hold back the waters."

"You were coming out of the firehouse," Mitch said. "Did you stop by to see us?"

"I did. Met your brother Geoff instead. And some woman named Eileen."

"His girlfriend," Jenna said. "What brings you to Iowa, Alex?"

"I wanted to get better acquainted with my stepsisters." She offered her most appealing smile.

Aubrey angled her head. "You don't say? After all this time?"

Alex was ready for their skepticism. She'd respond in kind if they showed up at her apartment in Century City to explore their kinship. "I'm worried about my father. I'm here seeking your help."

"Our help?" Jenna asked. "I'm intrigued."

"Me, too," Aubrey added. "But let's not discuss this out here in the parking lot. It's already a hot one. Let's go inside."

Not a good idea. Alex wasn't ready to run into that Eileen person again so soon. Especially since she hadn't asked for Jenna or Aubrey or mentioned her relationship to them. That Eileen was sharp. She'd see it as a subterfuge immediately, and Alex wasn't ready to go into her real reason for being in town. She had to get Jenna on her side first.

Think fast. Redirect. "You all look like you could use some downtime first. Change clothes, shower"— she gazed at Mitch, no hardship there —"and probably grab a nap. Why don't the three of us women meet for lunch somewhere, if you can spare the time?"

Jenna and Aubrey exchanged looks. "Uh, sure." Jenna took the lead. "Our next shift isn't until tonight, and hopefully, they won't need us any longer by then if the river recedes like they're predicting. Give us a couple hours to regroup, and we should be back to our normal selves. There's a tearoom just a few blocks from here, To a Tea. They haven't been affected by the flood and should be open."

"Noon?" Aubrey suggested. "We'll meet you there."

"Perfect. We'll talk then," Alex said. "It's about time I got to know my sisters."

ONCE IT WAS JUST the two of them, Eileen busied herself putting things away. "Your visiting chef may be able to whip up a mean dish, but she left a huge mess in her wake."

"What's with you? I've never seen you be so rude," Geoff said.

"She caught me off guard, that's all. But if I hadn't walked in when I did, who's to say how sick you'd be by now."

"You're overreacting. I can have eggs if I want them. And today, I did."

"Well, you're out of luck. I got here just in time. Why did you allow her to stay, anyhow? She was a complete stranger."

Good point, not that he'd concede as much. Nor could he tell Eileen he'd been so far gone with fatigue he hadn't even noticed his visitor had remained. "I, uh, assumed she'd left."

"Why did she get the impression you weren't feeling well? Is your multiple sclerosis acting up again?"

When they'd first started dating last summer, she'd been cool about his condition, unlike his brothers, who freaked if he didn't provide a weekly update on his vitals. But over time, Eileen had taken an increasing interest in his ailment well beyond his brothers' concern. She'd done an extensive internet search, which led her to ask very specific questions. Who were his physicians? How often were his checkups? What was his treatment plan?

"I'm fine," he replied after a beat. He was. At the moment. His short nap had done wonders. He would have slept longer if Eileen hadn't shown up.

She rejoined him at the table, studied him a bit, as if attempting to make sense of his behavior. "Did you shower before you slept?"

He made a show of sniffing his armpits. "Do I smell?"

"No, but your appearance is off."

"I've been sleeping, Eileen!"

"I've never known you to just fall into bed, other than the times when we, uh, you know? You're usually so painstaking about your hygiene."

"If you recall, I wasn't alone."

She arched a brow. "You did know she was still here?"

Eileen had been hanging out too much with his younger brother, Mitch, the attorney. She was in full interrogation mode and had maneuvered him over a barrel. Either he admitted he'd let the woman stick around while he slept, which obviously was not going over well, or he had to come clean about his degree of exhaustion. Truth be told, he did know Alex was still there when he fell into bed. At that point, he hadn't cared. Actually, he'd welcomed her vigil.

He held up his hands in surrender. "Okay, you got me. I was more zonked than I wanted to admit. I don't do much physical labor these days and was out of shape. Happy?"

"It doesn't make me happy to hear you admit you were exhausted, but I'm glad you finally let down your guard."

He rose, hoping she'd take the hint and leave. "Now that I've *admitted* my fatigue, can we drop it? This whole line of talk is more tiring than sandbagging."

"Why do you do this, Geoff? Make light of your MS."

"I take my MS seriously, Eileen, but it's my MS, not yours, not my brothers'. I appreciate the support, really, but in the end, this is my life, my challenge."

She straightened, brushed off her slacks, tears evident though not flowing. "Sorry. I didn't mean to offend you. I'm just concerned about your welfare."

Damn, why was she doing this to him, guilting him for sticking up for himself? She was supposed to be his main supporter, not his conscience. Was he overly sensitive, or had Eileen begun to assume too much about their relationship?

"Do you like tea, Aubrey?" Alex asked as they were seated at To A Tea. The place offered a cozy ambience, cute, in a cutesy way. Navy-blue checked gingham curtains hugged the windows, and a navy tablecloth as well as a white or yellow Gerbera daisy in a flowerpot topped each table.

"No, I've never been much of a tea drinker, although this past winter being my first in the Midwest, I drank more hot tea than ever. Iowa winters can be brutal."

"I'll say," Jenna added. "I was a little girl when my mother and I left here for California, but all those memories of snow, ice and cold came rushing back during our first snowstorm last December. The first of many, which resulted in the flood we're now facing."

Alex glanced up from her menu. "You both seem to have settled easily into this town. According to my dad, your mother didn't think either of you would survive the winter."

"Mother takes our choosing the Midwest over California as a personal affront. She thinks we landed here just because she disliked the place," Aubrey said.

"I take it she hasn't visited?"

"Paige and I spent a week with her and your dad at Christmas, although you were probably aware of that," Jenna said. "I had rented my house out there by then, so it wasn't available."

"My mother and I spent the holidays on the Riviera, so no, I didn't know."

"The Riviera, huh?" Aubrey replied. "Not bad."

"Not my idea of fun, but she, uh, needed to get away. I agreed to keep her company."

"What about—"

"Mother's husband, Philippe? He claimed he was swamped with editing his latest film and couldn't get away."

"Claimed?" Jenna asked, her tone innocent.

They'd learn sooner or later about her mother's separation from the man who cuckolded their stepfather, but she didn't want to make a big deal of it. "Faithfulness has never been one of Philippe's strong points, but until recently, he's walked a fairly straight line with Mother."

"Sorry to hear that," Jenna said. "How's your mother dealing with his, uh, departure?"

Alex leaned forward slightly. "Truthfully, I think she's relieved. He'll either pay well to get out of the marriage, or she'll continue to live the life to which she's become accustomed without having to share her bed with him."

Jenna sank back in her seat, apparently not sure how to continue. Aubrey stared at her folded hands.

Time for Alex to get on with her plan. "Getting back to my reason for being here, I need help with my father. He's not been himself lately."

Aubrey bit. "Like how?"

"It's not like you might expect for someone his age. You know, forgetting things, slowing down." She halted, made sure they were following. "He's been actively seeking television roles. Not just guest appearances, which he's been doing for years since leaving his sitcom, but starring parts."

"Is that a problem?" Jenna asked.

Aubrey unfolded her hands and pushed a strand of hair behind one ear. "Several seniors have starring roles on TV shows."

"True, but they're playing to their age. Dad's aiming for heroic leads. The kind of roles written for men in their thirties and forties."

"Is his agent actually submitting your dad's name for these parts?"

"He's been circumventing his agent. Pumping other friends in the business for information, submitting himself without his agent's knowledge."

"Maybe his agent hasn't been doing his job," Aubrey suggested.

"If Dad doesn't stop, he will soon become the brunt of jokes. Hollywood operates on who knows who, who's hot and who's seen as bankable. At best, Dad's been operating on the periphery of this circle for years. If this keeps up, he can say good-bye to even that amount of interest."

They ordered, Alex insisted on treating them, they refused and she won.

Jenna returned her menu to the waitress. "So your dad could be jeopardizing his career. Where do we come in? If he won't hear what his agent says, he's not going to listen to us."

"When I approached him, he acted pretty coy, which isn't like him. I thought, well, I hoped, maybe you could ask your mother about what's going on. I would, but—"

" ... you're not on the best of terms with her," Jenna said.

Alex hung her head. "In a nutshell, yes."

Jenna glanced at Aubrey. "Buddy's always been good to us. We'd like to help, but there's no telling with Mother. If she suspects you're behind this, she might clam up."

They could talk to their mother or not; Alex didn't care. She was feeding them a line. A line she'd cleared with her dad after explaining why the minor deception was necessary. She wasn't exactly lying to them. Her dad could conceivably be submitting himself for roles outside his sphere, although that wasn't the case. But she was up against a deadline and a demand, which, if not met, could have dire results.

"You both know how to phrase your questions with your mother, which buttons to push. I don't."

Aubrey shook her head. "Mother and I have just started renewing our relationship this past year. I don't want to risk her ire by pumping her about Buddy."

Jenna removed the silverware from her cloth napkin and placed it on the table. "The same goes for me. When I told her to stop meddling in my career, she was really put out with me. She might consider my questions about Buddy's career hypocritical."

Alex hadn't expected either one of them to jump on the band-wagon. But she didn't want them to turn down her request outright. She needed an excuse to stick around town. "Think about it. I don't need an answer today. I've decided to remain in town a bit longer. There's a young singer I've heard about in some town near Sioux City. I'm thinking about representing her."

The teenager had won some regional contest and was slated to appear at the national version of the contest later in the year. Although Alex had her hands full with her three current clients and didn't relish the idea of catering to another temperamental singer, the quest to sign the young woman proved a viable cover story.

She reached across the table and patted Jenna's hand. "This was fun. I've never had sisters or even a brother to talk to about my dad. I didn't expect to arrive in the midst of a flood, but other than that, Burlington is growing on me."

Two

Gray showed up at Geoff's apartment around noon with a sack of burgers and fries. "How'd your appointment go this morning? Do we have a hot new prospect?"

"All that rush to get back here and clean up by nine, and then the guy called and cancelled at quarter to nine," Geoff replied.

"Did he at least reschedule?"

"That's the worst part. Said he'd changed his mind about buying a coach for his company."

Gray unloaded the bag's contents on Geoff's small kitchen table. "Glad we hadn't gotten any further than a phone call from the guy, and we weren't banking on his sale."

The client didn't exist, had only been a ruse so Geoff could escape the sandbagging operation and catch up on sleep. Still, Gray's easy dismissal of the make-believe lead rankled. Even though Gray did the books, at the moment, his brother seemed oblivious to their continuing struggle to find new business. Blinded by love?

Geoff selected a burger from the pile of fast food. "Nothing for Mitch?" He checked the small wall clock. "Where is he, anyway? Orville got him working round the clock now?" In the past year, Mitch had transitioned from their full-time to part-time to retired mechanic

as he picked up increasingly more of the workload from Orville Drum-
mond, his law partner, mentor and friend.

"Something like that. With Aubrey and Jenna off having lunch at
the tearoom with their stepsister, he's catching up on some cases he
put aside to sandbag."

Geoff raised a hand. "Back up. Aubrey and Jenna are with their
stepsister?"

"Yeah. Would you believe we just ran into her on the street? The
girls had no idea she was coming to town. They hardly ever see her."

"Brunette with a short, kinda chiseled haircut that covers one eye?
Eyes big and brown that dare you not to get swallowed up in them?"

"Yeah, I guess. Met her briefly when I took Jenna and the coach
back to California last year. She's their stepdad, Buddy's, daughter.
You've met her?"

"Showed up here this morning looking for you."

"Me? Why me?"

"Didn't say."

Gray went to the fridge and returned with two sodas. "Don't tell
Jenna I had fast food. She's been watching my diet lately."

"She should. You've put on, what, ten pounds since the two of you
shacked up?"

"And don't use that term around her. She's real sensitive about
how we're defining our relationship."

"Uh-oh. She pushing for a ring?"

Gray stuck three fries in his mouth at once. "The opposite. Still
gun-shy about marriage after what that jerk of an ex did to her. You're
the one who should be wondering about a ring. You've been with
Eileen longer than I've been with Jenna."

"Eileen and I are just fine the way we are. Unlike you and Mitch
and your women, we're not even living together."

Gray gazed about Geoff's tight quarters. "Like you could here. This
was plenty of space when it served as Mitch's office and workout
room, but it was never meant for two people."

"Works to my advantage. She knows cohabitation would involve a
new place. A real commitment."

"So?"

"So neither one of us wants one."

Gray shook his head, his dark blue eyes merry. "Don't fool yourself. She's laying low, waiting for the right opportunity to spring the idea on you when your defenses are down."

Was that why Eileen was becoming progressively more involved with his condition? Debating if she could live the rest of her life with a man suffering with MS? Or was she trying to cure him before marriage? He hoped not. Marriage and family weren't in his plans. He wasn't going to tie Eileen or any woman to a marriage where his life expectancy was unknown. "Wonder how Mitch is faring with Aubrey," he said, to change the subject.

"What about Aubrey?" Mitch asked from the door. He wandered in and helped himself to Geoff's other burger and remaining fries.

"Hey! Those are mine."

"These on your list of acceptable foods?"

"Geez, what's the big deal about what I consume? Eileen wouldn't let me have scrambled eggs this morning."

"Eggs of any kind make you queasy," Gray said.

What had possessed him to bring up the eggs? Now he'd have to explain how they appeared. "I'd built up an appetite sandbagging and wanted more than my usual cereal. Is that a crime?"

"Okay, okay," Mitch said. "Don't be so sensitive."

"I'm not. That's your stock reply whenever I object to discussing my health."

Gray turned to Mitch. "You can't avoid the subject of you and Aubrey by stealing Geoff's food. What's up, man?"

Mitch helped himself to more of Geoff's fries and dipped them in ketchup. "Couldn't be happier. Aubrey seems to have found her niche here, and Orville keeps me more than busy."

"No talk of marriage?" Gray asked.

"No." Mitch attempted to stare down two pairs of doubting eyes. "Okay, once. Maybe twice. The word comes up occasionally."

"Well, well," Geoff said. "Baby Brother seems to have outdistanced us a—"

"Again," Mitch finished for him. "It's okay to bring up Diane. Our breakup was for the best. I wouldn't have found Aubrey if I'd remained engaged to Diane."

"Thank God for Aubrey. A year ago we couldn't say Diane's name without you wincing."

"Diane seems happy out East, and I no longer resent her for leaving. Even exchanged an email or two lately. With Aubrey's full knowledge."

"And approval?" Geoff couldn't help asking.

Mitch offered a sly smile. "Never attempt to bait an attorney, bro."

Geoff shook it off. "Ooh. Sor-ry. Did we hit a nerve?"

"Let's move on from the topics of our women and marriage."

"A little too close for comfort?" Gray asked.

Mitch's shoulders sagged. "Maybe. But let's drop it for now. Okay?"

Geoff exchanged a look with Gray. Apparently, they both recognized that hypnotized expression on their brother's face. They'd seen it there before. Just before he proposed to Diane.

"So, Doc? What do you think? Is my MS getting worse?" Geoff had managed to snag a four o'clock appointment with his neurologist that afternoon.

Dr. Roettger checked his tablet computer once more, then switched his attention to his patient. "It's been unusually hot and humid for May. Plus, you've put in several hours sandbagging. Since you've only noticed this extreme fatigue the last few days, most likely that combination pushed your body to the limit."

"That's what I thought, hoped it was nothing more than that but wanted to run it by you."

"Always wise, even if you think you're imagining things. MS is a tricky animal. We may know the basic symptoms, but like I've told you more than once since we diagnosed your case, MS is different from one person to the next. Even different for the same person over time."

"What about my fatigue?"

"That's a no-brainer. No more sandbagging. Despite your call to civic duty, you shouldn't have gone anywhere near the levee. Take it easy for a couple days. Work from your apartment, if you can."

"Since I now live at the firehouse instead of my folks' place, the latter should be easy." It was the "take it easy" part that would be difficult to accomplish without his brothers or Eileen catching on. "What about sex?"

Roettger lowered his eyeglasses on the bridge of his nose, then returned them to their usual position. "Have you been experiencing problems?"

"No. Just checking." He and Eileen had sex on occasion, but he suspected less frequently than his brothers and their ladies. His interest in sex had decreased since the onset of his condition—but not necessarily as a direct result. He and Eileen just didn't do it that often. Why was he even asking?

"Call me if the fatigue continues beyond a week. Call right away if anything else occurs, like tingles or trouble with your eyesight."

"Yeah, I know the drill."

"No trouble with your meds? No negative reactions?"

"No."

The doctor rose, indicating his consultation was over. "Thus far, you've been lucky not to experience the full spectrum of symptoms some MS patients encounter."

Lucky. Yeah, that was him. Mr. Lucky.

He'd just reached his car when his cell rang. "Geoff? This is Pam Sutton, Kyle's wife." He and Kyle, diagnosed with MS about the same time, had attended a class together on dealing with the disease. About the same age, Kyle two years younger, they'd met several times for coffee or beers the first couple of years to compare notes, cheer each other on and commiserate. In more recent months, though, their meetings had fallen off as Kyle experienced more frequent flare-ups. When they had managed to get together, Geoff came away depressed and disheartened, both for what lay ahead for Kyle but also with trepidations about his own future.

"Hi, Pam. What's up?" Must be bad news, since it was Pam and not Kyle calling, but still, he hoped.

"Kyle's in the hospital. He told me not to bother you, but his condition is deteriorating, and I thought you should know."

"I'm glad you did. I'll get over to see him today."

"Thank you, Geoff. Your visits always pump him up."

Before he could visit his friend, though, he needed to rest. For reasons he still didn't understand, Kyle seemed to thrive on Geoff's good health. The guy never groused about his own failing health compared to Geoff's.

Back in his apartment, Geoff set the AC a degree lower, turned down the lights, and settled in for a nap. He was almost asleep when loud knocking brought him back to a waking state. Probably one of the guys, since Eileen was still at work. He didn't want them to know he was napping, or they'd get suspicious, and if they found out how he'd been feeling, they'd hover again. Then Eileen would find out, and she'd more than hover. From all indications this morning, she'd take over his life. With great effort, he dragged himself from bed, swiped back his hair with both hands and went to the door.

"Hi. Sorry to bother you again," Alex whatever-her-name said.

Not the worst distraction, although he was still dead tired. How had she gotten into the firehouse? Hadn't he locked up before succumbing to nap time?

"Heard you found Gray, although it was really Jenna you were seeking." He let her know right away he was on to her.

She lowered her eyes. "Uh, right. She's my stepsister."

"Heard that also." Why was he giving her a hard time? Because she'd interrupted his sleep?

"Could I come in?"

"Uh, sure." He opened the door and indicated his couch.

She surveyed the room. "Kinda dark in here, isn't it?"

"Just got back a few minutes ago." He parked himself in one of the two club chairs that faced the couch.

"I did find Jenna, and Aubrey, too. We had lunch at a tearoom down the street."

"Then you're not still looking for her." Lame. But if he didn't say something, he was afraid he'd embarrass both of them by continuing to stare at those huge brown eyes. And lashes—thick, black lashes.

"Actually, I'm looking for my good pen. I seem to have misplaced it and returned to see if you found it."

"No." He rose. "But I'll check. You were only in this area, right"

She gazed away and nodded.

He returned after a few seconds, empty-handed. "Sorry."

She reached in her purse and pulled out a business card. "Here's my contact information, in case it shows up later. It might have rolled under something."

He accepted the card.

"That pen has sentimental value. Probably shouldn't carry it around with me, but I feel it's a good luck charm. My first client signed with it."

"Client?"

"I manage the careers of several celebrities."

"No kidding? What's that involve, getting them bookings?"

She ran a hand through the bangs covering one eye. No sooner had she pulled the hair away than it sprung back. "Bookings, no. Agents do that. I handle career management stuff, like getting them matched up with songwriters, record producers, stylists, that sort of thing."

"I'm impressed. So what are you doing here in town? Got some new talent you're trying to sign?"

"Thinking about it. Plus, it was a great opportunity to spend time with my stepsisters. We're virtual strangers with just my dad, Buddy, in common." She leaned forward. "There's another reason also. Can I trust you to keep this just between us?"

Geez, he'd only been making conversation, but her wanting to share a secret so soon after meeting intrigued him. *Watch out, guy.* Women with secrets could be dangerous. "Uh, I guess. But wouldn't you be more comfortable talking to your stepsisters?"

"It's about them. Jenna, anyhow. But since she and Aubrey seem to have repaired their rift, I don't feel I can share this with Aubrey, either."

"But you can with me?"

"I need a confidant. Someone who's connected to my family but not one of their men. You're it. I feel like I already know you … a little anyhow … after spending time with you this morning."

Eileen's concerns returned to him. "While I slept? My God, woman, did you watch me the whole time?"

She had the grace to glance away before responding. "No, it wasn't like that … exactly. I told you, I wasn't sure if you were okay or not. I don't think it was just fatigue from sandbagging like you told your girlfriend. But you're okay now, aren't you?"

"Just needed a few winks."

She eyed her surroundings. "That's why it's so dark in here. You were trying to sleep, and I interrupted you. Again." She rose. "I usually have a better sense of timing. I'll come back later. Let me know when you're available."

He slid in front of her. "I suffer from a mild case of MS. I'm not supposed to overdo, which I did last night trying to show I could hoist sandbags with the best of them. Haven't had to demonstrate those skills since I was in college. I wanted to relive the glory days and forget my physical limitations for one night."

She didn't respond. Instead, she simply sank back onto the couch, her expression changing to something on its way to pity.

"Sorry. Too much information. Wanted to shock you in retaliation for watching me sleep."

"I didn't watch you sleep," she replied a little too fast. "Well, okay, I sorta did, but I'm no weirdo. I was worried. I stayed to make sure you didn't have trouble breathing or something like that." Only then did his words appear to hit her. "Wait, you said you have MS. I was right. You were more than tired."

"No, just tired. Muscles, whole body throbbed. MS makes fatigue all the more acute. It was a stupid move. Never should have signed on for the physical labor. There were other jobs I could have done. But my brothers are worse than nursemaids. They never stop worrying about me. Just wanted to show them I was up to the task."

"Which you weren't."

"Beside the point."

She smiled. "Actually, that is the point. You were trying to convince yourself, and you wound up failing miserably."

Had Eileen not taken so poorly to this woman, he'd swear the two were double-teaming him. "Hey, I'm not at death's door. Just tired." Enough. As easy on the eyes as she was to look at, right now he needed sleep more than her company. "As much as I've enjoyed talking to you, you've kept me from sleep twice today." He glanced at her card. "I'll give you a call once I've gotten my z's. How much longer will you be in town?"

"At least until you and I have chatted. In the meantime, sleep. I'm staying at a motel on Roosevelt Avenue. Any chance the floodwaters will make it out there?"

He chuckled. "Not unless the place you're staying springs a water-pipe leak."

GEOFF HAD ALMOST DRIFTED off to peaceful sleep, finally, when his outside door clicked open. "Geoff? Geoff? Are you in here?"

Was there a plot afoot to keep him constantly awake? As he had with Alex only a short time before, he rose from his bed, slicked back his hair and padded into the living room. "Eileen? Didn't think I'd see you again today. What's up?"

"Did I wake you? Is that why all the lights were off?"

"I've tried to catch up on sleep all day without much luck."

She brushed past him to check his fridge. "A not-so-subtle hint for me to leave." She pivoted to face him. "Which I'll do, as soon as I make sure you have something nutritious in here."

"Still a few eggs left."

Her eyes went wide. "She missed some?"

"Sorry. Couldn't resist the dig. You were pretty upset to find Alex making me breakfast."

"Alex, is it now? Thought you barely knew her. What was I

supposed to think, finding you here so early in the morning with another woman taking care of you?"

"That again? Thought we'd beaten that topic to death."

Eileen removed a small container from the freezer and stuck it in the microwave. "Did she really misinterpret your condition, Geoff? She seemed pretty sharp. Not someone easily confused between run-of-the-mill drowsiness and heavy-duty fatigue because you hadn't paid better attention to your MS."

"That why you popped in unexpectedly? To check on me again?"

Her shoulders rose, then immediately fell. "Of course not!" Pause. "Okay, maybe I was just a little concerned. You skirted the issue when I asked you this morning whether your MS was worsening."

"I told you I'm fine, but apparently you aren't buying."

"You shouldn't have gone sandbagging. I begged you not to, but you were too fixated on proving to your brothers how independent you are."

"You're psychoanalyzing me again. Ever since Mitch joined Orville's law firm and Gray started doing architectural projects on the side, you've worried about me feeling deserted."

"Well, don't you?"

His brothers no longer working alongside him did bother him a little. This was their family business, launched initially to pay off their dad's debts trying to sell RVs. It had become their own as they branched into customizing motor coaches. But Gray and Mitch had given up promising careers to establish something that would provide him an income when his condition forced him to stay off the road with his sales job. He couldn't expect them to continue their sacrifices forever. "How could I feel deserted with Gray here part time and Mitch underfoot helping Aubrey finish the interiors?"

"You're not trying to prove you can take care of yourself and the business so they won't worry and rearrange their lives for you?"

He threw up his hands and flopped on the couch. "We've been through this before. I don't like them hanging around, just waiting to come to my aid if I show the slightest sign of weakness."

She joined him but kept her distance on the other side of the couch. "Are you're afraid they'll commit you to an institution if you appear the least bit reliant on them?"

"They've got a right to worry about the business. I get that. But there's a difference between overseeing operations and watching out for me."

"Maybe so, but your condition isn't like the chicken pox, where all you have to do is tough it out, take your medicine, and within a few weeks, you're back to your old self. You have a lifelong illness, Geoff. An illness that plays with your head when it lets up and makes you feel like yourself again. As much as I hate to say it, your periods of remission may only be temporary."

He couldn't remain seated any longer. The room and Eileen were closing in. Was it going to be like this from now on—Eileen checking on him every few hours, lecturing, swooping in and coddling him at any sign of relapse?

She studied him a few beats, as if debating how much more she could say before he kicked her out. "I'm only concerned about you. But apparently, the more concern I show, the less you want me around."

"You knew about my MS when we started dating. When I brought it up, you said not to worry. You were okay with the special lifestyle it dictated."

"I'm still okay with the fact the guy I'm seeing on a steady basis deals with a life-threatening disease. But if there's any future for us, I need to know you're fighting to stick around as long as you can."

God, she did want to get serious, like Gray had suggested. As much as he'd told himself they were keeping things casual, there'd always been this niggling worry at the back of his mind that this conversation might arise someday. But not today. Not when he was so tired he could barely keep his eyes open.

Maybe if he stalled, played dumb, she'd drop it. "Us?"

"C'mon, Geoff. We've been going together as long as Aubrey and Mitch. She's been living with him since last summer, and I still live with my mother. That doesn't mean I haven't thought about something more permanent between us."

So much for playing dumb. "Look, Eileen—"

"I've been taking my feelings about you for granted. Enjoying our time together, not really considering what lies ahead. But the time has come to establish some kind of understanding."

"Understanding?" he couldn't resist asking, like the moth drawn to the flame.

"I'm a patient woman, Geoff. I realize your MS makes you question your future, but this unsettledness between us can't go on forever."

"I've appreciated you not pushing. I assumed that's all you've wanted."

She came to him, placed a hand on his forearm. "Maybe so. At first. But we've been seeing each other almost a year. We need to think about the future."

Future? Was there some unwritten rule that said once your relationship passed the twelve-month mark, things had to change? If that was the case, that change might not be to her liking. He couldn't see his future. At least with her.

GEOFF DIDN'T GET to the hospital until seven, thanks to the interruptions that kept him from sleep. Pam and two older adults, presumably Kyle's parents, were seated around the room, but they all excused themselves when he appeared.

"Told Pam not to call you, but damn, I'm glad you're here," his friend said.

"Figured if you could take a vacation here in the hospital, I might as well get in on the action."

"Too bad this bed's only built for one. You'll have to pull up a chair."

Geoff would keep up the banter as long as his friend did, but he sensed things would get serious soon. "Pretty cool way to get out of sandbagging, although a little extreme."

"Don't tell me they got you out there on the levee?"

Geoff recounted how he'd snuck out early that morning due to exhaustion. Kyle was the one person besides his doctor with whom he could be truthful. "I overdid it, man, but while it lasted, it was great. But now I'm paying for it."

"Gotcha. You've gotta go for it while you can. My days of physical labor are over, but you've still got many good years ahead."

Even though they kidded each other, without ever laying out the guidelines, they'd tacitly agreed early on to give it to each other straight. So Geoff plunged ahead. "How you really doing?"

Kyle glanced away momentarily, then returned his gaze to Geoff. "I'm on the home stretch. Pam's being as brave as she can, but she knows it too."

"How can I help?"

"Coming to see me is plenty. But there is something else you can do."

Geoff was prepared for Kyle to ask him to look in on Pam from time to time. "Don't let this sucker defeat you. Live your life to its fullest. Get married, have kids," Kyle said instead.

He didn't know how to reply. Marriage? Kids? Despite Eileen's latest tactics, he didn't think so. This could be him in a few years. Pam might be putting on a good face for her husband, but Geoff didn't want to leave any woman a widow. "I'll, uh, try."

Kyle scrunched up his forehead. "Don't humor me, man. We've never done that before, and I sure don't want that now."

Why argue the point and disillusion his friend? "I hear you. I'll do my best."

Three

Geoff had just finished dressing the next morning when Eileen showed up again. This time, she wheeled in a suitcase. A large suitcase.

"Good. You're up." She floated over to him, and before he had a chance to duck, checked his eyes with a thumb and forefinger, then kissed him. "You still look a little peaked."

"I'm fine." He swept past her to check out her luggage. "Going on a trip?" Did he sound too hopeful?

"This is my destination, actually. You won't take care of yourself, so I'm here to do that for you." Her smile reminded him of his mother's smile when she thought she knew what was better for him than he did.

His stomach took a nosedive. Eileen was moving in? Just like that? No discussion. Or was this what she'd been building up to the day before? He wheeled the luggage back to the door. "I appreciate the gesture, but really, it's not necessary."

"It's for your own good, Geoff. You've been living in a fantasy world where your MS is as easily treated as an upset stomach."

"There's no room for two of us here. That's why Mitch took over the upstairs rooms when Aubrey moved in."

Eileen charged past him and moved her bag farther into the room. "You're right about closet space, with that large wardrobe of yours. I'll probably have to live out of my suitcase temporarily, until we find a larger place."

"We? *We* haven't discussed living together."

"You weren't just tired yesterday from sandbagging. Your MS is manifesting, and you're in denial. It would be irresponsible of me not to recognize what's happening and not force you to deal with it."

"How many times do I have to say it? I'm fine. I saw my doctor yesterday, and he agreed."

"You admit you weren't feeling well?"

"Fatigue. That's all it was. No more sandbagging."

Eileen hauled the suitcase into his bedroom. "I have to get to work. I'll be back at five," she said when she returned. She gave him a peck on the cheek, then was gone.

He allowed her a few minutes to depart the building, then made his way upstairs in search of Mitch and Aubrey. He could still manage the stairs. Just couldn't run up and down them like he did at one time.

He found his younger brother at the kitchen table. "Did you have anything to do with Eileen's moving into my apartment?"

Mitch almost choked on his cereal. "No kidding? Funny how we were just talking about—"

"Not funny at all. She's using my MS as an excuse to make herself at home. Or if she's really serious about my condition, she's not only completely mistaken, she's also presumed a little too much about our relationship. Didn't even stop to discuss it. Just delivered her suitcase and took off."

The smile disappeared from Mitch's face. "Calm down. She's envious of Aubrey and Jenna living with us. Told them as much."

"You don't believe I need a *keeper*? You didn't put her up to this?"

"Hell no. Check with Gray, but I bet he'll say the same."

"What am I going to do?"

"If she hadn't just showed up with her stuff, would you be okay with her moving in?"

"No! I thought she was happy with the way things were."

"Then you'd better clear things up with her as soon as you can."

Mitch's advice sounded logical. But that was the thing. The only logic Eileen would listen to at this point was her own. "She brought me out of my funk last summer. I don't want to hurt her, Mitch. Not like her last boyfriend did when he dumped her a week before Christmas."

"Ready to marry her so you won't hurt her?"

"No. It's just … no. I know what has to be done. Just don't like it. That's all."

"Understandable." Mitch finished his orange juice, while he apparently processed this new development. "Sounds like she's protecting her territory." He shot a direct gaze at his brother. "Given her any reason to be worried?"

"No, no way!" He may have played the field in his pre-MS days, but not since he'd started seeing Eileen. "The only other women I see with any regularity are Aubrey, Jenna, and Eileen's mother, Peggy." With the exception of Alex Appleby, who he met the day before. No, he barely knew the woman. Although her presence in his private domain had really torqued off Eileen.

His expression must have given away his thoughts, because Mitch asked, "What? What did you just remember?"

"Nothing. I may not be ready for a permanent arrangement with Eileen, but I haven't been two-timing her." He refrained from mentioning Alex since there was nothing to it.

Mitch rose. "Better be getting to work. Aubrey's already off for the day to check out upholstery fabric with a supplier in Davenport. So you're on your own. Maybe you could try calling that prospective client. See if he'll reconsider."

"Yeah. Sure. Won't hurt to try." In other words, find an actual client.

He returned to his office to ponder his dilemma with Eileen. He didn't want her to move in. Had to stop that before it got any further. But her moving in signified something even scarier: Eileen was taking over his life. No way was he going to let that happen. He liked her, or at least, he had liked her up until this morning. But he didn't love her. As Mitch had said, there was only one thing to do.

Forget about Eileen for now. He needed to find a real client. He pulled out the file where he kept business cards and other contact info he'd collected about possible customers, and considered the possibilities. A pro football team, a new Internet billionaire, a corporate party planner. One lone business card sat near the top of his desk. The one Alex Appleby had given him. He told her he'd get in touch after he'd rested. Hmmm. He'd now rested.

An idea took root in the back of his head, but he'd let it gel for the next few hours.

Around noon, he sent an email.

ALEX OCCUPIED a booth in a small mom-and-pop diner across the parking lot from her motel while she perused her client files.

"Would you like another iced tea, miss?" the waitress asked.

"Yes, thanks." She had finished her salad some time ago, but as long as the restaurant didn't complain, she'd be just as well off here as back in her motel room attempting to help at least one of her flock get a little closer to their lofty, unrealistic career goals.

Though the day before she'd told Geoff McKenna she was managing several clients, in actuality, she was balancing the careers of three—a wannabe cooking show host, an aging soap star and Loretta Kinsolver, rising country star. Managing the careers of the first two occupied half of her time, and managing Loretta claimed all of her time. Something had to change soon, or Alex was definitely going to lose it. Like she hadn't already *lost it* by coming to this town.

To be fair, she sort of liked Burlington. Certainly nowhere near the traffic that claimed so much a part of her daily life in Los Angeles, where it could sometimes take a half hour to go two miles on the freeway. However, though LA had its share of mudslides, she'd never witnessed a flood. She still hadn't viewed the river up close and personal, but she meant to rectify that before she left town. From a safe distance, whatever that was during a flood.

The waitress returned with a fresh glass of iced tea. "Here you go. I can take those plates, if you're done eating?"

A quarter of her sandwich still remained on the plate. "Yes, please. The chicken salad was delish. Guess I'm not used to such huge proportions."

"Happens a lot. Our cook is overly generous with his servings. We've tried to tell him to cut back, but that's just him." She gathered the plates and departed.

Time to check email. Alex had been putting it off, because all she seemed to receive these days was one demand after another from her exacting children. Gaylord St. Martin still wanted a spot on a particular national talk show, even after she'd told him in no uncertain terms the show's producers didn't want him. The man operated under some long-ago code, if one ever existed, where charming men were expected to come on to anything in skirts. It was like he'd never heard of Me, Too. A few years back, when he'd somehow wangled an appearance on the show, he'd walked uninvited into the dressing room of one of the show's cohosts and proceeded to put the moves on her. So far, his career had survived, but only barely, on the sidelines. He wasn't big enough for someone to charge him with inappropriate behavior.

Tyne Wheeler, frustrated with her lack of acting jobs, had gone to culinary school and emerged with a diploma and the belief she was now ready for her own cooking show. Nothing local. Had to be national or at least regional. Forget about having no experience. And after sampling some of her concoctions, not much talent either.

Then there was Loretta, who fired off a note to Alex every fifteen minutes. Usually about the same subject: Alex's real reason for this trip to the Midwest.

To her surprise, though, another name showed up in the unread queue: Geoffrey McKenna.

—*Slept out. Ready to finish talk.*—

Wow. She thought she'd been getting through to him on some

level, but she'd also been convinced he was under the influence of his watchdog. Maybe not.

Who would've guessed she'd pick a guy with MS as her ally? His condition shouldn't mess up her plans. Just added another element. He appeared to be a man of action who could no longer act, although that didn't seem to bother him as much as his fear of his brothers perceiving him as such.

Should she make him wait for a reply? Nah. Needed to move on this. The sooner she hooked her prey, the better. She wrote back.

—*Free this afternoon?*— She didn't have to wait long for a reply.

—*Want to see the sights? Where are you staying?*—

She arranged to meet him outside the motel in a half hour. Though she hadn't brought much in the way of wardrobe, that didn't stop her from going through the contents of her closet twice. In the end, she went with black jeans and a light gray pullover.

He was waiting for her when she walked through the lobby. "Prompt. I like that," he said as he helped her into his sedan.

He wore a light yellow golf shirt and chinos. Nice change from the dirty sweats of the day before. His freshly shampooed hair clung to his neck, didn't stick out in unbidden tufts as it had when she'd interrupted his nap. In all, he looked mighty fine.

"I'd just sent an e-mail to a client when I saw your note, so I was at a stopping point. The desk clerk at the motel suggested I check out Crapo Park to view the flood."

"Crapo Park. Good idea."

"Is it far?"

"Not by L,A. standards. Maybe fifteen minutes."

Once they'd left the main drag on the town's west side, they traveled through several neighborhoods of single-family dwellings. Most looked to be over sixty-seventy years old. At length, they entered what must have been the park, since a large shelter house appeared on the passenger side.

"This is Dankwardt Park," Geoff said. "It links with Crapo." Soon, numerous trees and bushes claimed the landscape. "Now we're in

Crapo. The town makes a big deal about this being an arboretum or tree sanctuary."

They emerged into the open, rounded a small hillock housing a band shell, and parked in front of two mounted cannons aimed across the river below. She didn't wait for him to get her door for her but instead jumped out and ran up the slight incline for a better view.

In the distance, water covered about as far as the eye could see on the Illinois side. A hundred yards or so from the farthest edge, a line of trees marked where the bank must lie in non-flood times. Only then did she understand the extent of the current emergency.

"At least the highway is still open over there," Geoff said as he came up to her. "There've been years when to get from here to the towns across the river, you had to drive miles out of your way north or south."

"How long will it stay like that?"

He shrugged. "Depends. The river level is supposed to go down today or tomorrow, but the fields may be filled for weeks. It'll be a while before the farmers can plant again."

"I had no idea how much the river affected everything."

"Life still goes on, but yeah, it does tend to put a crimp in things."

She turned to go back to the car, but he caught her arm. "You said you had something to discuss with me. We can talk on that bench over there."

Her body's reaction to the slight contact surprised her. After all, he'd simply touched her arm. She had to refocus her thoughts. "Oh. Okay." Time to put her cards on the table. She plopped down. "I need your help convincing Jenna to rent her motor coach to my client."

He sank onto the bench and turned to study her. Apparently, he hadn't expected this angle. "That's some request."

"Kept it short and simple."

"Short, yes. Simple, uh, no way. Jenna's coach is currently on the road, rented to someone else. That's the first problem. Second problem, I have nothing to do with her rental choices, so how could I help you? Since she's your stepsister, why don't you ask her yourself?" he added before she had a chance to reply.

"I'm aware the coach is currently in use. My client doesn't need it for a few months. As for asking Jenna myself, I already did a few weeks ago. She put me off. Didn't turn me down but said she wasn't sure what she wanted to do with it. Which is why I didn't bring it up at lunch yesterday and instead invented another reason for being in town."

"That's why you're here?"

"Also thought I'd check out a potential new client." She told him about the young singer she planned to interview. "Pretty far-fetched, isn't it? Coming all the way here mainly to rent a motor coach."

"Yeah, it is. Jenna's coach is special, but it's not the only luxury bus on the road."

She studied her nails. She couldn't tell him the "real" real reason, but to enlist Geoff's help, she needed to convince him why there was a compelling need for this particular vehicle. She'd been working out an alternate rationale for days. Time to try it out. "In the past year, my dad's wife, Iris, has lost both her daughters to your brothers. She's worried about their futures, especially Jenna's, since she put her concert tour on hold to move back here with Graham."

"Jenna's doing fine. She got herself an agent, who's sold both her children's books to a big-time publisher. More are underway. In the meantime, she's teaching music at a local school."

"I know. But it will be some time before she starts to see any royalties on her books, and her teaching job is only part-time at a private school. Iris is worried that's not enough to support her granddaughter, Paige, while Jenna has most of her money tied up in that monster bus."

Geoff scraped a hand across his jaw. "From what I hear, she's receiving a pretty nice fee from the current rental."

"But she could be earning more, much more, if she agreed to my client's proposition."

"C'mon, Alex. If you want my help selling this idea to Jenna, cut the bull."

On to her already? She released a huff, attempted to appear insulted. "Are you saying I'm lying?"

"From what I've heard about your stepmother from Jenna and Aubrey, there's no love lost between your mother and Iris Appleby, even though Iris wasn't even in the picture when your parents' marriage ended. So why are you now acting on her behalf?"

Besides his incredible looks, Geoff McKenna was also quite sharp. Not your typical Pretty Boy. She hadn't counted on that. "You're right. I've never been very close to Iris. But I'd like to get to know my stepsisters better."

Wrinkles creased his forehead. "Why this elaborate ruse? Why not the direct approach with Jenna?"

She attempted to respond, but his proximity to her on the bench, the scent of his spicy aftershave, clogged her reasoning. She needed to keep a clear head to gain his cooperation. She rose. "Let's walk." She headed for the street. "Thanks to my mother's continuing hostility toward my father, I hardly know Jenna and Aubrey. We're civil but certainly not close. Jenna might be more open to considering this deal if she believes the money to be gained from it will ease her mother's mind."

They'd reached the end of the semicircular street bordering the band shell and crossed over to a slightly higher hillock, on which rested a large fountain.

"Where do I come in?"

"You're the PR guy for the company, right?"

"Among other things."

"You can help her see the wisdom of this proposition better than I."

"No one's going to make her do something she doesn't want to do."

"You help her see she really does want to rent the coach to my client. It's a win-win. Even though my client gets the coach and I come through for my client, Jenna's the big winner, both financially now from my client's fees but also in the future, because everyone else will want to rent the coach when the entertainment world grapevine gets wind of my client's coup. Once Jenna's financial picture improves, Iris relaxes, which means my dad can relax."

He pulled her over to the rim around the fountain and they sat. "You've got this all figured out, except how I make it happen."

He wasn't jumping on this bandwagon as readily as she'd hoped. Nor was she prepared to answer his question. She had no idea how he'd execute his part. She had used up her bag of tricks convincing him to do the convincing. Time to punt. "Don't you all get together frequently? Socialize?"

"Not so much now that Gray and Mitch are both part of couples who do their own thing. Why do you ask?"

"The next time you're around Jenna, you simply ask about her current rental situation with the coach and build on that."

"What if she says she can't wait for it to end so she can begin her own tour?"

She bit a lip. "Is that a real possibility?"

"Beats me. She seems pretty happy with things the way they are, but she also spent a bundle to customize the coach just the way she wanted it. Someday she may want to enjoy the fruits of that decision."

Stick to the truth as much as possible. "According to my dad, it was Iris who was pushing for the concert tour, not Jenna."

He brushed debris off the section of rim between them. "Say you're right. How am I supposed to get around to her renting to your client if I'm not supposed to know about your prior offer? I don't even know who your client is."

She stood and strolled around the fountain. The base wasn't very deep. Less than two feet. A few stray leaves floated on the surface; otherwise, she could see the brick foundation below, scarred black over the years. Here she was in the middle of the day in an unpopulated park with a man she hardly knew. Yet she felt remarkably comfortable and safe with him. "All you have to do is ask in passing what she plans to do with the coach when the current lease runs its course."

"All." He joined her, flipped a coin into the water.

She raised a brow. "You don't strike me as the kind of guy who wishes on a fountain."

"I'm wishing the last ten minutes never happened."

"C'mon. This is a simple request."

"Yeah? What's in it for me if I agree?"

She figured this question would pop up at some time. For now, she'd appear to be obtuse. "My good will?"

"Nice try, but I'd be risking my relationship with Jenna. She might be my sister-in-law someday, and she's already a great friend. There should be some incentive for me to get involved."

Was he coming on to her? No, he couldn't be. He was taken. He didn't strike her as the kind of guy who cheated. "Incentive? Like what?"

THE WOMAN INTERESTED HIM, no doubt about that. Not only was she fantastic looking in an exotic sort of way, but here she was proposing he do her a favor for which so far he'd seen no advantage to himself. Yet if he agreed to help her and screwed up, he could offend his brother's woman and thus his brother as well.

The lady had gall. Though she'd explained why she'd asked him and why it was necessary, it still didn't ring true. But he was curious. And attracted.

Plus, he had his own agenda. She might be just the answer to his dilemma with Eileen. She'd laid her cards on the table, and now it was his turn. "As it happens, I could use your help also."

"Really?" She flipped her bangs away from her eyes. "Do tell."

"You met my girlfriend, Eileen, the other day?"

"Miss Warm Personality?"

"That's her. I need your help breaking up with her."

She gulped, retreated a step. "Me? I'm supposed to come between the two of you? Surely, you don't think—"

"No, of course not! I just want it to look like we've got a thing going." Although now that he'd denied the idea, it lingered in the back of his brain.

"I got the impression the two of you were serious. She was a bit territorial when she met me, but that's natural for someone who thinks she's got a right to her claim."

"Yeah, well, I'm not ready to be claimed."

"Oh."

"But I, uh, feel I owe her. She was the first woman I've seen on a serious basis since being diagnosed with MS. She helped me see I can live a nearly normal life, even with my disorder. She gave me back my self-confidence. But now it's just not working out between us."

"So just end things."

"I want this to be her idea, not mine."

"You think she'll break things off if she finds me sitting there holding hands with you in front of her? Why not find her another man?"

"Might have done just that, except you came along with this other proposition. Thought I could parlay it into a mutual deal."

"Surely you don't expect me to move in with you and, uh, other things?"

She'd done it again, planted an image in his head that wouldn't easily go away. "You mean sex? No. Although it would help if everyone else believed there was something going on."

She backed up a few inches, shook her head. "I don't know, Geoff. This will make me look like the 'other woman.' My relationship with my stepsisters is shaky enough."

"Might be your chance to get closer, if they come to your defense." He'd been banking on her initial negative reaction to Eileen to gain her agreement. Apparently her desire to make nice with her stepsisters was stronger than he'd realized.

Her phone interrupted their negotiation. When she checked the screen, her expression changed to one of forced tolerance, as if she had to deal with a pesky telemarketer. She stepped away to take the call.

"Yes, I'm working on it, but it's even more complicated than I imagined." For the rest of the call, Alex listened, although she opened her mouth a couple of times to say something, then didn't. He couldn't hear the other party. She pressed her lips together and glared.

Within minutes, it was over. Alex blew out a breath, then put her cell away.

"Client?" Geoff asked as she returned to where he had perched once again.

"Recognized the look, huh? If I didn't know better, I'd say you were in cahoots with said client."

"Tightened the screws?"

"Nice way of putting it." She stuck out a hand. "Looks like we have a deal."

Four

eal made, Alex was the first to speak. "Where do we start? You already said I don't have to move in with you, so how will your girlfriend see us together?"

"Still working on that part. My situation has changed since you saw me last. Eileen moved in with a suitcase this morning. Said she doesn't believe I'm taking care of myself. Used that as her reason."

"Are you?"

He blinked. "I'm a grown man who knows his limits."

Uh-oh, she'd insulted him. "Okay, okay. Cool your jets. Just wondered how she got that impression."

He scuffed his shoe through the grass, like a little boy who'd been called to task for breaking the neighbor's window with his baseball. "Even though both Gray and Mitch are living with their women, I thought Eileen was fine with our current arrangement. But now I suspect she's been looking for an excuse for us to do the same. My exhaustion the other day served that purpose."

"You're not ready for such togetherness?"

His chiseled jaw appeared to tighten. "I'm okay with seeing someone on a steady basis, but with my condition, more commitment than that wouldn't be wise. Plus, I don't like the way she's taking over. Like I can't think for myself."

Alex reached for a tree branch that must have shaken loose in a recent storm and swished it through the grass as she processed his statement. He'd essentially told her he didn't plan to marry due to his MS. Did Eileen know this? "Aren't you going to a lot of trouble just to avoid confronting her?"

He closed his eyes, appeared to consider her question. "The guy before me hurt her badly. When we first started seeing each other, she told me how it had taken her months to get over him. Maybe telling her outright would be kinder, but I thought I'd give her the chance to do the dumping for once." He stopped, booted a pile of fallen leaves from his path. "This all happened since she ran into you making me breakfast. Innocent as your visit was, that seemed to set her off. Thought I'd use it to my advantage."

"I don't know whether to be flattered or scared." How would she feel if her boyfriend manufactured a new love interest just because he didn't have the balls to tell her he didn't want to settle down? "But since I've already agreed to help you, back to my question of how we get started."

"Have you got any medical experience?"

She wasn't expecting that one. "Actually, I almost finished my first year of nursing school."

"That's great. Then the story will be that I've hired you as my health provider to relieve Eileen of those duties. You're not really going to take care of me. But it'll be your excuse to hang around the firehouse and ace her out of acting as my personal doctor."

"I was just planning to be in town a few days. A week at most. What you're suggesting is longer term. I can't afford to stick around that long, unless you're planning to pay me?"

He made a face. "Uh, no. Your compensation, if you recall, is for me to get Jenna to lease her coach to your client. Let me see what I can work out with Mitch as far as a place to stay. Who knows? Maybe we'll get immediate results with this plan so you'll only have to remain a few days."

Though that was her plan, why did the idea of leaving so soon bother her?

"What are you going to do about the suitcase that's already there?" Alex asked as they made their way to his car.

"Thought of delivering it to her mom's house this afternoon but didn't want to embarrass her in front of her family."

"Good. I broke up with a guy in high school—well, he broke up with me—and he stopped by the house to take back his senior picture when I was away. Our housekeeper, who knew we were no longer together, assumed I'd have no problem returning it, so she handed it over. I was furious when I got home. At her, at him for taking advantage of her, but mostly at fate, because I'd been robbed of the chance to return it myself, along with the appropriate vitriol."

"I also considered leaving it outside the door to my apartment for her to find when she returns, but I rejected that idea as being too public. My brothers, Jenna, Aubrey, or any customer could see it there."

She nodded. "With you so far."

"When she arrives, you should be there doing something very care-like for me. I'll move her baggage back to the living room from my bedroom so she'll know the score immediately."

She wrinkled her nose. "Score?"

"That I don't want to ruin our relationship by depending on her to oversee my health. So I've asked you, because you have nursing experience, to drop in daily and make sure I'm following my treatment plan."

She considered his idea. How would she react if she were Eileen? She'd see red, no matter how logical his rationale. She'd either call it quits immediately, which was what he wanted, or she'd pretend to accept the arrangement and go underground to sabotage the arrangement. On the other hand, she wouldn't have pushed her man into the corner in which Geoff now stood. Would she?

Geoff took Alex back to her motel so she could pick up her rental car and return to the firehouse later in the afternoon to be on hand when Eileen arrived after work. Meanwhile, he called Mitch and asked him to meet him there.

"I see the suitcase is still here," Mitch said when he arrived at Geoff's apartment.

"Yeah, but I moved it into the living room so she'll see it as soon as she arrives." He laid out his plan with Alex.

"And she agreed?" Mitch's voice rose an octave.

"Yes, although there's a catch." Mitch raised an eyebrow.

"I'm hoping Eileen will flip out as soon as she sees Alex on the premises again. Especially when she hears she's been replaced as chief health-care worrier. But if it takes continued exposure to Alex's presence, Alex needs a place to stay."

Mitch backed away. "Uh-oh. I sense this is where I come in. And Aubrey."

"You've got Gray's old bedroom you're not using. This shouldn't be for longer than a few weeks."

Eyes narrowed, Mitch studied him. "How did you ever get her to agree to help you? It was one thing for her stepsisters to leave L.A., since they were both under the spell cast by Gray and me, but she barely knows you. Unless ..." Again, he raised a brow.

"No! Get over that idea right now. Nothing's going on between Alex and me, although that's the picture you're going to witness. But it's all just made up. Okay?"

"Sure, bro. Whatever you say. However, it seems pretty fortuitous that only a few hours ago you were beside yourself trying to figure out how to dump Eileen and already you've come up with a plan. And a willing conspirator."

"Fast-moving issues call for fast-moving resolutions. That's all." It was just a coincidence using Alex had come to mind so quickly, wasn't it?

"I'll talk to Aubrey tonight. Gotta get back to the law office now."

Alone once again, Geoff wondered if he'd outfoxed himself. He'd put this plan in motion to remove one female from his life by bringing another into it. Nah. Alex knew how things stood. Plus, unless the prediction of the West Coast falling into the ocean came true, the odds against three women from L.A. falling in love with Iowa guys were astronomic.

"YOU'RE LATE," Geoff said as he opened his apartment door to Alex later that afternoon. "I was afraid Eileen would arrive before you."

"I had to make a call and got delayed. Do you happen to own a blood pressure cuff?"

"Huh? Yeah, I keep one in the bathroom. Why?"

"When she arrives, I'll be checking your blood pressure. We'll continue to keep it out here in plain sight to add credence to my role. I didn't have time to purchase a notebook for keeping track of your vitals."

He left the room and returned a minute later carrying the device, which he set on the kitchen table. Then he retrieved a spiral-bound pad from a chest of drawers. "Here. I've got a minor storehouse in that drawer."

She fished a pencil from her purse and set it by the notepad on the table.

"Haven't found that pen of yours yet?"

"My pen? Oh, right. I keep forgetting to search my rental car." He stared at her, as if gauging her response.

Note to self: Buy new pen to claim as the one I lost.

The sooner she produced a pen, the sooner she'd no longer be caught off guard when he asked about it. She'd told him it was senti-mental because she'd signed her first client with it. Bull. There was no sentiment where Loretta was concerned.

"Should we practice?" he said before she could think of a good comeback.

"Practice?"

"Yeah, take my blood pressure."

"Oh. Right. It's been a while since I've handled one of these. Have to look authentic." He started to pull up his shirt, but she cut him off. "That won't be necessary. I can do this through your shirt sleeve." So he wasn't just a pretty boy. She'd seen enough of the light brown chest hair to regret there wasn't some vital sign requiring a naked torso. Or more.

She stretched the cuff tight around his arm above his elbow and fastened it. She'd barely touched him, yet the contact seared her insides. Maybe this wasn't such a great idea.

Had he been affected as well? He'd quickly twisted away from her.

"Uh, Alex? You need to hit the On/Off button."

"Oh. Right. The ones I'm familiar with aren't automatic." She activated the machine and waited for the readout to appear. "One-fifty over one-ten. That's higher than it should be. Is this normal for your condition?"

"Chalk that up to Eileen's moving in."

"Uh, okay. Maybe this pretend health-care thing has unanticipated benefits, like getting that BP down."

"I told you… Never mind. Fine. Suit yourself. I'd rather have you nagging me on a temporary basis than Eileen on a permanent one."

She let a smile go wicked across her face. "Sounds like my license to harass. What else can I add to my list of tortures?"

He stared her down. "Don't get carried away. Like you said, this should only last a few days."

She released the cuff, attempted not to actually touch him to avoid a second jolt, folded the cuff and laid it and the control box on the table before she recorded the reading. "Okay, we're set as far as you're concerned. What about my plan? Have you had a chance to arrange something involving you and Jenna?"

He related how he'd asked Mitch if Alex could stay in Gray's old room in the second floor apartment. "Took care of the first step. Now I'm waiting to hear if it took. Aubrey has to agree, and it's sometimes hard to predict your stepsister's actions."

"Does your brother know about your girlfriend?"

"Yeah. At first, I thought he and Gray had put Eileen up to this so she could keep an eye on me. But when I confronted him, he denied all knowledge. I told him it was time to end things, but I needed a way to do it without hurting her. After you and I talked, I let him in on our plan."

An uncomfortable lump formed in her stomach. This was getting out of hand. All she'd wanted was Jenna's signature on a lease agreement. Now more and more people were getting involved. She'd had immediate bad vibes about Eileen, but those were no reason to play out this farce. Mitch would probably feel obliged to tell Aubrey and his brother, and one of them would inevitably tell Jenna. She didn't want to turn Jenna against her until the lease was a done deal.

Geoff rose and picked up the blood-pressure apparatus. "We need to set this scene better. Make it look more like a doctor's office." He placed the BP equipment on a small side table in the living room, then headed back to the bathroom. A minute later, he returned with a white towel, a handful of tongue depressors, and a thermometer. He moved the BP cuff aside long enough to drape the towel over the table and then arranged all of the other items on top.

She brought him the notepad and pencil. "Let's make sure she knows about this, but keep it in your pocket or somewhere she can't grab it and check the data," he said. "We'd better record actual numbers, just in case she gets her hands on it. She's slick like that."

"Good idea."

While Geoff continued to set the stage, Alex consulted the internet, seeking information about the care of patients who presented with mild cases of MS.

"Curtain going up in about five minutes," he said at length. "Time to get that cuff on again as soon as I haul that suitcase out here."

They didn't have long to wait. Two minutes later, Eileen swept into the apartment. "Honey, I'm home."

Unaccustomed to the role of The Other Woman, Alex took a deep breath and focused on her "patient."

"You? What are you doing back here?" No question who she meant.

Geoff answered for her. "You remember Alexandra Appleby, don't you? As it turns out, she has training as a nurse. You've been concerned I haven't been taking good care of myself, so she's going to be stopping by daily to make sure I am."

"But ... but—"

"I was concerned about taking you away from your family to play nursemaid to me, so I worked out this deal with Alex." He nodded toward the door, where he'd moved her luggage. "Good thing you didn't have time to unpack this morning."

"I, uh ..." She turned to Alex. "I thought you were looking for Graham."

"Actually, I'm in town to see Aubrey and Jenna. They're my stepsisters. The only address and name I had were Graham's."

"You're related to them?" Eileen's voice assumed an incredulous tone.

"Their mother is married to my father."

"Oh."

Eileen seemed to consider the revelation. Process it. "And you're a nurse?"

"Actually, no. I didn't finish my training. But I know the basics, enough to monitor Geoff's day-to-day vital signs."

"But I'm able to do that."

Geoff moved closer to Eileen. "You've got your job to consider. Didn't you tell me last week how they're assigning you to a new project where you could really make a name for yourself? I don't want to eat into the time that's going to require."

Once again, Eileen's gaze drifted over to Alex. "But she tried to feed you eggs."

"We've been through all that, Eileen. There's no need to be concerned."

Eileen pursed her lips. After a few beats, she straightened her shoulders, stood a little taller. She moved closer to Geoff, threw an arm around his shoulder. "This really isn't necessary. I wouldn't have minded doing the same things she seems to be doing. But since you've got this all set up, thank you, Alex, for helping my man stay healthy." Even though she was attempting to be friendly, her voice had become even more possessive.

My man. Couldn't be plainer. "I'll do my best," Alex returned in her most noncommittal tone.

"I'll, uh, take your suitcase out to your car for you," Geoff said a little too helpfully.

"Thanks. But then you need to change clothes so we can get over to Mom's. She's fixing barbecued pork tonight."

"That's tonight?"

"You forgot? I reminded you the other day."

"I need to beg off. Alex and I are still going through the protocol."

"Surely, you can pick up tomorrow?" Eileen's eyes bored through Alex, even though the question was addressed to Geoff.

Geoff hesitated. He apparently hadn't planned for this tactic. Eileen may have been surprised to have been replaced as his health-care aide, but she had no intention of giving up the role of girlfriend.

Alex waited for Geoff to dig himself out of this one. There wasn't much she could do.

Geoff turned to Alex. "I'll walk Eileen out to the car with this. Wait here, if you would."

Not much choice, unless she wanted to make a scene or break her agreement.

Geoff was gone about three minutes.

"Now what?" she asked once he returned.

"That damned suitcase is gone. One point in my favor. And I've made it clear I want someone else monitoring my vitals."

"But she also made it clear all she had to do was remind you you're still dating and you snapped to attention."

"Then that's our objective tomorrow."

"Don't you have a job? You've spent most of the day with me."

"Good point. Maybe we can do both. Are talent managers any good at finding motor coach customers?"

Five

Alex's phone rang the next morning as she ate breakfast.

"We need to talk. Can you meet me somewhere near where you're staying?" Geoff asked.

"I'm at the diner across the street from my motel. What's up?"

"Got good news and bad news, but I don't want to talk over the phone. I'll be there in ten minutes."

True to his word, he breezed through the door nine minutes later. "Haven't been here in a while. They serve great down-home food, which I now try to avoid."

"Like eggs?" She couldn't help asking.

He nodded, his lips curving upward. "I like your sense of humor. Actually, one serving would've been fine. Smelled great, by the way. Wish I'd had the chance to see if the taste matched the scent."

He ordered a cup of coffee, black, then planted his chin in his clasped hands. "Good news first. Aubrey, and thus Mitch, is fine with you staying at the firehouse. At least temporarily. You can move in today."

Her spoonful of oatmeal stopped midair. "Guess that's good news. Certainly will cut down on my expenses, unless … Do they want me to pay rent?"

"No, although if you wouldn't mind cooking on occasion or helping out with housekeeping, the gesture would go a long way to helping you fit in."

She replaced the spoon in her cereal bowl. "Aubrey is really okay with this?"

"Didn't talk with her directly. Only got the go ahead from Mitch. But she must've been willing to give it a try."

"I hope so. I want to improve my relationship with my stepsisters, not go the other direction."

He lifted a brow. "That's pretty much up to you, then, wouldn't you say? Are you prepared to back away if Jenna continues to refuse to rent her coach to your client?"

She avoided his gaze and aligned her cereal bowl with the smaller bowl of fruit next to her plate of dry toast. "No. I have to make this happen."

He removed his chin from his hands, settled back in the booth. "Why does this mean so much?"

She resumed aligning the dinnerware.

"Alex? Is it some big secret or something?"

He wouldn't be content until she supplied a reason. "It's pretty much get my client the coach or I can find a new client."

"Might not be a bad idea. Why would you want to keep such a client?"

A reasonable question. But then, Loretta wasn't reasonable. "I'm building my career on my client's. If I lose her, I not only lose my management fee but also my credibility in the business. I've worked too long and hard to get to this point."

He sipped his coffee a little too long, as if attempting to swallow her words as well as the liquid. Finally, he set down his mug. "Okay. I get all that. But why is this person so fixated on this particular motor coach?"

"My client wants something of Jenna's in return for something Jenna supposedly took from my client last summer. Sounds crazy when I put it in words, but that's my client. Insecure, illogical and vindictive."

"What did Jenna do to this person to generate such ire?"

"I, uh, can't say any more. Client confidentiality, you know?"

Geoff scrunched up his face. "Oh, yeah. Sure."

"How does this person even know about Jenna's coach? It was hardly in California before Jenna leased it."

Alex gave a wry smile. "When we first started discussing my client's upcoming tour, I mentioned having seen this incredible tour bus at my dad's place last summer, and truth be told, I tried to impress my client by disclosing that the owner was my stepsister. Suddenly, my client got interested. Wanted to know everything there was to know about Jenna, her tour and especially the motor coach."

What had appeared to be a simple though needless objective when Alex first described her mission was rapidly taking on an unsavory tenor. Even though she'd provided some background about her client's interest in the coach, the bottom line still didn't wash with Geoff.

His palms itched, and this wasn't his MS acting up. He was getting bad vibes just listening to Alex's story. "Do you think this person would destroy the coach?"

"I keep telling myself their motives are purely aboveboard. They just want to right their personal karma."

"You don't sound convinced."

"Even if there's more to my client's obsession, Jenna will be protected by her lease provisions and insurance."

But that didn't cut it. Maybe this mutual arrangement with Alex wasn't the smartest move. But it was the best thing he had going at the moment, especially given Eileen's latest countermove. "Just be careful. Your client sounds like a nut case."

Alex glanced away, stirred her remaining oatmeal. "More a superstitious narcissist. But don't worry. No harm will come to Jenna, personal or otherwise."

She seemed to be telling him subject closed. At least for now.

"What's the bad news you wanted to discuss?" She beat him to his other topic.

He rubbed the bridge of his nose. "Since I made it clear to Eileen I didn't want her to move in, she found another way for us to be together. She wants to go away to celebrate her birthday next weekend."

Alex didn't reply at once. Instead, she finished her toast. "And you don't want to go?"

"Of course not. That's sending the wrong signal."

"Then you have to find some way to get out of it. What did you tell her?"

"That I already had plans."

"Let me guess. She wanted to know what they were and why you couldn't change them."

Did all women think alike? "Told her you'd asked me to go with you to meet a potential client."

She set down her water glass so hard some of the liquid sloshed out. "You what?"

"You mentioned something about visiting with some young singer, right?"

She mopped up the spill with her napkin. "Yes. Where do you come in?"

"Told Eileen the kid is only available Saturday night. And she lives just outside Sioux City, a six-hour drive each way. We'll need to stay over and return on Sunday."

Alex seemed to digest his words before responding. "Did she buy it?"

"She wasn't a happy camper, although I'm not sure which bothered her more, the fact I'd be spending time with you or missing her birthday. To tell the truth, I'd forgotten about it being her birthday. Even though I talked myself out of a weekend away with her, I can't avoid her big day. The guy she was with last called it quits a week before the holidays."

"Lousy timing, McKenna."

"I'll do something to remember the day. I'll get her flowers, a gift."

"You do that and you'll once again be sending a mixed message. But to neglect doing anything would be really low. You're not that kind of guy."

He tilted his head. "Really? You know me that well after just a few days?"

"I know you wouldn't hurt her. You've told me as much."

He raised his hands in surrender. "What do I do, then?"

"Offer to take her out to dinner Friday night. Give her some kind of ambiguous gift, like a book or a plant. No jewelry, flowers or anything personal."

When had he lost control of this discussion? Oh, right. He'd asked for her suggestions. "Won't she get the wrong impression, even spending one evening alone with her?"

"Not if I call in the middle and make you end the evening abruptly. My possible client is going to move up the time we can see her, so we'll need to leave earlier than planned Saturday morning."

Not bad. Not bad at all. But scary, too, how fast she'd come up with the plan.

"What's the best restaurant in town?" He told her. "Is it her favorite, or is there another?"

Eileen called another restaurant her favorite.

"Neither will be available Friday night. I'll leave the reasons to you. I'm just giving you the overall plan. You're going to wind up at a so-so place."

"You're enjoying this, aren't you? Making what little time I spend with her miserable."

"You could always call her right now and tell her you're ending things. Won't help me get the lease from Jenna, but it would be a whole lot more humane than this increasingly more complicated scheme to avoid hurting her."

She was right, dammit. "Okay. I'll set up some kind of celebration as soon as I leave here. You can check out of your motel and bring your things over this afternoon, if that works for you?"

He slid out of the booth, stood.

"Hey, McKenna? If you and I had been a couple the last several months? You wouldn't have forgotten my birthday."

Her smile was a challenge, but the batting of her eyes defied him to find out.

Geoff wasn't around when Alex returned to the firehouse with her things, but Aubrey emerged from her office when Alex called out.

"Geoff asked me to help you move in." Her greeting wasn't exactly welcoming, but she was civil.

"Do you have anything other than your suitcase?"

"Just my computer and purse."

Aubrey took those and went ahead up the stairs. "The apartment is sparsely furnished since Graham moved most of his personal things to the McKenna house to be with Jenna. But it's much more comfortable than a motel room."

"I really appreciate your agreeing to let me stay here."

"I was outvoted, two to one." Pause. "Oh, God, you took me seriously. No, I was just kidding."

Really? People often hid their real feelings behind humor.

They passed through the living room to Graham's rooms. "We all share the kitchen and living room. Each bedroom has its own bath and small alcove for a study. No television, though. Graham took his with him."

"No problem. I can watch TV on my notebook, if I feel the need."

She inspected her new temporary home. Not bad. King-sized bed, respectable closet. "This looks great. Much better than where I was staying. I'll start unpacking immediately."

"Could you put that off a bit and have a cup of coffee with me in the kitchen?" Aubrey said as Alex opened her suitcase to unpack.

Coffee? What did that mean? "Sure." She followed her stepsister out of the room to a nice-sized kitchen with a table that seated six.

"Would you prefer a bottle of water? I'm not a coffee drinker myself. The guys take their coffee black, but there's milk in the fridge and sugar-free packets on the table."

Alex accepted her mug. "I drink mine black too."

Once seated, Aubrey didn't waste time on formalities. "Why are you really here, Alex?"

Though they weren't related by blood, Alex still felt a certain kinship to this woman. They both liked to cut to the chase. However, in her immediate case, she couldn't go there. At least not yet. "You're not buying that Geoff invited me to stay here so it would be easier to monitor his condition?"

Aubrey took a sip of her water, then set down her bottle. "I understand that's the story he's telling Eileen."

"I am actually checking his condition each day. And I do have some medical, well, nurse's, training."

"Because Geoff didn't want Eileen doing it and using it as an excuse to move in."

So Mitch did tell her. She'd figured as much. "I met Eileen the other day, just prior to running into you out back," Alex said. "She got needlessly territorial about Geoff, although she had nothing to worry about."

"That's why he tapped you to make her jealous."

"Not jealous. To force her to break up with him."

Aubrey lifted a brow. "I get the plan, but why not just tell her it was over? Why all the intrigue?"

Alex grabbed a paper napkin from the holder on the table and folded it over once, then twice. "I can't really say. I hardly know the man. But he told me if I stuck around a few days to go through with this scheme, he'd ask you and Mitch if I could stay here instead of wasting my money on a motel."

"And that's why you agreed? To save money?"

"Partially. But like I told you and Jenna the other day, I want to get to know the two of you better. Staying here seemed like a good way to do it."

Aubrey rose and crossed over to the kitchen cabinets. "I get the munchies in late afternoon. How about you? Want some chips or cookies?"

"How about a piece of fruit?"

"Even better." Aubrey searched the fridge and returned with two apples, offering one to Alex. "How's this? We rinse them off before refrigerating them."

Alex accepted the fruit and took a bite. "Umm. Nice and sweet.

Hits the spot."

Aubrey returned to her seat. "It's my turn to cook tonight. Or should I say order something or get takeout? How'd you like to go to the grocery store with me? You can pick out the kind of cereal you like and other things."

"Sure. I'd be happy to use the money I'm saving on a motel for groceries."

"Good. I was hoping you'd offer. We can talk along the way."

Was her younger stepsister actually offering them a chance to get better acquainted, or was she just trying to chip her armor?

Fifteen minutes later, they were pushing a shopping cart through the aisles of an upscale grocery store.

"The guys prefer the no-frills, supposedly cheaper place a mile away, but this reminds me of the super groceries we have in L.A., especially with the fresh produce they stock," Aubrey said.

"Do you miss L.A.?"

"Some. For bonanzas like this. Shopping for everything is more limited here, but it's not like we're on a desert island."

"Otherwise, you're content?"

Her stepsister tilted her head, considered. "Content? Guess I'm always striving for something more, but I am happy. I've never met a man like Mitch. He's so intelligent and loving."

"And a hunk."

Aubrey's lips curved up. "Yes, he is that."

"Graham's no slouch either," Alex added.

"And Geoff? Or haven't you noticed?"

How could she not notice the man's looks? He wasn't a hunk like Mitch or handsome like Graham. No, this one was a bona fide pretty boy with grit. "Not bad on the eyes. But I'm used to that kind of guy on the coast. Usually, they turn out to be a disappointment. No substance."

"You're looking for substance?"

They stopped in the middle of the produce aisle. Aubrey examined three different kinds of tomatoes before selecting heirlooms.

"I'm not looking for anything at the moment," Alex said.

"Even if *anything* just falls into your lap, so to speak?"

She stopped and stared at Aubrey. "Is this what it's like having a sister?"

Aubrey returned a smile. "You mean the harassment and personal questions? Yes. What do you think? You still up for this getting-to-know-you thing?"

Six

"Give it some thought, Joe. Once you consider the benefits of having your own rig at your disposal, you won't be able to rest until you've made this purchase."

"You've certainly presented a good case, Geoff. But I can't make any promises. I've got my bottom line to consider," Joe Adler, owner of a regional baseball team, said.

Geoff hung up, figuring the chances of making the sale were somewhere around forty-sixty. Adler really wanted his own custom motor coach. Geoff could almost hear the guy salivating through the phone. But the team had come off a less-than-stellar season last year. Would the guy feel justified spending money on his new toy when it should be going to recruiting new players?

"You talk a good line, McKenna." Alex stood just outside Geoff's office. "I stopped by to take your daily vitals. This door was open, and I overheard."

"Moved in yet?"

"Took all of ten minutes, with what little I have with me. I've been spending my time getting to know Aubrey. I accompanied her to the grocery store and picked up some of my favorite foods."

"At her invite?"

She nodded. "After first offering me coffee. Can't tell yet whether she really wanted the company or she's attempting to figure out my motives for being here."

"Not to burst your familial bubble, but her first reaction to your being here wasn't what I'd describe as overwhelmingly positive. I suspect she checked in with Jenna before she came around. The two of them may have decided the best way to handle your presence is to keep tabs on you. 'Keep your friends close, and your enemies—', you know?"

"Closer. You could be right. But your offer was too good an opportunity to turn down. Besides, that saying works for my purposes as well as theirs."

He closed the cover of his client file, stuck it inside a desk drawer and locked it. "I've come to care a great deal for both your stepsisters. They'll probably be my sisters-in-law someday. I don't want to see them hurt."

"Not my plan."

"I'm serious, Alex. If I get the slightest hint you're going to bring any kind of harm to them, our deal is off, and I'll put them on to you."

His words didn't send her running. Instead, she ambled into the room and took a chair opposite his desk. "Message received. For what it's worth, I have no intention of making their lives miserable. I really do want to get closer to them. But we have years of issues between our mothers to overcome, if that's even possible."

He folded his hands, like a doctor receiving a patient. "Ready to check my vitals?"

"I also need to know what our plans are for this weekend. Are we really going on the road, or do we just keep a low profile where Eileen is concerned?"

"I can drive around town, but I'm not able to go long distances, like to Sioux City. So I need you to to be my chauffeur. Are you up to that?"

"Okay."

"I've made reservations for Saturday night at a nearby midclass motel. Two rooms, but I requested they be next to each other, just in case Eileen were to check."

"She'd do that?"

He raised his hands. "I don't know what to expect from her anymore. But I wouldn't put it past her. I can't get over the change in her recently. I hardly recognize the woman I started seeing last summer."

She rubbed her hands. "Did you hear yourself? You could have said something like, 'the woman I was attracted to last summer' or 'the woman I thought I loved.' Instead, you described your relationship as 'seeing her.'"

Was she right? Funny, even after the words were out of his mouth, the significance of what he'd said hadn't struck him until Alex brought it to his attention. Had he ever come close to thinking of Eileen in terms of loving her? He'd liked her, at least until recently. Last summer, they'd spent countless hours together, discovering what they had in common. But even when they had sex, had he ever confessed deeper feelings for her? He couldn't remember. A guy should remember stuff like that.

"I hit a nerve, didn't I? Look, I'm no fan of the woman—she didn't exactly greet me with open arms— but consider my observation before you go any further with your plan."

"I don't love her. Okay? I would have realized this sooner or later, but her behavior of late opened my eyes."

"What did you wind up getting her?" Alex asked.

Huh?"

"Her birthday gift. You did buy her something, right? And you made a dinner reservation?"

He forked a hand through his hair. "Damn! I knew there was some detail I was forgetting. I made the reservation, but I hate shopping. Put it off and then forgot about it." He offered her an entreating expression.

"Surely, you don't expect me to do your dirty work?"

"Gimme a break here, Alex. I've got to have a gift by tomorrow night. Not much time to figure out something that meets the criteria you dictated."

"What's it worth to you? Enough to set up some kind of family get-together where I can get closer to Jenna?"

She had him by the short hairs. And she knew it. "What kind of get-together?"

"Offer to provide tonight's meal. It's supposed to be Aubrey's turn, but if you check with her soon, you'll catch her before she makes the order," she said.

"Thought you said you went to the grocery store."

"We did. We bought breakfast and sandwich fixings, fruit, snacks, and a couple pies to bake. One thing I learned about my stepsister, like me, she isn't much of a cook. But she places dinner orders like a pro."

"And in return, you'll go gift shopping?"

"Give me the address of the best mall for my GPS and I'm off." At the door, she swiveled. "This is going to cost. Okay?"

"Whatever. Just make it believable." He handed her several bills.

"Ah, yes. Not too little, not too much."

WITH THE ADDRESS Geoff gave her, Alex made her way to the mall and found a major department store. Not an exclusive women's boutique, as she'd hoped, but the department store came through. She purchased an exquisite silk neck scarf, not the most expensive but well beyond middle range and completely the wrong color for Eileen. As the cherry on her sundae, she had customer service handle it with their complimentary gift wrap.

She had a little over an hour before she had to be back at the firehouse for dinner. More than enough time to power shop and pick up a few items for herself. After all, she was going to share an overnight with Geoff in two days. A girl needed to be prepared.

"Where are the serving bowls kept?" Alex asked Aubrey as they set the table for dinner later that day.

"Second cabinet, top left," Aubrey said, still focused on opening containers.

Alex retrieved two medium-sized blue bowls and a large platter and set them on the counter next to open cartons of food.

Aubrey shoveled mashed potatoes into one of the smaller bowls and green beans into the other. She leaned over to sniff first one, then the other. "Umm, these smell wonderful. We've never gotten takeout from Halpern's before." She carried the bowls to the table. "Put the fried chicken on that platter, if you would. There's a basket on top of the fridge for the rolls."

"You realize I can only convince Geoff this one time to spring for dinner for all of us?"

Aubrey chuckled. "Every time it's been Geoff's turn to plan dinner, he's either finagled an invitation for all of us to Eileen's house where Peggy, her mom, provided an incredible spread, or he's unloaded one of Peggy's frozen goodies from his freezer. Now that Eileen appears to be out of his life, it's only fair he procure dinner on his own dime."

"Something smells great," Mitch said, entering the kitchen. He examined one of the sacks for the containers. "Halpern's, huh? Looks like we've moved up in the world." He turned to Alex. "Do we have you to thank for this meal?"

"I only ordered it. Geoff paid the bill."

"Now he's got you taking care of dinner for him?"

She didn't tell him about her excursion to the mall. Neither his brothers nor her stepsisters needed to know. That was her special detail to hold over Geoff's head. "I offered. I had no idea you all considered this Halpern's so la-di-dah. The name came up first when I searched for a restaurant that delivered takeout."

"Aren't Gray and his ladies here yet?" Mitch asked. "We should eat while the food is hot."

"Jenna just texted. They're on their way."

"Just enough time for me to change out of my suit."

"Better hurry, bro. We're here," Graham announced from the doorway.

"Wow, look at all that food," Paige, Jenna's teenage daughter, squealed. "Not that healthy stuff you've been making us eat, Mom."

As the girl bounded into the room and grabbed a seat at the table, Alex shot a glance at Jenna. "Is this the wrong stuff? I thought this was the kind of food you all ate here."

"Whenever we feel the need for comfort food," Graham said. "Which I do tonight. Jenna has Paige and me eating salads and fish as much as possible."

"Except when I can convince someone to go out for burgers and fries," Paige added.

Good grief! The awkward teen from last year had grown into an attractive young lady. Not quite the same features as her mother but just as tall. "You're Paige, right?" Alex asked. "Until your mother decided to relocate here, I used to see you every so often at my dad's house."

Paige didn't exactly smile, but she didn't scowl either. "Yeah, well, I was there at the same time you were sometimes, but you weren't exactly friendly."

"Paige!" Jenna said. "That was unnecessary."

Alex put up a hand. "No, it's okay, Jenna. She's right. My style has been to pop in to see my dad briefly and then rush off. I avoided your mother as much as I could, which sometimes spilled over into keeping my distance from you and Paige also."

"Paige can be rather blunt at times," Jenna said.

"One of the benefits of the teenage years. Candor comes with the territory," Alex replied. "But I have to say, Paige, you look a lot differ-ent. You're almost as tall as your mother. You've become a lovely young lady."

"*Lady,* not so much," Graham put in, "but she is quite a cute kid, isn't she?" He placed a fatherly arm around her shoulder, his pride evident.

Aubrey returned to the table carrying the platter of chicken. "Hey, you guys, dinner's on the table and getting cold. Let's sit before we continue this conversation."

"Where's Geoff?" Mitch asked. "Thought this family reunion was his idea."

"I'm here." Geoff entered the room holding two boxes. "Wasn't sure if we'd taken care of dessert, so I picked up cupcakes."

Jenna rolled her eyes. "More carbs? I see extra workout sessions in my future."

"Yum." Paige rubbed her stomach.

Alex stifled a chuckle. Apparently, the teen wasn't too grown up to reject dessert.

Geoff placed the two boxes on the counter and took the seat next to Alex. "So? What have I missed?"

The other six exchanged looks. Mitch took it upon himself to summarize. "We've established that Paige is growing up and that Alex has offered the olive branch to make up for ignoring her at the Appleby house. That about it, everyone?"

"Where's Eileen?" Paige asked. "She usually joins us for these family things."

Alex raised a brow Geoff's direction.

"Eileen won't be joining us tonight," he said.

That apparently didn't satisfy Paige. "Oh? She has to work?"

Geoff swallowed. "No. We didn't invite her."

Paige blinked, then shifted her gaze to the plate of fried chicken. "Could I have a drumstick, please?"

"Alex is going to be staying here at the firehouse for the next several days," Geoff said. "She wanted to have this time with us tonight so she could get to know everyone better. Eileen didn't hit it off with Alex when they first met, so I thought it best she not attend."

That seemed to appease Paige, who continued to fill her plate.

"I thought maybe we could catch up? Like, what is each of you up to these days?" Alex asked.

Silence.

Were they each waiting to hear what the other would say? Or were they not willing to share? She let the silence extend a few beats.

Fortunately, Aubrey came to her rescue. "I'll start, although we sort of caught up already when we went grocery shopping. I'm finishing up the interior of the motor coach for a recent ten-million-dollar lottery winner. One of his brothers has inoperable cancer, so our client's trying to reunite his brother with the rest of their siblings before it's too late. They haven't been particularly close for several years."

"That's so sad, Aunt Aubrey," Paige said.

"Yes, it is, hon. But our client wants to think positive, everyone being together one last time. He thinks the lure of traveling in a luxury coach will be the incentive for his siblings to arrange their schedules around the trip."

"He couldn't just pay everyone to come along?" Paige asked.

"Paige, that sounds so callous," her mother said.

"I don't think he wanted to offend his brother, so instead he's offering this carrot."

"Instead of a large bedroom, like your mom has in her coach," Graham said, "our client had us install special sleeping compartments along both sides that fold up during the day to provide more space in the living area. I'm sure glad we found Don Jensen when your mom and I took her coach west last summer. Don's proven he's not only a great mechanic, he's also got great ideas when it comes to customization."

Alex turned to Aubrey. "I never realized customizing these rigs involved such personal stories."

"Nor did I until Aubrey met Mitch when she worked on my coach," Jenna said.

"A-hem," Graham put in. "How about what happened between you and me when we returned your coach to California?"

Jenna turned to him and patted his hand. "How could I forget the *personal* nature of that trip?"

Alex hit pay dirt with this discussion. Hadn't even had to steer them around to this topic. Perfect opportunity for Geoff to bring up the future of Jenna's coach. When he didn't jump right to it, she kicked him under the table.

Geoff blinked but then seemed to grasp her message. "You no sooner arrived in California than you decided to put off your concert tour and rent out the motor coach. Still considering that tour one of these days?"

Paige came out of her seat. "You're not still planning to go on the road, are you, Mom?"

Jenna's eyes grew wide, apparently caught off guard by the attention. "Uh." She stole a quick glance at Graham, who shrugged in response. "It's always a possibility, I guess. In the future."

Paige's eye narrowed to slits. "Future? Like, when? This summer? Next year?"

It occurred to Alex Paige could help her win the lease. Best to sit back and let this little family drama run its course.

Jenna reached over and placed her hand over one of Paige's. "I really don't know, Paige. I haven't made any plans at this point."

"That's what you said last year every time I asked about your tour, when you already had decided to do it."

"Paige," Jenna said in a controlled tone, more to the rest of them than her daughter. "Let's table this discussion for now. We'll talk about it later."

Paige erupted, stood and burst from the room, knocking over her water glass. "I'm no longer a child you have to shield," she called, contradicting herself.

"I'm so sorry," Jenna said to no one in particular. "Teenagers." With that, she went after her daughter.

Aubrey fetched several paper towels and mopped up the spilled liquid. Mitch lifted Paige's plate so she could wipe under it.

Graham rose halfway, apparently debating whether to go after them. Finally, shaking his head, he took his seat again.

Geoff turned to Alex, both brows at full mast, as if saying, "Happy now?"

Happy? No. Nothing about this assignment gave her pleasure. But she had to do what she had to do, and if making an ally of that teenager helped her achieve her goal, then that's what she'd do.

Seven

S pill cleaned up, Aubrey ditched the soggy paper towels and resumed eating as a signal for the rest of them to do the same. Mitch, Geoff and Alex obliged, but Graham kept glancing every so often at the door to check whether mother and daughter were coming back. Muffled sounds came from the living room, punctuated at times by an increase in volume that immediately drifted off.

"I never meant to set this in motion, Gray," Geoff said. "It was an innocent question, meant to stimulate conversation."

Maybe Geoff hadn't meant to cause Paige's strong reaction, but he'd accomplished Alex's objective. He'd raised the topic of the tour.

"It's okay, bro. Happens every so often, although this is the first time in months it's been about the tour. Paige is no longer the precocious kid who listens at doors, but her teenage hormones flare up occasionally. You just witnessed one of those explosions."

"Poor Jenna," Geoff returned.

Mitch leaned into Aubrey. "I'm proud of you, babe. You didn't jump into the fray. You let your sister handle this on her own."

She released a muted chuckle. "To tell the truth, I didn't get a chance. It all went so fast."

Graham pushed away from the table. "I'll check on them. They've been away longer than it usually takes to settle these outbursts."

"Go back to your meal, everyone," Mitch said. "We can't help them, and those mashed potatoes will congeal if we don't hit them soon."

They ate in silence for a couple minutes, the only sounds those of silverware clanking against their plates.

"This is crazy." Mitch released a frustrated breath and set down his fork and knife. "No need for us to act like we're in church. Let's resume answering Alex's question about what we're each up to. Although I guess that just leaves me, at the moment." He directed his gaze at Alex. "I'm working full time with my mentor and now partner in a local law firm. It's taken months to complete the transition, while I've been here part time bringing our new guy, Don Jensen, up to speed as our mechanic, which I've been the last three years."

"You're an attorney who's worked as a mechanic?" Her dad had only briefed her on the legal aspect of Mitch's background.

Mitch exchanged glances with Geoff. Geoff answered for him. "Mitch gave up sitting for the bar and practicing law our first few years in the business as his way of paying us back for handling his college bills. If it hadn't been for Aubrey here"—he shifted his attention to her stepsister—"it would have been some time before Gray and I figured out the sacrifice he'd made."

Alex put down her fork, attempted to absorb Geoff's statement. "You did that for your brothers?"

Mitch focused on his food. "I never would have finished law school had they not helped. We inherited a pile of bills from our dad's ill-fated RV business, bless his heart. When I graduated from law school, I joined the guys in this company."

"You never sat for the bar?"

"This past winter," he replied.

Aubrey squeezed him. "And passed on his first try."

"Thanks, babe."

Aubrey hugged him again. "I'm proud of you, you big lug."

Mitch's eyes glowed, obviously proud of his accomplishment and pleased at his woman's admiration.

"Congratulations, then." Alex meant it. These brothers helped each other, and in so doing, seemed to share something she'd never experienced and probably never would if her stepsisters discovered her real reason for being here. "So you're no longer working for the company?"

"I'm still one-third owner and do the legal work. And every so often Don needs another pair of hands to help him."

"The plan was for Mitch to hand over his mechanic duties to Graham, but now that he's gotten involved doing sets for the local theater group, whatever time he can spare for the company goes into the rehab planning," Aubrey added.

"Graham's involved in local theater?" Alex asked. Her dad would be interested in this news.

"He's an architect by training, you know?" Geoff spoke up. "Customizing coaches isn't really a full-time job, at least until we're doing more business. His goal is to design auditoriums and stages, so he's starting small. Getting to know the ropes as well as the people in the community who can help him."

"That's ... fascinating."

"Yeah, well, the rest of the story is really Gray's to tell," Mitch said.

Graham reentered the kitchen. "Did I hear my name?"

"We were giving Alex the headline version of your new career," Geoff explained.

Graham turned to Alex. "Ah, well, a subject I love to expound upon, but not right now. I think it's best if the three of us make it an early evening. Sorry to cut out like this, but Jenna and Paige are involved in a deep mother-daughter discussion that shouldn't be interrupted."

"We understand," Aubrey said. "I'll wrap up some of this food for you. We have more than enough."

Graham held up a hand. "Don't go to the trouble. We've got plenty at home."

"No problem." Mitch went to the cabinets and removed paper plates and aluminum foil. Within a few minutes, Graham had meals for three packed away in the discarded Halpern's bag.

"Thanks, guys. We'll do this again soon. Maybe send Paige to a movie with friends."

And then they were once again four.

Mitch turned to the other three. "That was fun. What have you planned for the rest of the evening, bro?"

"How about dessert and coffee? I couldn't possibly come up with anything more entertaining than the opening act."

"How about you, Alex?" Aubrey asked. "We've all shared what's going on in our lives. Now it's your turn."

Crap. She hoped they hadn't noticed how she was flying under the radar. "Not much, other than this visit to the Midwest."

Aubrey eyed her. "That in itself needs further explanation."

Alex shot a pleading look at Geoff, but he rose and cleared away plates. "Let's load all this in the dishwasher and then have our cupcakes and coffee in the living room."

At least he'd given her time to prepare her story. She picked up her own plate and took it to the sink.

In the living room, she settled into one of the easy chairs. The room was quite comfy and attractive with cream-colored walls with touches of red and brown for accent. Perhaps she could forestall the inquisition if she got them talking about their furnishings. "I was expecting a man cave. This definitely is not."

"Thanks to your stepsister," Mitch said. "The guys and I couldn't afford much when we first converted this second floor to two apartments, so we settled for odds and ends that friends donated or what we could find at garage sales. It was a hodge-podge of styles and pretty uncomfortable."

"I really like what you've done, Aubrey." She could butter up her stepsister and actually mean it.

"Thanks. It took a while to come together, because I picked things up as I shopped at various warehouses for my coach projects."

End of conversation. Silence.

"Did you do Geoff's apartment downstairs?"

"Still on my to-do list. It's such a limited space, we found him the necessities and left it at that for now."

Alex nodded, waited for Geoff to jump in and defend himself. But he didn't.

"So, Alex, back to my question," Aubrey said. "I know you're a talent manager out in L.A., but what do you do, who do you represent?"

Okay, she could get through this. Skim over the details. "Celebrities deliver the talent. Whether it be on TV or film or in the music industry. Their job is to concentrate on maximizing their performance. My job is to see that the other aspects of their career— promotion, appearance, finances, career direction—are addressed so the celebrity doesn't have to worry about them."

"You set up appearances for them on talk shows? Things like that?" Mitch asked.

"If they have the budget, we contract for a publicist. If not, then yes, I handle it or work with their agent."

"Sounds like a lot of work, although I bet you get to rub elbows with a lot of famous people," Mitch added.

"Not as much as you'd think. Mainly, I deal with the other people who work with celebrities."

"Tell us about your clients, or is that confidential?" Aubrey said.

"You may know about one, because my dad announced her name to everyone when Jenna and Graham brought Jenna's motor coach to California last year. My client is Loretta Kinsolver, the country music star."

"Loretta Kinsolver, huh?" Mitch seemed surprised. "She's really come up in the world the last few years. That because of you?"

"Loretta's really talented. I'm mainly in the background, helping her strategize her career moves. As her star has risen, we've brought more people on board to augment her image. Like a record producer who not only helps her pick her music but also works with her label to get her the kind of musical support she needs."

"Loretta Kinsolver? Where have I heard that name before?" Aubrey tapped a finger on her chin.

"You probably heard her on the radio or some talk show, babe."

"No. I think it was Jenna who mentioned her."

"Probably like Alex said, her dad announced the name of her client when Jenna was in California last summer," Mitch said.

Aubrey clapped her hands. "I know! She's the one who received Jenna's costumes last summer. They had the same designer, and somehow their orders got mixed up. I remember it clearly because it was the day I first arrived here. Jenna had forgotten to let you guys know about me. The costumes were all she could talk about when I called to hassle her for not warning you."

Those damn costumes. They'd turned Loretta against Jenna. "I was on the other end of that mix-up. Spent several days tracking down the right shipment."

"That's one of your jobs? Sorting out messes?" Aubrey asked.

Alex thought about it a moment. What did she do exactly? "Guess you could say that, sorting out messes and creating messes for others. Both under the umbrella of making things happen for my clients. The things they want to happen, obviously."

"Who are your other clients?" Mitch asked. "Are you able to say?"

"Not really, although I can describe a couple in broad terms." She had only two other clients, but she decided to keep that number indeterminate. "One wants a big-time food show, even though she has very little experience as a chef. The other is a bit of a lech who wants national exposure, even though no one wants him due to his reputation."

"Wow," Aubrey said. "Sounds challenging."

"Speaking of which, I have some late-night emails to send to keep my children happy. Do you need help cleaning up in the kitchen?"

"All taken care of," Aubrey told her. "There wasn't much to do, except load the dishwasher."

Geoff walked her to her room, all of ten feet away. "I have a busy day tomorrow, and tomorrow night's my dinner with Eileen. So I probably won't see you until we leave early Saturday morning. Meet you in the parking lot out back."

Alex said good night and entered her new room. She leaned against the door, took in her latest temporary home. Huge bed. Plenty of room to sleep on one side and use the other for a makeshift desk. A couple of easy chairs. A bare-bones desk in the corner she could use to apply her makeup.

First item of business: change into something more comfortable for the next few hours of work. She hadn't been in touch with her charges in the last day or so. More to the point, she needed to formulate action plans for Gaylord and Tyne. Something that moved them at least one step ahead in their career aspirations, as unrealistic as they were.

Tyne's should be the easier of the two impossible goals. After all, unlike the aging soap star, she hadn't offended anyone else in the business. Yet. Except Alex. Tyne wanted to cook for the camera. On her own terms, of course, which meant she wanted to head right up to the top kitchen. Twin tasks with this one: first, create some buzz for Tyne herself; and second, much more difficult, convince Tyne she might have to cross first, second and third bases before hitting home.

Now into his sixties but still retaining a healthy mane of silver hair, Gaylord had aged well. His ego convinced him all he had to do was appear on a late night talk show and he could revive a career whose pulse had just about stopped. After he'd come on to the cohost of the show in question, he'd been severely chastised by the executive producer of his show, but for reasons no one could fathom, he had not been fired. Rather than reform his behavior, her client had interpreted the outcome of the incident as validation of his staying power on the show. These days, though confined to secondary story lines, he was striving for one more run at the big time.

A quick check of her phone clock showed it to be nine twenty. Two hours earlier in California. Tyne first. "How's it going?" she asked when her client came on the phone.

"It's about time you called. I've been sitting here all week waiting for something to pop. Please tell me you've got something lined up for me."

"Back up. Tell me what you've been doing while you've been sitting around. I sent you a prelaunch plan. You were to set up a website as well as get more involved in social media and develop a treatment for the kind of show you want to do. What progress have you made?" She'd bet money Tyne had done nothing.

How was she going to convince the woman she had to do some of the work?

The wannabe chef didn't say anything for a few beats. "I'm, uh, working on them."

"What does that mean?"

"Get real, Alexandra, where is any of that going to get me?"

"We've been through this before, Tyne. Even the best chef needs fans who spread the word about their food. That doesn't happen in a vacuum. These days, you've got to generate buzz about yourself. That's where social media come in."

"But I'm no techie. How am I supposed to create a website on my own? Isn't that something you could do for me?"

"Content, Tyne. I can't do anything to help you until you decide what you want your website to say."

"But, Alex—"

"Did you at least check out the list of other food websites I sent you? Don't copy them, but they should give you an idea what other chefs think is important to emphasize about their food concepts."

"But—"

"Complete just that one step in the next few days."

She said good night and signed off before her client realized Alex had placed the burden back on her. The woman wasn't going anywhere until she took stock of who she was as a chef and where she wanted to go with her career. Of course, that meant little money coming in for Alex, too, until Tyne got her act together.

She lay back on the bed, gazed at the ceiling, wondered how much longer she would be able to keep up this farce of a career. Did she really care if Tyne ever got her stuff together? Her lazy chef and randy soap star were just sidelines to keep Loretta from monopolizing her time. Though why she even tried, she had no idea, because Loretta demanded so much from her, there wasn't really time for other clients. Or energy.

Her phone pinged. A text. Not Loretta again. She closed her eyes for a nanosecond and prayed for strength.

—*Thanks for tonight.*—

It was from Geoff.

How had he known she needed encouragement?

Right at this moment, no less. She texted back.

Thanks for the thought. Perfect timing. Clients frustrating.

Too many irons in fire tomorrow to go out for a drink?—

Did she dare? Why not?

Maybe this weekend?

She waited. Nothing more. Oh, well. Nothing ventured … Another ping.

Great idea.

Eight

In his darkened bedroom, Geoff lay back on his bed, phone still in hand. Why had he done that? Things had been fine between Alex and him when he said good night earlier. But he hadn't been content to let it rest there. No, he had to check in with her one more time.

Why? And why had this evening seemed so different than previous family gatherings this past year? Obvious answer: Alex had replaced Eileen. Not exactly replaced. That would say she was the new lady in his life, which wasn't the case. They were business partners, of sorts. More like coconspirators. Although Alex had engineered the dinner, she'd needed him to steer the conversation around to Jenna's future plans for her coach. Which he'd done, and she'd used to her advantage.

He hadn't counted on Paige reacting so strongly that the three of them had to go off and discuss her tantrum elsewhere. The girl's feelings about her mother going on the road were still close to the surface. To her credit, Alex hadn't jumped in and suggested Jenna rent to her client instead. No, Alex had been more subtle. She'd struck pay dirt with Paige's reaction and had very sagely decided to sit back and allow the mother-daughter friction to percolate.

Maybe he wouldn't have to do anything more to further Alex's case with Jenna. Still, he didn't like the way he felt about manipulating his family. By extension, he didn't appreciate Alex putting him in this position. Truth was, though, he'd willingly put himself here. Sure, she made her proposal first, but rather than turn her down, he'd used it to negotiate her helping him with Eileen.

Eileen. Yet again he asked himself why he was hesitating to end things instead of pulling Alex, his brothers and their ladies into this ridiculous farce. Because he owed her. It kept coming back to that reason. But how much?

During the first years of his MS, he'd put any kind of social life on hold, fearing he might relapse in the middle of a date, not wanting to put himself or any woman in that situation. But last summer, he and Eileen had landed next to each other in the bleachers as they watched Gray and Mitch battle it out in a baseball game. Though aware of his disease, Eileen hadn't retreated. They'd started talking that day and had been great companions ever since. Until these last few days.

Alex. His family. Eileen. Events were coming at him so fast he felt as if he was treading water in the middle of a whirlpool. And about to go under. He was smart, adept at adjusting to changing circumstances. Normally. But he was also juggling two other larger issues—sluggish sales and his health. One current project was in the garage, and two more were lined up. But he'd picked up those sales a couple months ago. Lately, he'd been coming up dry. He'd exhausted his first and second round of cold-call contacts. Maybe two or three possibilities bore enough potential as callbacks, but he needed a different approach, had to tap new markets.

This year, his condition had presented faster and stronger than it had the last few years. Was this a sign he was moving on to the next stage of the disorder?

No wonder sleep eluded him. He had more on his plate than he'd allowed himself to realize until now. He'd been too blown away by Eileen's actions to do much but react the last few days. Tomorrow, he had to start taking charge.

"I've switched locations, Dad. Thought you should know, although my phone goes everywhere with me," Alex told her parent the next morning when she checked in with him. "I'm staying in the firehouse where Aubrey and her guy, Mitch McKenna, live."

"They've taken you in? Didn't think you were that close with your stepsisters."

"Working on it. In the meantime, I've agreed to play nurse, well, home health aide, if you want to get technical, with Mitch's brother Geoffrey. He has what appears to be a mild case of MS and hasn't been doing such a great job monitoring his condition."

"Health care? Thought you said good-bye to that life years ago. Never understood the sudden switch to talent management, but you were hell-bent to go that direction."

And if she had anything to do with it, he never would know why she gave up nursing. "I'm not spending more than fifteen minutes a day at this, but he thought it would help if I was nearby." She explained how Geoff had prevailed upon Mitch and Aubrey to let her stay in Graham's old room.

"Have you had a chance to mention my so-called foray into romantic leads?"

"First day. Laid it out to both Aubrey and Jenna. Despite their uneasy relationship with their mother, neither was ready to go to her on my behalf. Iris would be pleased, although I have no intention of telling her, and I hope you remember your promise and don't tell her either."

"No, sweetie, your secret's safe with me. Although I have to admit, ever since we cooked up this plot, I've considered actually trying it. Put myself up for just one of those leads. Or two."

"Dad, we talked about this. Your life is so much easier if you can pick and choose guest-starring roles. If you were to snag something ongoing, you'd be tied down. Right now, you've got all the flexibility in the world."

"Sometimes all the flexibility in the world gets rather boring, Alex."

Ominous statement. Not at all like her generally positive father. "Everything okay, Dad?"

"Your old dad's just feeling sorry for himself. Since Aubrey and Jenna have been gone, Iris has thrown herself into one activity after another. Can't say she's enjoying any of them, but she's gone a lot. You'd think a guy would relish all the quiet, but after a while, even all that downtime can get old."

"Let's have lunch when I get back. We'll talk about that downtime."

"Hey, kid, I wasn't trolling for sympathy. Well, maybe a little. Don't worry about me, though. You've got enough on your mind."

That she did. She'd check back with him in a few days, see if his outlook was any more hopeful. Maybe her cover story about her dad wasn't so far off, after all.

"THEY SAY the fish is pretty good here. Especially the salmon." Geoff pretended to scan his menu while he surreptitiously observed Eileen's reaction to his choice of restaurant. Extra Innings made its reputation on its down-home cuisine and ballpark location. He'd never eaten here himself but had read good reviews online, reviews that warned it wasn't much for ambience, although the service was good.

"Salmon? Actually, I was thinking more about steak tonight. It appears there are only three selections in that category."

"How about beef stroganoff or lasagna instead?" He kept his tone helpful.

She continued to study the menu, every so often releasing an audible sigh. At length, she chose salmon but not before quizzing the waiter about the origin and freshness of the fish as well as how it was prepared.

Had she always been this picky about her food? In all fairness, she'd been expecting a much fancier place. She was disappointed.

Probably had a right to be. Maybe he shouldn't have followed through on Alex's advice. On the other hand, what had happened to Eileen, the good sport who took things in stride?

"How's your wine?" he asked to make conversation.

She brought the glass close to her eyes and stared at the contents. "At least there's nothing floating in it."

"That bad, huh?"

"Tasteless, actually. What can you expect from a box wine?"

Ouch! "I like some box wines. They've gotten a bad rep."

"Perhaps they've been aging this particular box beyond its time."

He motioned the waiter to their table. "The lady's wine appears to have gone flat. Have you got something better behind the bar?"

"Never mind. I'll have water."

The waiter eyed Geoff, who nodded him off. Might as well get the rest of this show underway. He reached inside his sports jacket, pulled out a narrow package, and placed it to the side of her plate. "Happy Birthday."

Her eyes widened as she spotted her gift. "Ooh, what's this?"

"You didn't like the boxed wine. Maybe you'll like this box better."

There was nothing delicate in the way she ripped into the present. She didn't even glance at the note he'd carefully crafted: "Thought this would look great on you."

Meanwhile, Geoff sat back and waited. Not for long.

Eileen lifted the top of the box, separated the tissue paper, and … slumped in her seat. She sat forward almost at once, but her reaction was clearly evident. "A, a neck scarf. How … nice."

"Thought it would go well with all those suits you wear to work."

She removed the item from the box, although she didn't wrap it around her neck. Instead, she made a show of examining the pattern and feeling the fabric, but it was obvious she was seeking the label. Her lips parted briefly. "Oh, Geoff, this is such an expensive brand."

"Wanted to give you something special for your big day."

She continued to turn the fabric one way, then another, still without placing it around her neck.

"Put it on," he urged. "I want to see how it looks."

She pursed her lips, lifted the accessory over her head, and drew it together under her chin, all without actually wrapping it around her neck.

How long would it take her to exchange it tomorrow? Okay by him. She should get something she really liked. He didn't wish her ill. Just out of his life without having to hurt her.

"Hey, a perfect match for your eyes." He settled back, folded his hands, and in general, offered a broad smile, as if completely pleased with his selection. In reality, Alex had done a great job of finding something completely wrong for Eileen's coloring.

"Really?" Her tone was incredulous.

"You don't think so?"

"It's your opinion that counts."

Could she be any clearer about what she thought of the gift?

She made a show of carefully folding the neckwear exactly as she'd found it in the box, tucked it back inside the tissue. "I actually expected a gift certificate of some sort, knowing how much you hate shopping."

"For you, I made the effort."

She nodded. "Uh-huh? Did you have help?"

He returned an innocent expression. "From the store clerk."

"Not what I meant. I thought perhaps your new health aide went with you."

"Alex? No. She may have provided a few suggestions ..." He let his explanation trail off.

"Really? As to color? Pattern?"

Had to hand it to Alex. She'd called this perfectly. The question now was how seriously Eileen would take this.

"She's been busy moving into the firehouse," he said. Coup de grâce.

Eileen dropped the box onto the table. "She's moved in with you?"

"With me? No. Why would you think that?"

"Why wouldn't I? She seems to be there quite a lot these days."

"Alex moved into Gray's old room. Temporarily. She's not going to be in town long. But it didn't make sense for her to spend good money for a motel room when she could be getting better acquainted with her stepsister instead."

"Getting acquainted with Aubrey? That's why she moved in?"

"Have to admit, it's a lot more convenient for her to check in with me daily if she's on the premises. Why'd you think she moved in with me? There's no room for two people. I told you the same when you arrived with your suitcase earlier in the week."

"I, uh, right. Things aren't getting cozy between the two of you, even though you're going with her to see this new client?"

Important not to answer her directly. Let her speculate. Let her jump to the wrong conclusion. "I told you. Alex needed someone who's familiar with the state to help her find the little burg where this young singer lives."

Their meal arrived. He dug into his beef stroganoff.

Eileen stared at her plate.

"What's wrong? You're not eating," he said.

She picked up her fork, took one bite, and put the fork down. "I'm sorry. I seem to have lost my appetite."

"Are you sick?"

She shook her head. "I just … I … could we just go?"

The waiter, who'd hovered to check on their meal, came immediately. "Is there a problem?"

"Think we're going to skip dinner tonight. Could you get me the bill?"

He paid for their meal, and they left, without even waiting to have their meals boxed up. His phone rang as they stepped outside, Alex's call telling him they'd have to leave early in the morning. No longer necessary. He let it go to voicemail.

In the car, he adopted his most conscientious manner. "I'll take you home. You probably just need rest and your mom's attention."

Eileen didn't say anything during their ten-minute ride. After they pulled up at her mother's house, she turned to him. "Is there something you want to say to me, Geoff?"

He resisted the temptation to end this once and for all and stuck to his resolution to let her do the dumping. "Happy Birthday tomorrow, Eileen. Have a good one." He smiled as if nothing was amiss.

"Don't worry about walking me to the door. I'm fine." She scooted out but didn't immediately close the door. Instead, she stared at him for what seemed like eons. "Have a good trip," she finally said.

Nine

At ten minutes after seven the next morning, Geoff stuck his duffle bag in the backseat of Alex's rental car, where it joined her own small bag, borrowed from Aubrey, and her computer bag. He slipped into the passenger side of the front seat.

"I'm impressed. I didn't take you for an early riser," she said.

He thumped his chest. "You insult me."

"Sorry."

"I'm usually up by seven thirty."

"Oh, well, I stand corrected. I've set the GPS, but I'll feel a lot more secure having you along to navigate."

He adjusted the seat, slid it back to accommodate his length. "I don't get it. You drive around L.A. all the time. The only places we might see traffic like you're used to would be in Des Moines and Sioux City."

"I can deal with traffic. It's the geography that scares me."

"You're kidding. It's not like you'll be driving through high mountains or trying to stay awake on straight desert stretches. This is Iowa. Flat at times, rolling prairie otherwise. Mostly fields."

"And livestock. Right?"

"Well, sure. Cattle and hogs. But they're usually way back from the road, behind wire fences."

"Oh. Good." She twisted to face him momentarily.

"Promise you won't laugh."

"Okay. I won't laugh. What's got you spooked?"

"Iowans."

He jerked forward. "You're kidding?"

"You said you wouldn't laugh."

"I'm not. I'm amazed. You've been in the state almost a week. You've never shown the least bit of hesitation or trepidation the whole time. Why now?"

"I'm not accustomed to niceness. Angelinos aren't necessarily mean and malevolent, but they're usually in a rush to get somewhere since the area's so spread out. They don't take much time with each other. Not so much the case here."

"Never noticed."

"But as nice as everyone comes across, a lot of people I've met so far demonstrate a sort of boys' club mentality. If you weren't born here, you're an outsider."

"Aubrey's never mentioned it."

"Aubrey's been pretty much into Mitch since she's been here."

"Good point."

"So you needed a, what, a translator?"

She hadn't planned to go there, let him in on her weak spot. But it was true. These people scared the hell out of her. "Yeah. How 'bout that? My tough façade

doesn't work here. Plus, I wanted company."

"I'm flattered."

"Don't be. Who else was there?"

"Won't let that discourage me. You gave me an excuse to skip Eileen's big birthday weekend."

"How'd your early birthday dinner go last night? I called to tell you we'd have to leave earlier than planned, but you didn't answer."

"From my perspective, couldn't have gone better. We were already leaving the restaurant when you called. Eileen was that disillusioned. I didn't see a need to tell her our departure time had been changed."

She almost felt sorry for the woman. Almost.

He gave Alex a blow-by-blow account of the gift opening. "She wasn't even that subtle checking the label to see how expensive it was."

"I spent everything you gave me."

"Made me cringe, spending that much on a scarf. She'll probably hit the store as soon as it opens this morning to exchange the thing for store credit. You should've seen how carefully she refolded it so they'd take it back. Before she got out of the car, she hesitated, like she was expecting me to call it quits there and then. Even if I'd decided I'd have to be the one to do it, I wasn't going to end things just before her birthday."

"Then you're getting close. Maybe she'll call while you're on the road and do it?"

They drove in silence for a few minutes, Geoff apparently processing her comment. "Told her about your moving in too."

"Oh? Bet that went over well."

"Let's just say she wasn't pleased." They passed a road sign. They were approaching their turn-off. "Keep going on US 34 through Mount Pleasant."

"But my GPS says to turn onto 218 North."

"We can come back that way. I want to go up through Pella."

"Pella? What's there?"

"Breakfast goodies. Some great bakeries in that town."

She gave him a dubious look but continued on rather than turning as her GPS had indicated. "We're going out of our way to appease your appetite?"

"No, we're taking an alternate route."

"Just so we're not late reaching our destination."

"Not to worry. We got a great head start. We'll have plenty of time. Maybe even to eat inside one of those sugar heavens rather than mess up your car."

"Maybe you. I'm not so much into doughnuts."

"Uh-huh. We'll see." He licked his lips. "Personally, I can't wait."

She didn't hear his next words. She was still reacting to the lip action. Had he done that intentionally, just to see what she'd do? She gripped the steering wheel tighter, stared ahead and focused on the surrounding landscape while she wondered why just that one gesture had her lower parts clenching.

Conversation drifted off. Geoff pulled out his notebook computer and concentrated on reviewing some document. After about ten minutes, he shut the lid.

"Done?"

"Just getting started. Problem is, I'm stumped."

"Want to bounce whatever it is off me? According to your earlier statement, we have plenty of time."

He rubbed his chin, ran a hand through his hair, then shifted in his seat. "Guess it couldn't hurt. I'm working on a list of new leads. The well seems to have run dry."

"I thought you were such a hotshot salesman. What's the problem?"

"I'm good at sales. And that's not just ego talking. It's my track record. But my skill set doesn't kick in until I've got a prospect to go after. This part of the job requires someone who's a good researcher."

"Would it be a breach of confidentiality to tell me who all you've contacted?"

"Can't give you names, but I can describe the types of people and organizations I've approached." He listed professional sports franchises, athletes and local and regional companies.

"Logical targets. So tell me about your pitch."

"I start with our introductory brochure, along with a cover letter. A few weeks later, I call. Invite them to town to inspect a current project."

"What percent actually come for a tour?"

"I'll bet over the last year I've sent at least a hundred brochures. Only four showed any interest in the tour. Three actually came."

Discouraging numbers. "Did you consider those returns good?"

"Hell, no!. During these first years of operation, we've mainly dealt with people who either contacted us or were referred. We've pretty much exhausted that source, which is why I'm making a concerted effort to revise my methods."

Concerted? Sounded like a shotgun approach. She didn't want to insult him. They still had the rest of the trip ahead. Had to approach this carefully.

Before she could come up with a response, he pointed to the sign ahead. "We're closing in on Pella."

She was struck immediately by the town's appearance. Everything —the yards, the houses, the streets—screamed spic-and-span. The closer they got to the downtown area, the more signs of the small town's Dutch heritage appeared. Many of the houses had incorporated the Dutch stair-step-façade motif.

"Nice town."

"This place is the model of neat and clean as well as the early home of Wyatt Earp."

She shot him a glance. "No kidding?"

"Burlington's famous, too. William Frawley. He played Fred Mertz on *I Love Lucy*. The guy who wrote 'Fly Me to the Moon,' Bart Howard, was also born there."

"I'm impressed."

"A lot of famous people were born in this state. Since we've got some of the world's most fertile soil, it's no wonder we grow great people."

"You're quite the spokesperson for the state. Maybe you should switch careers like your brothers have."

He released a sigh. "Exactly why I have to stay where I am. Some-one's got to keep an eye on things full time."

Since it was late May and breakfast time on a Saturday morning, they had to wait in a long line of pastry lovers once they arrived at the bakery. Not a problem for Alex, who hadn't been expecting so many goodies from which to choose.

Geoff leaned down. "No matter what else you select, we each have to get a Dutch letter, their specialty. Your taste buds will never be the same."

"I'll keep that in mind," she said, since it was clear Geoff was a fan of these pastries.

Besides the Dutch letters and coffee, Alex ordered a cream horn and Geoff chose a giant cinnamon roll. He also bought a bag of cookies for the rest of the trip.

They wandered over to the town square and found a park bench from which to devour their goodies. Dominating the landscape were two tall white pillars atop an outdoor stage joined at the top by what appeared to be a Dutch emblem. A nearby sign designated it as the Tulip Toran. Remains of tulips of many colors surrounded them.

Geoff pointed out a huge windmill about a block away. "Largest operating windmill in the country. Two weeks ago, we wouldn't have been able to get through town because of the annual tulip festival. About this time of morning, there would've been a parade of town residents marching down the street in wooden shoes. Klompen."

"Wooden shoes. Of course, it wouldn't officially be Dutch if they weren't featured. You know, I think there's a place in California a little like this. I visited there once. Solvang. No, wait. It's Danish."

Although her Dutch letter in the shape of an *S* appeared enticing, she saved it for later in the day. Perhaps she'd be able to eat it to celebrate signing a new client, if she decided that's what she wanted.

"Hold up," Geoff said after they'd discarded their trash. He bent and swiped the sides of her mouth with an index finger, his coffee-laced breath tickling her face, but his touch sending a shiver down her chest. "How much of that cream horn made it into your mouth? You've got most of the powdered sugar on your face."

The same involuntary reaction she'd had earlier when he licked his lips assaulted her again. What was up with her? This was a pretend relationship. She wasn't supposed to have feelings for this man. At least not feelings like this.

Geoff backed up a step. "Sorry. Did I startle you?"

"Uh, yeah." One way of describing her reaction.

He apparently remained unaffected by their contact as he continued on to where the car was parked across the street. He was no sooner inside than he jumped out again. "Hold on. I'll be right back."

What? He needed more sweets? Was that good for his condition? Of course not. All of those carbs wouldn't be good for anyone, healthy or not.

Geoff returned in five minutes, carrying a small brown bag. "Here you go. Something to remind you of Pella."

Now he was giving her gifts? She reached for the package, but he continued to hold it. "Not so fast. Let's wait 'til later. It'll mean more then."

Intrigued, she didn't question his motives but instead glanced at the car clock. Time to hit the road.

"Tell me what you were trying so hard not to say before we hit town."

He could read minds, too? She attempted to stall. "Refresh my memory. I'm still on a sugar high."

"My approach to generating clients stinks. You probably wouldn't have put it quite like that, but that's the gist."

How much farther to their next stop? She really didn't want to burst his bubble, although from the sounds of it, he'd already pricked it himself. Reluctantly, she proceeded, though she tried to express her concerns with diplomacy. "Let's talk goals first. How many annual customizations are you shooting for?

"Haven't set a number. So far, we've taken on as many as we could get as fast as we got them."

No goals. Not good. But rather than lecture him on the point, she asked another question. "How many coaches can your company handle at a time?"

"Optimum, four. Two in the garage and two parked out back, although it would be more efficient to work on just the two inside."

"Next question, how long does this customization process usually take?"

He considered, ticked something off on his fingers. "Varies. As brief as a couple weeks if they don't want major changes, and up to two months if the changes are major and involve special orders."

"Say the average conversion time is five weeks, a midrange between the two- and eight- week time periods you cited. That would allow for about ten five-week periods in a year and two weeks for either spillover or shutdown to regroup. Ten times two coaches at a time would be a possible twenty coaches per year as the optimum schedule you described."

He sat forward, rubbed his hands together. "Wow! That's way more than we've handled in total so far."

"My point. Now that the company is up and running and you and your brothers have proven its viability, it's time to move into the growth phase." God, was that her speaking? She'd had one business course in college. Had she actually learned something? "If you weren't aware you've reached that stage in the cycle of a business, you sensed it intuitively."

"You really think we could do twenty a year?"

"Just projecting based on your estimates. Depends on how accurate they are. But when you get back, you can check your numbers and revise the projection accordingly."

Geoff was still for several minutes. At one point, he dug into the bag of cookies, as if consuming more sugar would clarify his thinking. "I knew all that, although it's been a while since I've thought of increasing business in those terms," he said at length. "Thanks for getting me back to the basics."

Yay! She'd helped and not offended. However, according to the road sign she'd just seen, they still had another twenty-five miles to go until they reached Des Moines. She had to come up with something else to talk about before she started thinking about his touch again.

"I suppose you have our lunch stop planned already?"

He lifted a brow. "Hungry so soon?"

"Gosh, no. Just curious. We're supposed to be taking I-80 west once we reach Des Moines. Thought I should ask now if there's another detour ahead."

"We didn't detour. We simply took another route. But once we reach the interstate, we'll stay on it so we get there on time. Tomorrow, when we return, I hope you'll let me show you some of the back roads."

There was more behind her tour guide's proposal than simply the desire to show off his state. "Do you miss traveling?"

He shifted position to stare out his window. "At times. I miss witnessing seasonal change happening around me day by day. I took for granted seeing the fields sprout, the corn shoot up, the leaves turn. Even the snow was a comfort, until it made the roads slick or got too high."

"I assumed you were happy to get off the road. Didn't realize you might miss it."

"I also liked the independence."

"Didn't you have certain clients to visit at set times? Quotas to meet?"

"Sure, but within those parameters, I was my own man."

Interesting. She'd thought he was his own man at McKenna Custom Coaches. "Don't you have that now?"

"It would appear that way, but not really. Once the client signs on the dotted line, Gray picks up the client-liaison role from there. Mitch handles all the legal issues, except in his mind that also covers management and fiscal issues. I'm relegated to the administrative stuff, mainly following through on what the other two have set in motion."

An undercurrent of dissatisfaction? "Even though you're there full time and they're not?"

"Probably why. I've, uh, been absorbing more and more of their unwanted duties as they've been out of the firehouse more frequently. It's not easy to feel you're on your own when you're staring at someone else's to-do list."

Who'd have thought it? A road trip where the toughest challenge she'd imagined to be finding the small town where her potential client lived had now taken on consideration of one man's happiness. She couldn't catch a break with whatever topic she chose.

But she was in there now. Couldn't turn off this stream until she helped him find some kind of resolution. "Stupid question, Geoff, but why do you accept their to-do lists?"

He swiveled around to stare at her, as if she'd told him she was dumping him at the next cornfield. "I can't exactly refuse."

"Because—"

"Because … well … because if I don't, they can no longer do their full-time jobs. Someone had to pick up the slack."

"That someone being you? Why not Aubrey? Or your new mechanic? Or even someone new you hire as your assistant?"

He appeared to think through her questions before answering. "Aubrey would have balked. She's a bit of a fixer. She suggests, she doesn't follow through. The new mechanic is a nice guy. Too nice. He'd crumple if asked to hassle a supplier. And an assistant? Great idea, but no budget. But I'll stick that one in my file of dreams."

"So they, and you, just assume you'll pick up the slack? I can understand why they might be that obtuse, but why you? You don't strike me as the kind of guy who'd be quiet when it comes to defending your best interests."

He faced the window again. "We should be reaching the outskirts of Des Moines in a few minutes. We'll come in on the east side. It'll meet up with I-235, which we'll take through the city to the West Mixmaster, where we'll turn onto I-80."

Changing the subject. She'd hit a nerve. No problem. She'd put this topic as well as the subject of generating new clients on hold. She had enough on her own mind, anyhow, framing her pitch to Allison Corley, who she'd meet in just a few hours.

Ten

As Geoff had promised, traffic picked up as soon as Alex pulled onto the freeway. Late morning on a Saturday in the state capital. While she concentrated on her lane, he stared out the window. This trip was turning out totally different than he'd imagined when he'd invited himself along. Alex was brash, sophisticated, into the moment. At least that's who he'd told himself she was. But in the short period of their forced companionship today, she'd proved she had much more substance than he'd credited her.

For months, his life had been filled with cold calls and internet searches, schmoozing, cajoling, purring, whatever it took to sell their product. In less than half an hour, attempting to answer her questions, he'd discovered he'd been doing it all wrong. He was bummed and excited at the same time. Didn't really know how to change, but Alex had some great ideas. For some reason, though, she'd pulled back, changed the topic. Had he been so far afield in his approach she didn't think he'd get it, even if she spelled out a new strategy?

Had he overstepped when he brushed the powdered sugar from her mouth? It had just been one friend helping another, right? Although he hadn't expected the brief contact to send such shock waves through his body.

To end his speculation, he reached for his phone to check messages. Two from Eileen. One last night, thanking him in a round-about way for her birthday dinner and gift. The other had been sent this morning, wishing him a speedy and successful trip and suggesting they get together for dinner at her mother's on Monday night. Damn! She wasn't giving up. Wanted to be in his thoughts, even if only in text messages.

Before he had time to reframe his mind into a more positive outlook, another text caught his attention. Pam Sutton.

Kyle continuing to fade. Next step: hospice.

Already? They knew this was coming, but so fast? Without real-izing he was going to do it, he said a silent prayer. *Please, God. If this is his time, make it painless.*

"Geoff? Bad news? Those wrinkle lines across your forehead don't look good."

"Huh? Oh, yeah. No way to hide it, I guess. A friend of mine is fail-ing. A trip to a hospice isn't far off."

She twisted her head in his direction. Just briefly. Then returned her gaze to the road, where traffic was increasing. "I'm so sorry. Do you want to turn around and go see him or her before, uh …"

"Thanks for the offer. No. I can't do anything more for him at this point. I said my good-byes last week."

They each pursued their own counsel a bit. "Do you want to talk about it?" Alex said.

"Not really. It's just …"

"Just … what, Geoff?"

"Every time I let myself be fooled into thinking I can live a normal life with this condition, something pulls me up short. My friend and I both have MS, only that's where the similarity ends. At least so far. He's had one problem after another with his condition. Had to quit his job and go on disability over a year ago as his organs began to go. Meanwhile, other than an occasional setback when I don't pay enough attention to my health, I've continued to live a fairly normal life."

She didn't reply immediately. "That happens, doesn't it? The condition differs considerably from one person to the next?"

"Yeah. Our situations sure make that point."

"And you feel guilty because you're not suffering like he has." It wasn't a question. It was a statement, spoken with quiet authority.

"He's dying, Alex. Within days. And I'm still here."

"Have you ever told him how you feel?"

"Not in so many words. But he knows just the same. That's what he was trying to tell me when I last saw him. That he holds nothing against me. He's made peace with his situation."

"And he wanted you to make peace with yours?"

"Okay if we table this discussion the rest of the trip? I need time to digest this news, and I don't want to spoil things for you. You need to concentrate on this possible client."

She reached over and squeezed his hand. "Don't worry about me. I'll work this out, one way or another. If you receive any worse news while we're on the road, we'll turn around immediately and go back. Okay? This potential client isn't as important as your friend."

He cleared his throat. "Thanks." The word was garbled, but she'd know what he meant. They crossed the Des Moines River.

"Surely, this isn't a branch of the Mississippi?" Alex asked, the first to speak in minutes. "The Mississippi's on the other side of the state. Could be the Missouri. No, that's on the state's western border."

"Des Moines."

"I know where we are. What was that river?"

"The Des Moines River, Alex. It runs into the Raccoon south of the bridge we just crossed."

"Oh."

"No flooding here. They didn't receive as much snow in this area, and whatever they did get has probably drained off already and is now downriver."

"Will that be the case the rest of the way? Are there more swollen rivers in our path?"

"I checked the road reports yesterday. Everything's fine."

"Except when you get a hankering for some food item."

"Told you. We're good the rest of the day, except for finding lunch."

"It's barely ten o'clock."

"Aren't you getting hungry?"

She stole a glance his direction. "You're kidding, right?"

"Eyes on the road, Appleby. We're about to head onto I-80. Move over a lane."

"Mighty directive over there, McKenna."

"Yeah, well, didn't want to wind up in Minneapolis, which is where you'd be heading if you stayed in that lane."

She shifted lanes and went about a mile until the next exit, where she pulled off and drove into a fast food place.

"Hey, I was kidding about being hungry."

She turned off the ignition and twisted to face him. "Thought you might want to take the wheel for a while. Are you prohibited from driving on the interstate?"

He shook his head. "My decision after I ran off the road a few years back. Didn't want to take any more chances with my life or anyone else unfortunate enough to be on the road when I was."

"But I'm here to keep your eyes on the road. Why not drive the next fifty miles or so?"

Why was she doing this? "You trust me?"

She lifted her hands, spread them. "Wouldn't have offered otherwise. Besides, I could use a break, and I'd like to take in the landscape and not have to concentrate on the road."

He jumped out of the car, skidded across the back and flung open the driver's door before she could rescind her offer. "Okay. Just fifty miles. No more."

Alex nudged his shoulder. "I noted the number of miles on the odometer, McKenna." She stepped out of the car and whipped around to the passenger side.

As soon as he pulled off the entrance ramp and onto the interstate, he pushed the car up to seventy. Probably should've given himself a chance to acclimate to the higher speed, since he'd sentenced himself to town speed limits four years back, but he couldn't restrain himself. It was like he hadn't really been breathing all this time, just existing. This was fantastic.

He waited for Alex to tell him to slow down. She didn't. Instead, right elbow bent against the window, she gazed out at the passing countryside, just as she said she wanted to do. Nevertheless, he kept within the speed limit. Last thing he needed was a ticket.

Memories of his life on the road came flooding back. Mornings with the sun behind him, shedding its glow over young sprouts coming to life in the cornfields. Peaceful rainstorms that allowed him to think about his work goals. Heading for home or a motel at dusk as the world around him went progressively darker.

Though not by choice, he'd moved on to making new memories. Not bad memories, actually. Most days, he enjoyed selling customized motor coaches. But those didn't prevent him from remembering how it used to be.

The miles shot by. He'd gone at least ten of his allotted fifty before he moved into the passing lane, mainly because the vehicle in front of him was creeping along. But once he'd broken the passing barrier, he continued. He didn't take chances, though, didn't accelerate too fast, or pull in too close.

At forty-five miles, Alex turned to him, offered a sweet smile. "How's it going?"

"That code for five miles to go before I pull off the road?"

"Do you want to?"

"Hell, no! I don't want to. But that was our agreement."

"That was a suggestion only."

He shot her a quick glance. "You telling me I should keep driving?"

"Not at all. I wouldn't presume to know how you're feeling. How are you feeling, by the way?"

He cocked his head to consider. "Think you already have your answer. You just want me to say it out loud, admit it to myself."

"Deep, McKenna. Deep."

"I'm feeling better than I have in some time."

Her lips curled up. "I kinda suspected as much."

"Suspected? Hah! You made it happen. You knew I needed this."

She put a hand to her heart. "You're giving me more credit than I deserve. But thanks."

He reached fifty and continued on. Ten more miles. Then he'd do a self-check. Decide whether to relinquish the wheel. If he kept on, he'd check again at seventy-five. Or a hundred. A hundred miles. They'd almost be there by then. Good time to stop for lunch. Geez, someone would think he hadn't eaten in days the way he kept thinking about food.

Around a hundred miles, he turned onto I-29 to go north. He pulled off at the first exit and headed for a fast-food place. This had been fun. Best time he'd had in days. He sat back and slapped his thighs.

Alex returned an I-told-you-so look.

In response, without giving it further thought, he gripped her shoulders, brought her toward him and kissed her.

"That was unexpected," she said when he released her.

"For me, too. But not at all unpleasant."

She remained only inches away, her breath grazing his face. Her eyes didn't leave his. Without uttering a word, she invited him to return to the scene of the crime. So he did. Big time.

When she didn't back away, he increased the pressure on her mouth, drew her closer, his arms encasing her, his right hand massaging her back. His left hand remained at her waist, awaiting its destination.

Though spontaneous—yeah, there'd been some kind of vibes going on since Pella, but it wasn't like they'd been flirting or engaged in more serious sexual byplay—neither seemed shocked nor turned off by their actions. It was as if they'd both been waiting for some sign from the other since the day they first met.

When had he last made out in a car? Not since college. Maybe even high school. He'd forgotten how the intimacy of front seat lip-lock could give a guy such guilty pleasure. Could send his insides into overdrive, even in broad daylight.

Broad daylight. Right. *Get control of yourself, man.*

Alex beat him to the punch, shifted back in her seat. "Should I, uh, read anything more into it than a thank-you for having you drive?"

Hell if he knew what was behind it. The thought had hit him, and he acted on it. So why was he feeling so gobsmacked rather than just pleased? *Gobsmacked?* Had he ever used that term before? "Started out as pure joy. Turned into something else the second time," he said.

"I'll say. Got a name for that *something else?*"

"What do you want me to say? That I've got the hots for your body?"

One brow arched. "Do you?"

"Damned if I know. Don't suppose you'd buy that I was just bored from being confined in this car?"

"If that's what it was. I'm all for living in the moment, grabbing your pleasure as you can. But you'll let me know if you decide there was more to it than that? A girl likes to be prepared for these onslaughts." She seemed to be accepting it for what he thought it was, spontaneous combustion. So move on. "Want to eat inside or get our food to go?"

She checked the time. "Probably should eat in transit."

He didn't wait for further discussion. They changed places, and Alex took the wheel. Once back on the road, they spent the next several minutes devouring chicken sandwiches and iced tea. And some of the cookies from their bakery stop.

"You were right," she said at last, having finished her lunch and two cookies.

"Of course, I was. About what?"

"These cookies. They're great, and they do add to the trip."

He grabbed the bag and opened it. Instead of reaching for another sweet, though, he merely inhaled the bag's fragrance. "I do know my cookies. One thing I can do right."

"Fishing for reassurances?"

He considered. "Pretty needy statement, huh? By the time we're back in town, you'll probably regret letting me come along. I seem to be sharing a lot of my dirty laundry."

"So far, I'm glad you're here. I certainly haven't been bored. Plus, I've got my own dirty laundry I might be tempted to air on the return trip, but let's put those *issues* on hold until after I meet with this girl. I need to get my head ready to deal with her."

"Right. Sure. You want to go over your pitch?"

"Maybe. First, I need to talk through why I'm doing this in the first place."

He tilted his head her direction. "Why you're driving?"

"No. Why I'm seeking another client." There, she'd said it out loud, to another person. That made it real.

Geoff did a ninety-degree swivel toward her. "Understandable. Even if you've seen her videos, you need to see her perform in person before you decide whether to represent her."

"True. But not what I meant. I'm not sure I want another client."

"You're kidding. Thought you wanted to grow your business."

"Did I say that?"

"Well, no. But you seem so driven, especially to get that lease for your one client, guess I assumed."

"I am driven when it comes to my clients. Why, I swear some days I don't know, except I'm pretty good at what I do."

He didn't respond immediately, because he'd snuck another cookie. Maybe Eileen had been right to worry about his eating habits. As his so-called health aide, though her assignment was pretend, she should probably be watching what he consumed. But unless he went overboard, she'd hold back for now. He seemed to be enjoying himself. Why cut that short?

At length, he did follow up. "That why you gave up nursing, you enjoyed talent management more?"

She started to answer, then rethought her response. She might be growing to like this guy, but she wasn't ready to confide everything. "When my parents' marriage fell apart, it was public and ugly. Rumors flew about my dad forcing himself on other women. I was caught in the middle, not knowing who to believe. Just plain lost. I struggled with college a few years and then did a stint as a production assistant on a TV show. I thought I'd finally found my niche in nursing."

"Why did you change your mind?"

"Loretta prevailed upon me. First, to get a part on my old show and later to represent her."

"You gave up nursing for her?"

"Loretta can be very, uh, persuasive."

"How did she *persuade* you? Was her voice that great?"

She'd never forget that day, as much as she'd like to. Loretta had called the week before and attempted to set up a meeting. Alex had begged off. A mutual friend called next and pled Loretta's case. She'd finally relented and met Loretta at a diner not far from her small apartment. The future country star looked nothing like she did these days. Just hungry for celebrity. Hungry enough to suggest it would be a shame if Buddy's recovering career suffered yet another setback, one from which he would not recover, even with L.A.'s lenient tendency to forgive its stars.

"Actually, she wasn't singing then. She'd aimed her sights on an acting career. No stage or screen experience. Never took an acting class. Just thought she had it, and all she needed was a role and a chance."

"How long ago was that? She's been around for several years now. Singing, not acting."

Alex thought back. She'd been in her mid-twenties at the time and was now thirty-one, almost thirty-two. "Six, seven years ago. I agreed to manage her, actually acted as her agent at first also, as long as I could finish nursing school. But launching her career demanded so much of my time, I couldn't keep up. I had to leave with only six weeks to go." It had been her only option to avoid losing her mind.

He narrowed his eyes, readjusted his seat belt. "I'm getting a totally different impression of Loretta Kinsolver than your publicity machine has produced."

"I'll deny ever having told you any of this if you share what I've told you. Suffice it to say, dealing with her is not always easy."

"That the way it is with celebrities? Not the personality their promoters manufacture. Are you deliberately trying to get me off the topic of why you may not want another client?"

"My point in telling you about Loretta is to underline the time suck managing her entails." If only she could tell him how much she wanted to drop the woman as her client, but then he'd want to know why, and she couldn't get into Loretta's blackmailing efforts. "Over the past several months, I've grown weary of Loretta's demands, so I've attempted to expand my client list to replace the income I'll lose when I no longer manage her. My other clients come with their own challenges, but their fees have provided a cushion."

He rubbed his jaw, apparently processing her comments. "If that's the case, why aren't you delirious at the thought of adding another revenue source?"

"If she's the real deal, she could be just the ticket for ridding myself of Loretta. But I need to assess her in person before deciding. I want raw talent that can be readily shaped and groomed into a big-time star without the baggage my other clients have dragged with them."

"Baggage? Egos?"

"Those are just part of it. They have to be willing to work for their careers. I don't bring them on a silver platter. They have to behave themselves around other people rather than chase after every skirt."

"So rather than this girl and her parents interviewing you for the job, you're actually auditioning her?"

She fist-bumped his arm. "You catch on fast. I need your help as a second set of eyes, because I sometimes get so involved talking to them, I don't get a chance to stand back and observe. Willing to do that for me?"

"Yeah, sure, although I'm not a very good judge of raw talent."

"You deal with people all the time. You know when someone's telling the truth and when someone's handing you a line. That's what I need."

Geoff grabbed the bag of cookies. "One left. I won't feel the least bit guilty about taking it now that you've assigned me this new task. Hope my take on this girl is worth the price."

Eleven

Geoff savored the last few bites of his cookie as he considered his new assignment. He'd never been a talent scout before. Maybe he should've volunteered to stay in the car while Alex met with her prospect and parents. He didn't want to disappoint her. Too late now.

In the last half hour, he'd learned a lot more about his co-conspirator. More than he imagined she'd ever share about her dealings as a talent manager. The drive must be getting to her.

Within minutes, they turned off the interstate onto a county road that led them east through the loess hills, ancient bluffs that backboned the western border of the state.

"Could you check the note I left on the console?" Alex asked. "Mrs. Corley sent me directions to their house."

Geoff grabbed the paper. "Says here we go eight miles east on this road, which will take us through most of the town. Then we turn left on a Mulberry Road and go another two miles. When the road splits, we veer right. We pass a convenience store and then an auto repair shop, and turn right at the next road, which will be Porter Lane. Their place will be the second house on the left."

"Sounds complicated. I thought all we had to do was turn off this road and find their farm."

"From this description, I'd say they're townies."

"Oh. I just assumed everything around here was a farm."

"Snob."

"Not at all. Out of my element."

Yeah, right. But she had enough on her mind at the moment. No sense laying this on her too.

He read off the directions one leg at a time until they were turning into a long drive that led to a one-story white ranch trimmed in red brick. Looked fairly new. Alex pulled into the circular drive and parked near the sidewalk to the front door.

"Nice place. Not what I was expecting," she said.

"Do I want to know what you had in mind?"

"Uh, no. At least not until we're on the way back." She retrieved her lipstick and touched up her makeup in the mirror. "Ready?"

"When you are."

The woman who greeted them at the door had medium brown hair pulled back in a sleek ponytail. She wore designer jeans and a crisp white-and-black-striped overblouse. Not your typical Iowa housewife. really had to drop these pre-set notions about Iowans.

"You must be Alexandra Appleby." She turned to Geoff, smile still in place. "I didn't know you were bringing your staff." She extended her hand, first to Alex, then him.

"Hello, Mrs. Corley. This is Geoffrey McKenna. I asked him to make the trip with me. He's going to sit in on our discussion, if that's okay with you?"

"If what's okay with us?" a fortyish man in khakis, navy golf shirt, and an expensive pair of running shoes asked as he appeared from the back of the house.

"This is my husband, Jason. I'm Nicole," Mrs. Corley explained. "She brought a member of her staff with her, Jason. She asked whether it would be okay for him to join us rather than told us he was. I was about to agree."

Jason Corley shook Alex's hand, then Geoff's. "Oh, sure."

Alex looked around the room. "And Allison? Where is she?"

Nicole Corley exchanged a glance with her husband. "She's in her room, waiting for us to call her. We'd like to speak to you first."

Geoff was tempted to twist around and check Alex's expression, but he kept his eyes glued on the parents, as if the gauntlet they'd just laid down for her hadn't registered with him. How would he handle this if he had a talented fifteen-year-old daughter? Now that he thought about it, he could. He would've been twenty-one when she was born. Geez, he was getting old.

"Of course," Alex returned. "I don't have any children of my own, but I can still imagine your desire to be totally involved in her life decisions right now."

"Please, have a seat, both of you," Mrs. Corley answered. "I'm glad you understand our, uh, interest in Allison's singing career."

"We don't want Allison to go into the business before she at least graduates from high school," Mr. Corley said after a few beats. "She has tremendous talent, but she has no idea how her life and ours will change if she does this before she's eighteen."

"That's pretty clear, Mr. Corley, Jason. So why did your wife contact me and ask me to consider representing your daughter?"

"I called you to pacify Allison. She threatened to seek emancipation if we didn't let her pursue her singing career."

"Could she do that?"

"Not yet and not easily," Jason Corley replied. "She has to be sixteen and show proof that we agree to it or that her home life is that bad."

"But the fact that she was willing to even consider something so serious convinced us we had to work with her rather than against her," his wife said.

Alex, who'd been sitting on the edge of the davenport, settled farther back. "In other words, I'm here today merely for appearances?"

Nicole Corley pursed her lips, shifted her gaze away briefly. "I promised Allison I'd contact one potential manager, just to see how they might respond. I called you because your name was near the front of the directory. I was sure you wouldn't be interested, or on the off chance that you were, you'd only agree to see us in your office in California. I had no idea you'd be willing to come here."

Geoff stared at his shoes, curious how Alex would handle these people who really didn't want her here. Since she herself wasn't sure whether she wanted to be here, maybe she'd turn around and leave. Or maybe she'd be challenged to prove her worth, go after this client just to show she could turn these parents around.

"As it happens," Alex began, "I was coming to the state on other business, or I would have done just as you predicted, if I decided to even pursue her after listening to her tapes."

"It's not that we're discouraging a singing career," Mrs. Corley put in. "She has an incredible voice. It would be a shame to waste it. But we don't want her gobbled up by the entertainment world's machine. We've seen what's happened to so many young entertainers."

The way this meeting was going, Geoff doubted they'd even get to meet the young artist in question. They'd be leaving any minute. All those hours on the road for less than half an hour with the Corleys.

But Alex didn't rise. "You have every right to be concerned," she said instead. "I've lived in L.A. all my life. I've seen my share of teenagers as well as people in their twenties and even older crash and burn after they've been exposed to the life. Even if you and Allison thought I might be the one to manage her career, you have to know, I first have to be convinced I want to."

Ah, she was going that direction. Act like she didn't care. Make them want her. Had she decided to take on this girl as her client, after all?

"Then let me sing for you." A petite young blonde in a medium-blue dress stood in the doorway.

Nicole Corley sprang to her feet and went over to her daughter. "I thought we decided you would wait for your dad and me to call you?"

"I heard the car drive up, so I knew when she got here." She stole a glance at Alex. When she saw Geoff, her forehead wrinkled slightly. "I waited long enough for you to tell her how you feel about my singing career. But now it's my turn." She turned back to Alex. "I get why you want to hear me in person."

Alex rose and went over to the girl. "We haven't formally met. I'm Alexandra Appleby. You can call me Alex." She glanced over her shoulder at Geoff. "This is Geoffrey McKenna. He's assisting me in this interview. My West Coast approach to things can sometimes be offputting to others who aren't accustomed to that environment, so Geoff has tagged along to help facilitate our discussion. He's from Burlington."

Sensing this was his cue, Geoff rose and approached mother, daughter and Alex. "Hi, Allison. I've been looking forward to meeting you. I read about your success at the state talent contest."

Allison studied him, then Alex. He remembered the first time he met Paige last summer. He'd seen a similar look in her eyes until she got to know him and Gray. He'd learned to back off, give her time to get used to him. Perhaps the same strategy would work on this young woman.

"Let's all come back into the living room," Allison's mother said, leading her daughter.

Allison allowed herself to be steered toward a dark blue micro-suede easy chair, which appeared to be centered between two other easy chairs and a loveseat, on which Mrs. Corley indicated Alex and Geoff should sit.

Once everyone was seated, Alex took the lead. "Geoff and I would love to hear you sing, Allison. But before we have that honor, let's get to know each other a little. Your parents and Geoff can sit in, but I'd prefer this be between just you and me. Okay?"

The girl didn't even look at her parents. "Sure. What do you want to know?"

Alex didn't give Mr. or Mrs. Corley a chance to intervene. "Let's start with some easy stuff. Is Allison your real name?"

"Yes. Do you think I should change it?"

"No, I like it, even if we decided today we wanted to team up, and I'm not suggesting that will happen, determining whether to retain your given name or adopt another is a decision for another day." She paused. "I asked because I wondered if you were attempting to sell your image as an Alice instead of Allison, whether consciously or subliminally."

"Alice? You mean the girl who fell down the rat hole?"

"Rabbit hole. Right. You know? Long blonde hair. Blue dress."

"No." The girl raised her voice in protest, and her face assumed an expression of distaste. "That's a fairy tale. For little kids."

"Sorry. Just thought, well, never mind."

Damn, why hadn't he picked up on that? Now that Alex had pointed out the girl's appearance, it was as obvious as his own unshakeable sugar rush. Alex was good. How was she going to use this?

Allison appeared so surprised at Alex's observation she actually glanced down at her outfit. "No, I'm not that girl."

Alex drew in her lips, as if she'd just bitten into a sour apple, then rose, and gestured for Geoff to follow. Huh?

"That's too bad, Allison," she said, emphasizing all three syllables of the name. "Because if I took you on at this time, at the age of fifteen, that's the image we'd use. When you entered the room, I was sure you were that savvy. That you realized every other young female vocalist your age is promoting herself as a baby hooker. Wholesome is unique these days. It would set you apart from the pack, get you noticed. Your talent would do the rest."

She grabbed for her bag and took a few steps toward the front door. Then pivoted. "But since you are so blatantly opposed to the idea of selling yourself like that, which is the only way I'd want to handle you for a few years, our business here is finished."

She hustled Geoff to the car and drove off before either Allison or her parents could react. Before he could react either.

"What was that about?" he finally asked once they were back on the county road.

A LEX HEARD her passenger say something, but it didn't register. She wasn't exactly a zombie; she was alert enough to drive, but her brain was elsewhere. What had she done?

She spotted a mom-and-pop convenience store and pulled into the lot. Turned off the ignition. Her hands still framing the steering wheel, she bent forward to catch her breath. She was the only talent manager the Corleys had contacted, so at this point, she could have negotiated a great deal. Why had she walked?

"You okay?"

She shook her head to come out of her reverie. "Huh? Yes, I'm fine. Need to stop long enough to process that meeting."

"Want to talk about it?"

"Not yet." First, she had to figure out if she'd made the right move. No, even before that, had she wanted Allison as her client or not? She'd never wanted to manage talent. Loretta had pushed her into it. Loretta had been demanding and high maintenance from the start. But Allison Corley was the total package—looks, voice and a certain amount of desire. She was raw.

Developing her image would take work, and that was only if the girl—and her parents—had been willing to do so. But it would also be one huge rush.

"You want something to munch on? Or drink?" she asked Geoff. "I need to walk."

Geoff followed and got his own bottle.

They didn't return immediately to the car. Since they'd parked on the edge of the small town's two-block downtown, they wandered the street, peeking in store windows. Geoff kept silent, let her take her time to reflect on the last half hour.

"You think I've lost my mind."

"No, but I am curious. When a salesman walks away from a potential sale, there's a reason. It's usually to scare the customer into agreement. That your goal with Allison?"

"I don't know. I was undecided before we met her, and I'm now more undecided than ever. Whoever marched out of that house was acting on pure instinct."

They settled onto a bench outside a women's clothing store. "Want my read?"

"You've been able to make sense of my actions? Sure. Shoot."

"You walked into the Corley house seeing your visit as a courtesy call. When both parents told us they didn't want their daughter in the business, you had your out. But their objection also became a challenge."

"You think?"

"Then Allison showed up. Any teenager I know, based on my short acquaintance with Paige, would've have shown up in a tight miniskirt or tighter jeans, wearing way too much makeup, in part to impress you, but also because that's how they dress these days. But instead, she was squeaky clean in her little blue dress and long blonde hair. Something clicked inside you."

She considered his theory. "Something definitely did click, but I can't identify it yet."

"Possibly because your mind is fighting it? You want to represent this kid."

"Maybe. But every time I go there, I remember how little time I have to take on yet another's demands. Before you say get rid of Loretta, just know, it's not going to happen. My contract would be difficult to break." At least on her side. Loretta could change managers on a whim at any time, which she constantly threatened to do if she didn't get Jenna's coach. But Loretta's departure wouldn't happen without consequences. For Alex. And her dad.

She glanced at Geoff to find him staring at her.

"There's more to this than you're telling me, isn't there?"

So much more. But she didn't dare breathe a word of her predicament to anyone else. Not even Geoff, who she was coming to trust. "If I said yes, you'd wouldn't be content until you got it out of me."

"I wouldn't be happy about it, because I thought we were getting pretty close, but I'd be more concerned for you. You need someone to confide in." He twisted around to study the street. "Listen to me. I sound like a host on one of those women's talk shows."

She took his hand. "No, you sound like a good friend." Then the explosion of feeling she was experiencing from even this small contact hit her. She lifted their locked hands. "Maybe more than a friend."

Geoff turned his head back to her again, stared at her in a totally different way than he had just a minute before. His eyes grew smoky as they seemed to look inside her. "Let's get out of here." They walked back to the car. "Still want to stay over tonight rather than drive back? It's not quite three. We'd reach town around ten."

He was giving her a way out from the direction they were otherwise headed. But she didn't want an out. "We already have a reservation. Besides, you don't want to run into Eileen tomorrow, do you?"

"Uh, no. That's right. Not after that big production of a low-key birthday dinner last night."

Except for her occasional questions about road signs, they drove in silence. Once they reached the motel, they registered for two adjoining rooms. As soon as she'd flopped her overnight bag on the bed of her room, she went to the connecting door, unlocked her side, and knocked. On the other side, a similar sound of a lock being turned signaled the door opening, and then Geoff stood there as if waiting for an invitation.

"Come in," she said. "Are you here to—"

His mouth covered the rest of her question, providing its own answer. This was more than their kissing in the car like teenagers making out on their first date. Even more than the manly gaze that drilled through her back on that street bench. His arms tightened around her as the kiss deepened. Why should she hold back? She stepped farther into his embrace and returned the favor.

He backed them over to a sofa and pulled her into a sitting position next to him, his lips moving to the side of her neck to nuzzle. Tantalizing heat surged through her. She would have stripped for him there and then, but he continued to minister to her neck column, moving his lips slowly down to the curve just about her shoulders. He nibbled, then peppered the area with tiny flicks of his tongue.

Her breathing slowed as her pulse sped up. How was that possible? She was still fully clothed, and he had yet to touch any of the parts of her body where nerve endings waited to be addressed. Was it possible with his MS he could only go this far, pleasurable though it was? All he was accomplishing was to make her want more. Soon.

Maybe she needed to be more assertive? She ran a hand slowly up the back of his neck, fingered the edge of his hairline, which caused him to squirm and tighten his grip around her rib cage.

At length, he returned his lips to hers, his tongue now pushing its way into her mouth. Her tongue met his and jousted for position, the contact sending more waves of warmth down her chest and through her abdomen. She squirmed, her other hand threading down his side and around his front.

He pulled his lips away from her. "Getting anxious? We've got the rest of the afternoon."

"Are we going for quality or quantity?"

"At this point, I'd say you're more into finishing."

"I'm into proceeding." She broke away from his embrace long enough to unbutton her blouse and pitch it to the side.

His gaze dipped to her bra, a lacy leopard-skin number that left little to the imagination, including two rosy aureoles peeking through sheer beige netting. She decided to give him a better look by straddling him, her private region touching the hardness barely concealed by his slacks. "I wore this just in case. Hope it's worth the small fortune I paid for it before it's just a great memory."

His expression told her the investment had paid off. "If what you were after was to give me a hundred ways I want to admire it before it's history, yeah, you got your money's worth." Finally, he moved his mouth away from hers and brought it to one breast, still encased in its flimsy covering. He tongued the nipple with slow, deliberate strokes, which only added to her mounting need for more. As the nipple went hard, he drew away, cupped the breast, and with one finger, pulled down the fabric just enough to frame the mound so he could place lips to actual flesh and suckle.

The sensation was so powerful she almost shot off his lap, trying to push herself deeper into his mouth, but he held her firmly and forced her to be patient as he and her breast became better acquainted.

He pulled away, leaving the breast bathed in his moisture, and repeated his play with the other breast, both of them now protruding from the garment like warm, fuzzless peaches ready to be plucked. This time he nibbled as well, and his tongue and teeth worked faster. At one point, he drew her further into his mouth, moaning as he did.

Moisture pooled between her legs. She'd have to change her slacks if they left the room for dinner. Hadn't felt this turned on since … maybe never. He was good. Damned slow, but oh, so good.

He came up for air. "Enough of this. I've gotten my money's worth." His hands snaked around her back and unclasped the brassiere, threw it behind him.

"My turn." Unabashed by her nakedness, she lifted his shirt over his arms and tossed it the same direction. "Oh, wow," was all she could say in response to his naked chest. His pecs, firm and high, were feathered with light brown hair that tapered through his middle down to his waist. She couldn't resist touching him, marveling at the hard muscle beneath the surface.

"C'mere." He crushed her to him, naked chest to naked chest, setting loose her desire to rub herself into him while his hands massaged her back.

"Stand up," he said. She did so, expecting him to remove her slacks. Instead, he picked her up and carried her to the bed, where he laid her flat on her back in the middle. Then he removed her pants, leaving her clothed only in the thin strip of a black thong.

He climbed in beside her, rose above her on his knees. "You are one spectacular woman to look at, Alex Appleby. But I want to see more." In one swift motion, he drew the thong down her legs, where she kicked it off.

He straddled her, placed kisses on her forehead, down her nose. He stopped briefly to ravage her mouth and then moved down her chin to halt within her cleavage. Her back arched off the bed as his mouth connected with one erogenous zone after another.

His lips slid over her stomach and farther down. He glanced up. "Okay to proceed?"

"Good grief, yes!"

He obliged, spreading her legs apart, laving first one inner thigh with his tongue, then the other. Her own moisture mixed with his as his finger slid inside her with no difficulty. He probed the soft, warm interior until he found her sensitive area. The increased pressure served as counterpoint to the intense sensations building within her.

He slipped a second finger inside, now cooing to her. "Easy does it, babe. Just lie back and let me bring you through the haze."

His lips returned to her stomach as his two fingers worked their magic. In. Out. Press.

Her hips writhed in frenzied need for him to bring her to the edge. Within seconds, she climaxed and lay still, feeling sensational. Giddy. Pacified.

Rolling to the side, he unzipped his pants. He removed a condom from his pocket before dropping them on the floor.

She watched, fascinated. He wore only black knit briefs, which did nothing to disguise the package beneath. Before she could wonder further about said contents, the briefs hit the floor, and he stood before her, taking in her body with his eyes, his penis jutting forth for her admiration.

Oh. Yes. Fantastic as his mouth on her lips and breasts had been, as his soothing hands and insistent fingers had proved to be, this was what she wanted. All of that. Inside her, dammit. Now.

"Forgive the rush, but now that you've been satisfied, I need the same." He stuck on the condom, mounted, and entered her with one magnificent lunge.

"Oh, Geoff," she moaned.

"Too soon?"

"No. Just in time. I needed this so bad."

"Me, too." He didn't speak further as he moved in and out, starting with slow, luxurious thrusts, then increasing the rhythm until he pumped so fiercely she thought she would split. He filled her completely.

She lost herself in his parries, moaning his name, calling on the Deity, whatever. Her hands gripped his back, and he continued to rock back and forth until with one final shudder, he peaked. She came just after him.

Both lay flat on the bed, tried to regain normal breathing. Geoff closed his eyes. She remained slightly more alert.

Geoff released a breath. "That was spectacular."

"Yeah. Agreed." Was this why she'd gone along with his accompanying her on this trip—so she'd have her chance to seduce him, away from the firehouse? She'd been fantasizing about him since he'd fallen into her arms that first morning. If so, she congratulated herself on getting exactly what she wanted: Class A sex. Geoff was a master.

Twelve

They lay on the bed reenergizing, each of them retreating into their own private thoughts. Geoff simply savored the incredible feeling of completeness permeating his body and his brain. When was the last time he felt this way? Certainly not after any of the numerous flings he'd pursued prior to his MS and not at any time he'd been with Eileen.

Maybe after the first time he had sex—with Juliette Kaplan when he was a junior in high school—he experienced as much satisfaction as this. But that satisfaction had been purely from pride in his prowess and the newfound release it brought his body. What he felt now totally engulfed his senses, made him weak all over and yet believing he was the strongest guy in the world.

But he wasn't kidding himself. Once his body regrouped, his brain would come alive again and begin to question what the hell he'd been thinking.

But he wasn't going there just yet. No, for now, he was simply going to enjoy being with this woman. If that meant the sex was over, he'd live with it, though he'd regret not taking advantage of the rest of the time they had together this weekend. Maybe they could stay an extra day, spend all their time in bed. Yeah, right. Like that was going to happen. Alex had too much on her mind to just lie back and enjoy her time with him. For that matter, he had issues on his own plate, starting with getting back to see Kyle. It most likely would be the last time.

The next thing he knew, Alex was nudging his shoulder. "Geoff? It's six thirty. Are you hungry, or do you want to sleep longer?"

"Six thirty?" He'd been out over two hours? "Why'd you let me doze off like that?"

"I was a goner myself. For a while, at least. Guess the road time got to me."

As he came awake, he realized she hadn't dressed. Good sign, especially since he was sprawled out sans clothes, his guy quite relaxed. "How long you been awake?"

She glanced to the side, fingered the bedspread. "Not long." Her voice trailed away.

"How long?" He got the distinct impression she'd been ogling him. Just the thought of serving as the object of her inspection sent new life into his fellow, which apparently decided it had rested enough.

Alex traced a finger over the bed fabric. "I, uh, okay, if you must know, I, uh, studied you. Your body. Which is unbelievably sensational."

He studied her back. Normally so sure of herself, for once she came across shy. Maidenly.

"Thanks. Touch anything?"

She offered a knowing smile. "Parts of you would have been at full mast when you woke if I had." She leaned closer. "But there's nothing keeping me from doing so now." The smile was joined by the tip of her tongue coming to one side of her mouth as she drew her index finger down his chest, stopping just above the tufted hair on the edge of his entertainment system.

His body went from relaxed to alert in a heartbeat, as if someone had flipped a light switch in a dark room. "Whoa! You're playing with fire, you know."

"Really? That mean I could ignite a flame with little trouble?"

He pulled her on top of him. "Too late. A five-alarm is already underway. But now it's my turn to do the exploring and ogling." He stroked both buttocks. "Mmm. I like this much better." As he fondled, he drew her closer, crushing her mound to his growing hardness.

Alex wriggled beneath his grip. "I was just starting to enjoy my journey down your chest to unexplored regions."

"Ah, c'mon, admit you like this more. His hands drifted down the back of her legs into the crevice that led to her opening.

Alex squirmed at the contact. "Good memory. Your fingers are like a homing device."

"Welcome, I hope?"

In response, she lifted her chest above him, let her breasts hang less than an inch from his mouth.

Within an instant, he picked the one he wanted and brought it into his mouth. Just a minute ago, he thought he'd reached the pinnacle of his satisfaction quotient. Nuh-uh. This woman had found a way to heighten his pleasure even more. Once his fingers had done their work, she produced a condom from nowhere, sheathed him, and brought him into her as she began to rock up and down. Each move brought excruciating ecstasy. Her moist, velvet channel welcomed his hard penis and tightened around him.

When he could tolerate the titillation no longer, he swung on top of her and completed the job, bringing himself to climax just after she did.

Once again, he fell back, exhausted. Was his age catching up with him? Geez, he was only thirty-six.

"That was icing on the cake."

"Cake. Great idea. You hungry yet?"

He drew a hand through her bangs, which yet again covered her eye. "My *appetite* has been satiated for now. But I could stand to eat actual food."

"Then a mutual shower is off the table, if we want to find a restaurant before midnight."

"Damn tough choice."

She rolled off the bed, gathered her clothes and overnight bag, and headed for the bathroom. "Last one dressed has to pay."

Though he planned to pick up the check anyhow, he completed his shower in record time and was reading a magazine on her sofa when she emerged from her bathroom two minutes after he arrived. "That was record time."

"Reason why I keep my hair short." She wore a different pair of slacks, a knit pullover, and sandals. "Ready?"

"Was it this muggy earlier?" Geoff asked as they made their way to the car.

"It does seem more humid. But it could be our bodies are still overheated."

"Maybe that's it."

A cluster of eateries ranging from drive-throughs to a couple of high-end franchises was located about a half mile away. "What's your pleasure?" she asked from behind the wheel.

He presented her with a smug smile. "We just found out back there at the motel."

WAS he teasing or thanking her? She chose to go with the latter. She glanced at the various signs. "Steak, Mexican or Italian?"

"Steak. Need protein to restore my energy."

"I had the same thing in mind." She parked and opened her own door. This wasn't a date, although what did one call a postcoital meal?

Geoff must have been under a different impression, because as soon as she came around the car, he moved in, placed his hand lightly on the small of her back. When they entered the restaurant, he asked for a table, his hand remaining where it was until she was seated.

While he studied his menu, he released a chuckle. "This is ironic. Eileen expected steak last night, and I disappointed her. Here you are, and it seems to fall into your lap."

"Is one or both of us supposed to feel guilty with that statement?"

"Not my intent. In fact, the coincidence just hit me as we walked in." Finished scanning the menu, he put it aside and folded his hands.

"I sure don't feel guilty. In fact, I feel spectacular. I enjoyed our time together back there in your room."

"It was good sex, wasn't it?"

He studied her, his eyes narrowing slightly. "You're talking about it like we just saw a great flick."

Was he actually offended? "Oops. Didn't mean to step on toes. Did you see it as something more? Er, something else?"

A waiter appeared. They ordered and he reappeared with their beverages. "This afternoon wasn't just a spur-of-the-moment whim for me. I've been wanting to sleep with you almost since we met," Geoff said.

True admission or was he telling her what he thought she wanted to hear? She liked hearing him say it, true admission or not. She raised her eyelids, gazed back at him. "Almost?"

"I was pretty out of it when you first came knocking on my door. All I wanted was to go to bed at that point. Alone. Even when I woke up to Eileen's screeching, I was probably unaffected by your charms. But that breakfast? God, those scrambled eggs were like pheromones. Even though I didn't get to eat them, I wanted the cook who prepared them."

This wasn't just an admission. More a declaration. "That why you decided to break things off with Eileen?"

He opened his linen napkin and placed it on his lap. "Actually, Eileen took care of that herself, for all the reasons I've told you. But when you told me you needed my help with Jenna, it's like Fate brought you into my orbit."

"You've got a thing for me?"

"No, I wanted to sleep with you." He jerked back. "Did you think I just declared my undying love?"

"No, of course not. I knew exactly what you meant." Not. Now that the idea had been planted in her brain, it wasn't leaving on its own accord. No, not love. But something was happening between them. More than friendship. Not quite love. But apparently, he wasn't in the same place. Time to save face. "So if we're being totally frank with each other, now that I've seen yours and you've seen mine, the idea of getting it on with you occurred to me, too, once or twice in the last several days." She deliberately chose that phrase to keep things light and of the moment.

"Which is why you agreed to move out of that motel and settle into the firehouse?"

"Well, no. Saving money was the incentive then. But once I arrived, the idea grew. It's been a while, okay, months, since I've been with someone. Loretta's kept me pretty busy."

"Our time together was something of a release?"

"Let's go with that. You said spectacular." God, she remembered his actual statement. "A spectacular release of pent-up energy and emotions we couldn't restrain any longer."

Their salads arrived. He played with his. She forked her lettuce but didn't eat. He sipped his iced tea, she sampled her wine. He moved his knife a half-inch to the side. She pleated the napkin in her lap.

"Well," he said at last. "Now what?"

She glanced up, checked his demeanor. "Now what, what?"

"Did you, uh, get me out of your system? I, uh, scratched the itch?"

She flinched. "That what you think that was?"

He pressed his lips together, almost but not quite like a little boy told he couldn't go out to play. "Hey, I get it. You're only here a little while longer. I'm available, and if I do say so myself"—a hint of a smile appeared—"I make a great diversion."

She reached across the table and caught his thumb between her own thumb and forefinger. "That you do. But don't underestimate yourself. You're more than a sexy hunk and great in bed."

He raised a lascivious eyebrow. "Oh? Both of those sound pretty great to me. What else?"

"At the risk of boosting your ego beyond recognition, spending time with you has been fun. There's more to you than your looks. You're solid."

"*Solid* as in overweight?"

A corner of her mouth crooked up. "Don't get carried away." She left it at that.

Geoff sat there, studying her, but didn't push it.

Their steaks arrived, and talk changed to speculation about Allison Corley. "You think she'll change her mind?" Geoff asked.

Alex considered. She'd been wondering the same thing ever since they'd left the Corley house. Well, not the whole time. She hadn't thought of much of anything while she and Geoff were rolling around in bed. "Mom and Dad have her best interests at heart. Not like a lot of parents in the business, who're only interested in getting more money and exposure for their darlings. Allison's an only child. They'll either go overboard protecting her or give her what she wants." She raised her hand, palm out. "In other words, I haven't a clue."

"I think you made an impression on them. Didn't press them to sign anything. Nor did you promise anything."

"Time will tell. In the meantime, let's enjoy the rest of our trip, starting by tabling further discussion of Allison Corley, Eileen, changing up your marketing

strategy, dealing with my other clients, or—"

"Sex?" he suggested.

She finished off her wine. "For now. The rest of our meal, at least."

"Okay. I'm game. What should we talk about?"

"How about my stepsisters? What have you learned about them in the last year?"

"You should really form your own opinion of Jenna and Aubrey. But I'll play along. Aubrey came across at first as a woman with an attitude. Didn't help that she and Mitch got off to a bad start, although that soon turned out to be their libidos erupting. However, within a day or so, she knew more about our secrets than we did, not that she used them against us. No, Aubrey's a fixer. Once she picked up on our problems, she kept at us until we'd resolved them."

Interesting. Alex had always considered Aubrey a bit of a screwup, at least from stories she'd heard from her mother. Even Iris, Aubrey's mother, hadn't been all that positive when she talked about her younger daughter. "Wasn't she hiding out in town to escape a decorating mess in L.A. that turned into a lawsuit?"

"From what I've heard, she did a terrific job on the decorating part, but her client used the job to get back at her philandering spouse. Then when the client and her spouse got back together, the client lied about her part in the renovation project and sided with her husband in the suit against Aubrey."

Alex savored the last few bites of steak. Not bad. Especially for a chain. Aubrey was a pretty decent person. Good to know. "How about Jenna?"

He stirred his iced tea. Second glass. "Jenna? You know, now that I think about it, she started off on the wrong foot with us as well, especially with Gray."

"What's with my stepsisters and the way they relate to the McKenna men?"

"Apparently, neither wanted to be in Iowa but for different reasons. Aubrey didn't want to face her problems in California, so she agreed to finish the interior of Jenna's coach. Jenna put aside time rehearsing for her concert tour to come claim Paige, who'd taken off on her own to be with Aubrey."

He folded his hands on the tabletop. "Guess that's a good omen for you and me, huh? Since we got off to a pretty good start."

Could he be any clearer about his intentions? Or lack thereof. Not that she disagreed, but she wasn't going to let him get by with that statement without a little flack. "You immediately fell asleep on me. You call that a *good start*?"

That stopped him. He took a moment to regroup before responding. "Better than harping at each other like the other four." He thought some more. "You weren't seeing the two of us as a couple, were you? I thought we were keeping whatever *this* is casual?"

She fluttered her eyes, then lowered them as if caught unawares by his question.

"Alex? You okay? I didn't hurt your feelings, did I?"

Enough fun. "No, of course not. I couldn't resist making you panic."

"I didn't exactly panic. I was just surprised. I thought we were on the same wavelength, and I was right."

"Don't act so smug. If we both lived in the same place, who knows how that might change things."

He tilted his head. "Didn't stop the other four."

"Both my stepsisters gave up their lives in California to be with your brothers, neither of whom has yet even offered marriage. Aubrey transferred her decorating skills to motor coaches, and Jenna gave up her tour to write children's books. Although we've already established there's talent in this state and it's possible to conduct some business long distance, to be a successful talent manager, I need to keep my roots in the entertainment hubs."

Geoff took a last swig of his iced tea. "For the sake of argument, who says you'd have to remain a talent manager? You've already told me you aren't thrilled with the job. You could go back to nursing. That translates anywhere."

"Why are we even discussing this? We just agreed we're in this for the short term. Because we like each other's company and we had great sex."

He set down his glass with a start. "Right. Just an idle thought." He signaled for their waiter. "Ready to go?"

"Uh, sure." Her brain was still processing his *idle thought*. Why had he even mentioned it? Guys didn't mention things like that unless they gave them at least a passing thought. The strange part was she had been considering going back to nursing once she got Loretta off her back. How eerie. But changing careers as part of relocating to Iowa to be with Geoff? No way. Not gonna happen. She liked the guy, but she didn't have feelings for him. Did she?

Thirteen

Their waiter approached. "Sir? I have your bill ready. We're closing now due to the weather."

"What about the weather?" Geoff asked.

The waiter raised an eyebrow. "There's tornado warnings out for the area fifty miles west. Those could include us any minute."

Tornado? Why were they just now hearing about the warnings? Because they'd been otherwise engaged the last several hours. Even here, they'd been so engrossed in their conversation they hadn't paid much attention to how few customers still occupied the restaurant.

Geoff grabbed her hand, placed his arm around her shoulders and ushered her back to the car as soon as their bill was paid. No time to argue about who would pay. She'd reimburse him later.

Without discussing it, he took the keys and assumed the driver's seat. He turned on the radio, scanned stations until he found a weathercast, but static cut into whatever the announcer was saying.

"Are we in danger?" she asked. "I'm more familiar with earthquakes than tornadoes,"

"Hard to say until I see a weather map," he returned. "Even then, it's sometimes hard to tell if one or more will materialize. They mainly show air conditions and pinpoint areas most likely to be affected.

We'll check at the motel desk as soon as we get back. See what they advise."

The ride seemed to take forever. Alex watched out the window for swirling air columns. Though his mood had become more serious, Geoff didn't appear frightened. Probably used to these things. She, on the other hand, had little experience with this type of storm, although tornadoes weren't completely foreign to California. Most of her knowledge came from films and television shows, where girls from Kansas and cows were swept into the whirlwind.

Suddenly, the wind picked up. Trees swayed, leaves that shouldn't be dropping until fall flitted across the road. Even with the windows sealed tight, the air hummed with mounting energy.

Tiny drops of moisture dotting the windshield expanded into blobs and then became a steady downpour. The wipers struggled to keep up.

"I'll drop you off at the front door," Geoff said as they approached the building. "See what you can learn at the front desk. I'll park the car away from the building and trees."

"But you'll get drenched."

"Got dry clothes in my room."

She paused out of concern for him.

"Go! Every second counts right now," he said tightly.

She ran for the door, getting soaked in even that short distance.

No one was at the front desk, although she heard a television or radio somewhere close. "Hello? Anyone back there?"

A young man about twenty stuck his head out the door of a room off to the side of the desk. "Yes, ma'am? Are you checking in?"

"No, I'm already a guest. I heard a tornado might be coming this way. What do you know about that?"

"I been watchin' the TV weather guy. S'hard to tell how bad things really are. These guys get so excited, tryin' to show off their knowledge and beat the competition. There's a sign on your door tellin' you what to do in the event of a tornado."

"What does it say?"

"Mainly, go to an interior hallway since we don't have a basement.

Close the door to your room behind you so if the windows blow, the glass'll stay there."

"The, the windows blow out?"

"Never here. Just somethin' they warn you 'bout."

"When do we do this?"

"Keep your TV on as long as you can. I've got a battery-operated radio here. If one is actually comin' toward us, the sirens will sound outside."

The first thing she did when she reached her room was turn on the television, before she even grabbed towels to dry off. Fortunately, the TV was still transmitting. A good sign? She settled on the sofa and became absorbed listening to the meteorologist. A map came on, purportedly showing the extent of the storm. Since she wasn't familiar with many of the towns named, she didn't know whether to be concerned.

She kicked off a shoe, then changed her mind. Better keep those on, in case they had to move out fast.

Apparently, one tornado had touched down in a field over in Nebraska about a half hour before but didn't do much damage. The weather guy remarked how, due to the day's heat and humidity, conditions were ripe for one of these things, but even at that, it could stay aloft and move on toward the northeast.

Just as she was contemplating escape by driving off in the opposite direction, the guy cautioned everyone to stay put. "You don't want to be out in your car or outside period when a tornado is possible. One of these things could change direction at any time and come after you."

After the announcer repeated himself for the fourth time, she grew restless. How was she supposed to keep her sanity when they made such a production of so little information? She retrieved her cell phone from her purse and began recording her thoughts about the Allison Corley interview. Thunder in the near distance outside her window caused her to jump.

Shouldn't Geoff be here by now? How far away had he parked, anyhow?

In her room, Alex checked the time on her cell once more. Seven minutes at least since she'd entered the building. Where was Geoff?

The TV had flickered momentarily when the lightning struck but had come back on within a minute. It had been enough time, though, to send a chill through her body that had nothing to do with the room temp. She couldn't stop shaking. The only comfort she took in being alone in the middle of this deluge was the realization that if she perished, Loretta wouldn't get her lease. How bad was that as one of her last thoughts on earth?

Maybe she hadn't heard the siren. She went to the door and checked the hallway. No one there. In fact, the corridor was eerily quiet. Weren't there any other guests tonight? Had they cleared out when they heard the tornado warnings? If so, where had they gone? She'd certainly like to be there as well for as safe as she felt here.

She checked the cell again. Two more minutes gone.

Maybe Geoff was waiting in the car for the rain to slow. One way to find out. She fast-dialed his number. No answer. After five rings, it went to voicemail. Why wasn't he answering? There was still a signal if it had gone to voicemail.

She tried again. Same result. *Why are you doing this to me, Geoff?*

She returned to the television. A new map was up. Still didn't recognize many names other than Omaha down in the left-hand corner and Sioux City above left. But if vivid reds and fuchsias meant anything, the storm was much nearer and far from over.

She wasn't going to let this get to her. Nope, it was time for action. She made the rounds of the room, deciding what she would take with her when she evacuated. Didn't bring a raincoat, or any raingear, for that matter. But she did have a windbreaker. It was still in her overnight bag. Her phone. The charger. Billfold. What else? Would've been nice if she'd tucked a health bar in her purse or if there'd been any fruit in the lobby. Geoff had long ago consumed all the cookies.

Dry clothes. She searched the drawers and closet until she found the plastic bag they provided for laundry and wet swimsuits, and tucked her change of clothes in there. And towels. She wasn't sure for what, but it seemed like a good idea. Everything else went into the bag also.

Okay, she was set.

Now she waited. Tried to focus on the TV screen. Waited some more.

Then the screen went fuzzy. She waited for it to reappear. It continued to flicker until if went off completely, along with the room light and the rest of the electricity. Oh God, oh God, oh God! Now what was she supposed to do?

She couldn't stay here. In the dark.

She felt for the plastic bag and stumbled to the door. It wasn't much brighter out there, except for the few battery-operated lights along the ceiling every twenty feet or so. "Hello?" she called, her tongue sticking to the top of her mouth. "Hello?"

No one answered. Somewhere off in the distance she heard a noise. It didn't sound unfriendly, so she headed toward it.

It grew louder as she progressed. She increased her speed. If there was noise, it had to mean another human was here. She wasn't alone.

She was almost there when she smashed into a wall. No, not a wall. Walls didn't fall over on you. That was her last thought as her world went even darker.

SINCE THE PERIMETER of the motel property was ringed with small trees, Geoff was challenged to find a place where the car wouldn't be hit by falling debris. Finally, he spotted a small opening near the back of the building, but when he attempted to come in a side door, it was locked. His keycard would've gotten him in, but he didn't want to stop long enough to search his pockets.

Instead, he headed for the front entrance. Maybe the desk clerk would have some news. Just as he cleared the door, a bolt of thunder struck a tree down the street.

"Close," he said to the desk clerk peeking out of an internal door.

"The lighting strike or your arrival?"

Geoff released a nervous laugh. "Both, I guess.

What's happening? How close is it?"

"Come see for yourself."

Geoff followed the desk clerk into what appeared to be the guy's office off to the side of the front desk.

The place reeked of onions and garlic, most likely the main ingredients in whatever had once occupied the fast-food bags strewn about the room. In the corner, a weather radio blared and crackled.

"Is it still coming toward us?" Geoff pushed past the kid to catch as much of the broadcast himself.

"Best I can tell in all that racket."

Geoff didn't like this. Tornadoes were bad enough when you were hiding out in a basement, but all the occupants of this motel were sitting ducks. Not as bad as being out in a car, but not where he'd like to be at the moment. Alex! He'd been so into his own safety he'd briefly forgotten about her.

"Seen a gorgeous brunette with short hair?"

"Sure did. Sent her to her room. Best place for her unless the sirens go off. Told her to head for the hall if that happened."

Geoff pivoted to run back to Alex just as everything went dark. What the—

"Well, dammit all to hell," the clerk said from somewhere behind Geoff.

"This place have a backup generator?"

"Good grief, no. We got clean, comfor'ble beds, but no frills."

Geoff stood stock still, not trusting himself to make his way without some illumination. "How about a flashlight? I need to check on my friend."

Papers rattled, something heavy and metal hit the floor. "Got a couple here, if I can find 'em." A few seconds later, a bright circle of light hit Geoff in the face. "Sorry. Found this one. Gimme a sec to find the other. Yeah, there it is, near the back."

At the same time Geoff took hold of the beacon, a huge rumble sounded from somewhere out in the lobby. Not like a lightning strike.

More like something heavy had crashed to the tile floor. "What was that?"

"Oh no, no, no." The clerk rushed past him.

"What do you mean?" Geoff asked, not liking the tone of the guy's muttering.

The clerk didn't answer. Instead, he headed toward the corridor where their rooms were located. "Good God!"

Pulling up behind the clerk, Geoff could make out what appeared to be a long, rectangular cabinet surrounded by bits of broken pottery, greenery and dirt. And under it all? An unconscious Alex.

He shoved the clerk out the way so he could get to her. She was on her back, blood oozing from a mean cut on her forehead, one arm jutting out at a strange angle. "Alex? Can you hear me?"

No response. Dirt and plants as well as numerous shards of broken crockery covered her head, her arms, her upper body. He started removing them, until the clerk put a restraining hand on his arm. "Careful, man. That looks sharp."

He'd already discovered as much. The tips of his fingers were bleeding. "Call9-1-1. She needs medical help as soon as possible. And while you're back there, see if you've got any heavy-duty gloves so I can get this stuff out of her hair."

While the clerk was gone, he felt for a pulse. Weak, but steady. He breathed easier. "Alex? If you can hear me, don't move or you might get cut more."

Whether she heard him or not, she remained motionless.

"Her eyes flickered. Is she coming to?" a familiar-sounding male voice asked.

"Starting to, but this may take a while yet, as her brain returns to consciousness," said another voice. A female.

Were they talking about her? Before she could decide, everything went blank again.

After what seemed like just moments, sounds returned.

"She moved her hand."

"Shouldn't be long now."

She attempted to open her eyes, but it felt as if they'd been glued shut. She tried again, went a few seconds longer before they closed again. Finally, after several false starts, she began to focus. Not that she recognized her surroundings. She was on her back. When she turned to one side, she was bombarded with pain shooting through her arm, up her shoulder, through her head.

"Where?" All she could get out. Tremendous effort.

"Alex? It's me, Geoff." His warm hand covered hers.

Geoff. Right. Geoff, uh, McKenna. She'd been looking for him. Couldn't remember why. But now he was here. Wherever here was.

"Miss Appleby? I'm Tresa, your nurse. Don't try to talk yet."

"Nur—"

"You're in the hospital. We don't know all the details yet, but something heavy fell on you while you were in the dark."

Dark? Right. She'd been trying to find her way out of the nearly pitch-black hallway when she'd collided with something heavy, toppling it onto herself. Didn't remember anything beyond that.

"Alex?" Geoff squeezed her hand. "I'm so sorry. I shouldn't have left you alone so long."

Alone? Where had he been? All she remembered was the dark.

"You have a concussion, Alex," the nurse said. "Along with some cuts to your hands, arm and face. And a broken arm, which we've set and placed in a cast. Take your time coming to. I just wanted you to know your situation. I'll be back in a few minutes to check on you again. Meanwhile, Mr. McKenna will keep you company."

Geoff came into view. The usual scruff on his face had grown fuller. He still looked mighty fine, probably why the nurse was letting him stay. But his forehead showed lines, and those beautiful dark blue eyes were narrowed. Worried. About her.

"You gave me a scare, lady. All thoughts of the tornado vanished when I found you lying unconscious in the hall."

Tornado? Now she remembered. They'd returned from dinner amidst tornado warnings. The wind had picked up, and the heavens had opened just as she'd come through the motel doors. Things were coming back to her now. Then she blacked out again.

"Ah, you're back."

She blinked a few times, and this time she felt more awake. "Groggy."

"The nurse said to expect that for the next several hours. You may be going in and out a bit but not to worry."

"Tornado?"

"Didn't touch down, on its way northeast, although it's fast losing velocity, they say."

"Didn't hit … motel?"

He scrunched up his nose briefly, apparently not tracking. "Oh, right, the power failure," he said, catching on. "No, lightning hit a nearby tree, which fell on a power line."

"Oh."

"How are you feeling? You were covered in plants, dirt and broken pottery when I found you."

"What?"

"What was it? A large ceramic planter on top of a wooden base. It's usually tucked neatly behind a corner in the lobby but had been moved temporarily so they could mop the tile floor earlier in the evening. Some kid had puked. Unfortunately, it wasn't moved back when they finished. You would've walked right by it when the lights were on."

Attacked by a planter?

"Needless to say, the clerk was beside himself because he should've noticed the stand was out of place."

"Fired?"

"Not yet. Maybe not. He was a big help getting those broken ceramic pieces off you without nicking you or us. We had you pretty well cleared from the debris by the time the EMTs arrived."

They'd brought her here by ambulance? "Broken arm?" She'd never had a broken anything in her life, let alone been unconscious.

"Clean break, but it requires a cast and a sling for now. It finally dawned on me to look in the bag that was partially tucked under you.

Found your wallet, which contained an insurance card. But since you were out, they wanted to talk to your next of kin. Got your dad's name from Aubrey."

"They know?"

"Had to let them know we wouldn't be back tomorrow."

That was news. She attempted to sit up but quickly discovered it a bad idea; the various tubes and other paraphernalia connected to her impeded her progress. "Why aren't we leaving?"

"The doc wants you under observation for at least twenty-four hours. Here in the hospital. You're also pumped with a bunch of meds that need time to work their way through your system. For toppers, you can't drive, not with your arm immobile. Despite our adventure getting here, I can't drive all the way back."

She'd only been hospitalized once. When she was eight and her appendix had been removed. She didn't want to be here, but she didn't have much choice. She could barely hold her head up. Besides, she was still having trouble keeping her eyes open.

"Go back to sleep. I'll be here. They said I could camp out in this chair since you don't have any family with you."

His sticking around comforted her.

ALEX SLEPT THROUGH THE NIGHT, although the nursing staff woke her every so often to check her vitals. By morning, she was feeling much better and much worse. The dizziness from the night before had muted into a dull ache, but her arm hurt so much she wanted to pull it off.

Geoff sprawled in one visitor chair, his feet propped up in another, snoring softly. This was the third time she'd watched him sleep. She liked what she saw. He seemed so vulnerable and simultaneously peaceful. She couldn't believe he'd stuck the night out with her and not gone back to the motel, where he would've been much more comfortable. But she was damn glad. His presence made her less apprehensive about being here.

When they brought in her breakfast, he awoke. While the aide propped up the head of the bed so Alex could reach the tray, he excused himself to use the facilities down the hall.

Eating with one hand, her left when she was righthanded, wasn't easy, but she managed to feed herself. She hadn't been hungry, but after the first bite, she continued to work her way through the cereal and toast.

"Think you could get by on your own a few hours?" he asked when he returned. "The motel has offered me a free room and meals as long as I need to stay. Thought I'd take them up on their deal so I can shower and grab a few hours of sleep in a bed."

"By all means. I'm apparently not going anywhere."

"I'll bring your things back later. I kept your wallet. You won't need it while you're here."

"My phone?"

"Later. You need your rest this morning."

"But—"

"Only a few hours, Alex." He came to the bed, bent and kissed her. He grinned. "More of that when your body heals."

Her breakfast finished and Geoff gone, she drifted off to sleep until sometime later when the nurse woke her to check her vitals another time. A tall, red-haired man of about thirty stood next to the bed, reviewing something on his computer tablet. "Ah, you've joined the living again. I'm Dr. Whittaker. I'll be handling your case, since the doc you saw last night in Emergency doesn't carry a caseload."

His bedside manner reassured her. "What's the verdict, doc? Am I going to recover from this concussion?"

"All signs are good, Ms. Appleby, but with concussions we don't like to take chances. The brain is a funny thing. Doesn't always evidence a problem until later."

"You mean I could suddenly drop dead someday six months from now due to my run-in with a planter last night?"

"Remote possibility. But that's why we're keeping you here for observation today, even though the rest of your injuries have been addressed. Mainly, you just need time to heal."

Time to heal. Just what she didn't have. She needed to get back to Burlington and convince her stepsister to lease her motor coach. Then she needed to hightail it back to L.A. to babysit her other clients. "How much time are we talking?"

"I understand you were staying in the area overnight. That you drove up from the southeastern part of the state. So I've contacted a colleague there I'd like you to see next week. You've got a nasty cut on your forehead. It should heal with minimal scarring, but you may want to consider cosmetic surgery down the road. On the other hand, they tell me your hair normally covers that side of your face. You may opt to leave it alone."

She brought her good hand to her face to confirm the doctor's statement. Sure enough, a bandage covered over half her forehead. Plastic surgery? Not like there weren't thousands of surgeons she could turn to when she got back to the coast, but she'd never seen herself being part of that culture. "Guess I won't be changing my hairstyle for a while."

"I want you to stay here today," he continued. "I'll stop by tomorrow morning and decide then if we can release you or if you need to stick around a little longer. If the latter, I'll go over my reasons with you at that time."

"What do I do in the meantime? Can I get up and walk around?"

"You can sit up in bed and walk to the bathroom, but that's all for this morning. This afternoon, you can sit in that chair over there, walk the corridor. No heavy exercise."

She wasn't one for watching much television, but that seemed to be her best option for now.

"Officially, you're a casualty of last night's foul weather. But you weren't the only one affected by the blackout. We've got a woman here who fell down her basement steps when the lights went out and a guy who cut himself on a power saw. Fortunately, there've been no reported fatalities."

Someday, her being attacked by a ceramic planter and thus suffering an injury thanks to the storm might make an interesting cocktail-party story, as if she ever attended those dreary events. But right now, the doctor's words left her with cold comfort.

Bored, but not enough to turn on the TV, she watched the nurse go through her routine. The medical world had moved on since she was in nurses' training, and the age of electronic medical records had arrived. Doctors and nurses now carried computer tablets. Didn't reduce the need to enter data correctly, but there was much less potential for confusion from illegible script.

"How do you like using one of those?" she asked the nurse. Tresa?

The nurse lifted her eyes from the computer screen. "This?" She chuckled. "It was one big pain at first. I kept forgetting to save my input. I was trained on a clipboard and paper documents several years ago."

"How about now? Does it make your job easier?"

Tresa considered a moment. "I s'pose so, now it's become second nature. And from a total hospital standpoint, it's much better. I can pull up stuff in seconds now that would've taken much longer to retrieve before."

"Do you like being a nurse?" The question was out before Alex realized how inane she sounded.

The nurse placed a blood pressure cuff around Alex's upper arm. "You know, you're the first person to ask me that in a long time. Mostly, I'm either invisible doing my thing or not around when a patient thinks they need me. But I do enjoy the job, other than the havoc it's starting to play on my feet and back. Gonna have to find a desk job soon."

"Your patients' loss. I certainly appreciate the care you've given me."

"Thanks."

"I was in nurses' training once."

"You didn't finish?"

How much to reveal? Even though Tresa was a stranger she'd probably never see again, the full story behind her career switch was still too painful. "No. What seemed like a better offer came along near the end of my first year."

Tresa stopped what she'd been doing long enough to glance at Alex. "Regret it?" Sometimes. Yeah, I do."

"You're still young enough to go back and finish, you know."

Sounded so easy coming from the other woman. All Alex had to do was end her relationship with Loretta and her other two clients. All. Not gonna happen. Not as long as Loretta had the ace in the hole. "I've considered doing so. Just not yet."

"Take it from me, it's worth the investment in education."

The nurse left her alone with her thoughts. Thoughts about the future and how she wanted to shape it. She hadn't controlled her own destiny for some time.

Oddly, unlike most hospital patients, she felt at home in this room, even with all its tubes and monitors. Actually, because of them, most of which she recognized.

"Hope you don't mind a visitor?" Buddy Appleby stood in the door, an unsteady smile attempting to cover an anxious expression.

"Dad! What are you doing here?"

"Checking on my little girl. Heard you went and got yourself banged up." He made his way over to the bed. "Okay to hold your hand?"

"Of course. The arm hurts like hell, but the hand is still fine. How did you get here?"

He bent and kissed her forehead. "Aubrey called last night right after you'd been admitted. Said they found your insurance card in your things but wanted your next of kin to know you'd been hurt. Your mother couldn't be reached, so they called me."

"Geoff McKenna—he was with me—told me as much. But he didn't say you were on your way. Surely, the hospital could have gotten your consent or whatever it was they needed from you over the phone?"

He wandered around the foot of the bed, came over to her "good" side. "I only have one child of my own, kiddo. When I heard she'd been injured in a tornado, nothing was going to keep me away."

"Not even—"

"Iris? She's the one who agreed I had to come, and drove me to the airport." He picked up a package he'd dropped on a chair and handed it to her. "Insisted I bring this along. She didn't have time to shop before my flight, so she sent along her newest purchase for herself."

"You open it," she said. "Haven't mastered use of my left hand yet."

The package contained a light blue silk bed jacket. So Iris. Alex had never owned such a garment and probably never would have, but now she did. "Thank her for me. No, when I get my phone, I'll call and thank her personally."

"She'd like that. She'd like it even more if you wore it long enough for me to snap a photo and send it to her."

After they took care of appeasing Iris, he settled into the visitor chair where Geoff had spent the night. "Catch up your old man. Last I heard, you'd moved into the same firehouse where Aubrey lives with this Mitch guy. How did you wind up across the state in the path of a tornado?"

She related her experience with Allison Corley.

"Did you at least sign her for all this trouble?"

"No. I walked out on her and her parents."

"That bad, huh?"

"No, that good." She owed him some sort of explanation, even though she didn't want to reveal her hesitation about taking on another client. She told him how the Corleys had sought her out only to mollify their daughter.

"You didn't give the kid a chance to change her mind about her image?"

"To tell you the truth, Dad, even if she had been willing to go along with my assessment, I'm not sure I was ready to take on another client." Okay, now she'd done it. No way would he let her drop the topic until he knew the reason.

He surprised her. "Hallelujah! I'm happy to hear you say that, sweetie. You've got your hands full the way it is."

She tried to sit up further, but the shooting pains in her arm reminded her she could only go so far. "You, you think I'm in over my head?"

"Alexandra, you can accomplish anything you set your mind to. But lately, you haven't seemed happy with your job. I'm guessing it has something to do with Loretta Kinsolver, even though her star just keeps on rising, mostly because of you."

"True, but the more famous she gets, the more she demands. This ridiculous insistence that her motor coach for next fall's tour must be Jenna's is the most recent, but not the only one." Only Buddy knew the identity of the client who wanted the motor coach. She'd had to tell him as much to get him to back up her cover story about his seeking parts too young for him. He shook his head and continued doing so for several seconds. "Which is why you went to Burlington, even though you told your stepsisters it was because you were concerned about me."

"I also told them I wanted to get to know them better. That began as simply my entrée into their lives, but the longer I've been there, the more I believe it. They're nowhere near the bitches Mother has described over the years."

He released a laugh, the worry lines around his eyes fading. "I could've told you that years ago, but I'm glad you got a chance to see for yourself. Back to this mission to get Jenna's motor coach, have you gotten any closer to her consent?"

"I got Geoff to intercede with Jenna at a family dinner a few days ago where I was present. He asked about her future plans to tour. Jenna's daughter, Paige, erupted and left the table when Jenna said she was still considering a tour sometime down the road. I hate coming between mother and daughter, but it appears that issue predates my interference."

Once again, he shook his head several times. "I don't like your being in the middle. I've heard more than my share about it since last summer. From both Paige and Jenna, and especially from my own wife."

"Sorry, Dad. If I find another way to do this, I will. I'm really coming to like Jenna. And Aubrey. At times, I've actually felt like I have two sisters."

A broad smile stole across his face. "I like hearing you say that. I think Iris would too."

"The only problem is that they're both living in Iowa for the foreseeable future, and I'm returning soon to L.A."

"You don't sound all that excited at the prospect."

If he only knew what, or who, she'd found in this state. But Geoff was just a fling, a casual hookup while she was here. "I hate to think of returning without getting the lease. When I first got here, I told myself I wasn't going back until I had it, but now I'm not so sure."

"Is there no other way to satisfy Loretta? Like finding her a coach even grander than Jenna's?"

"In Loretta's warped sense of justice, it has to be this coach." She related the costume incident of the previous summer and how Loretta had taken that as such an insult from the upstart, even though it wasn't Jenna's fault.

"The more you reveal about this client of yours, the less I like her."

And he only knew part of Loretta's threat. "She's not the easiest person to manage."

"Then why don't you drop her?"

And there was the question of the year. Problem was, she couldn't tell him why. "I'm earning my keep from Loretta, Dad. The other two clients aren't bringing in much money and won't for some time, if ever."

Wrinkle lines crept across his forehead. "Then why don't you get out of the business entirely?"

Was it the drugs they'd given her for the pain, or was he just wearing her down? She wanted so much to confide in him. "It's not that easy. I signed contracts with Loretta and the others." Plausible. Her dad understood contract commitments.

He rose, poured her a glass of water.

How had he known she needed hydrating? Scary.

"How long you been managing Loretta?"

"Six, seven years. Why do you ask?"

"Tryin' to recall how it all came about. After high school, you bounced around for a while, trying to find yourself."

Bounced around. Nice way of saying she'd screwed off for nearly seven years after her parents' messy divorce. "That I did. I was just telling my nurse how I'd gone to nursing school for almost a year at one time."

"Did you tell her why you quit? Because you never told me, at least gave me a reason that made sense."

Thin ice again. How to skate over it without falling through? "We shared a mutual friend who I'd worked with when I was a production assistant on *Down with the Upps* the previous year. She wanted help getting into the business."

He sat there nodding. "Uh-huh. Heard all that before. But it's preamble. How'd she talk you into leaving school and managing her?"

She sighed inwardly. She was fast losing energy. "I don't recall," she lied. "She talked a good line. I'd just done poorly on some test, and before I knew it, I agreed."

Her father rose, found another glass in her bathroom, and poured water for himself. His way of saying he didn't believe a bit of her story.

At length, back in his chair, he said, "There's more to that story than you're letting on. You're hiding something for some reason you don't feel comfortable sharing with your old man. So I won't push. But when you're ready, I'll be there."

"Dad—"

"Shh. Don't say something you don't mean. Let's just leave it at that. For now."

Tears behind her eyes fought to make themselves known. "Have I told you lately how much I love you?"

He stood, leaned over her, encased what he could of her upper torso in an embrace without hurting her arm. "Feeling's mutual, kiddo." His voice choked as the words emerged.

"Hey, what's this?" Geoff ambled into the room, carrying her overnight bag in one hand and a vase of flowers in the other. "You've made friends fast. Thought you were going to sleep most of the morning."

"I did. For a while. Then I got this wonderful visitor. This is my dad. Geoff, Buddy Appleby. Dad, this is Geoff McKenna."

The two men shook hands, and then Geoff put her bag aside and located a place to put the flowers. "Had no idea what kind you liked, so I went for roses."

"They're beautiful. Thanks."

Geoff and her dad continued to stand, eyeing each other. "So. You accompanied Alexandra on this trip?" her father asked, as if expecting a full explanation of their relationship.

"It's a long drive from the southeastern part of the state to the northwest. Alex asked me if I'd come along to keep her company. And I needed to get out of town for a few days. Long story."

Her dad pointed a finger at Geoff. "Long story, huh? Care to share a few details?"

Geoff sneaked a glance at her. "Uh, there's this woman, see?"

"Ah. Got you."

"We've been seeing each other for several months, but lately, she's been moving into my life uninvited. I don't want to hurt her by being the one to break things off. So I'm keeping my distance."

"By going off for the weekend with my daughter. Staying in a motel together."

"We booked two rooms, Dad."

Now her father glanced at her. "No need to explain. Two rooms or one, I was just curious why he was here." He turned to Geoff. "Had you not been there in that motel, Alex could have been out cold on the floor longer than she was." He held out his hand again. "Thank you, man."

Somewhat surprised, Geoff readily accepted her father's hand. "I'd say it was my pleasure, but it wasn't. She scared me out of two years' growth, if I was still growing."

Buddy Appleby, who was just under six feet himself, raised his eyes to the man facing him. "You stopped right in time."

"Thanks. So I'd say a trip to the Midwest wasn't necessary. Alex is doing fine and should be released in the next day. But since I haven't had the privilege of being a father yet, I can only guess you had to see her for yourself."

"About the size of it. So what's the scoop on her stay?"

"Hey, guys. I'm right here, you know. I'm the one the doctor spoke with this morning."

Both swiveled to face her. Her dad was the first to ask. "And?"

"Yeah, and?" Geoff added.

"He'll stop by tomorrow morning. If nothing more to do with my head injury shows up between now and then, I'll be free to go. I'm supposed to take it easy for at least a week. It looks like I'll be staying on a little longer in the firehouse than the original plan, provided that's okay with your brother and Aubrey. And you?"

"I've already alerted them to the possibility, and they'd love to have you stay longer. As soon as I give him the word, Mitch and Aubrey will come up and get us, since neither of us can drive. We'll drop off your rental car here."

Her father raised a brow.

"Geoff has MS. He can only drive for short distances," Alex said.

"I, uh, could drive you back?" her dad said.

"You, Dad?" Alex said perhaps a tad too fast and too skeptically.

"Yeah, me. I'm a veteran L.A. driver. Driving across this flat state should be a snap. The traffic here can't be anywhere near the I-5 at any given hour.""Flat? Not from what Alex had seen. And I-80 and I-35 were major thoroughfares and truck routes through the rest of the country. On the other hand, he sounded like he could use his own adventure right now. Why not?

It wasn't exactly the return trip Geoff had envisioned. Alex's father drove them back to Burlington in Alex's rental car. Geoff played navigator in the front seat while Alex spread across the backseat, napping. Her doctor had told her to expect grogginess over the next few days from the pain meds she was taking for her arm and head.

Sex was probably out of the question for a while. God, he hoped not the rest of her stay. With her dad along, they couldn't even make out in the car as they had two days earlier.

Who'd have thought back then his fake health-care aide would need medical care of her own by the end of the day? Real medical help.

Once Geoff had directed Buddy out of town and back onto the interstate, they rode in relative silence a bit, Buddy acclimating himself to the car and the road, Geoff wondering what lay ahead as far as he and Alex were concerned.

"Tell me about yourself, Geoff." Buddy threw him an interested gaze before returning his attention to the road.

"You already know the basics. I'm a one-third-owner of McKenna

Custom Coaches, along with my two brothers, Graham and Mitch. Our business, my apartment and Mitch's are located in a renovated firehouse. I'm the front man. I seek out clients. My brothers are gradually cutting back on their time to pursue other careers. Mitch is an attorney and Gray an architect. I was a sales rep for several years until I was diagnosed with MS a few years back."

"Nice to have family. I often wished Alex had other siblings, but it wasn't in the cards for her mother and me."

"Alex told me you went through a difficult divorce when she was in her late teens."

"It had been going sour for years. We stuck together for Alex's sake and my career. Well, Deidre did. She liked being the wife of a sitcom star with a certain amount of public recognition. Until she met Philippe Guilbert. At the time, the guy was directing a few episodes of my show, but he had big plans for going into film. By some twist of fate, his first film struck gold."

"Your wife had an affair?"

Buddy glanced over his shoulder to check on Alex. "On the down-low. Philippe was still making a name for himself. Didn't have much money. Deidre wanted more than her share of our joint bank account, so she decided to smear my name. Started a rumor that I'd forced myself on one of my young costars. Totally untrue, but the rumor mongers in LaLaLand don't always check their *facts*."

"You got a raw deal."

"One way of putting it. The starlet I supposedly raped never testified in court, but she didn't deny the story either. Later, she wound up with small roles in several of Guilbert's films. Affairs are an accepted way of life in some entertainment world circles, but rape or even the rumor of it was considered pretty bad back then, and that was before the more recent attention sexual harassment has received. My story line was dropped the following season, but the stigma stuck with me. I had a tough time getting parts for the next several years."

"Alex told me a little about your story, but hearing it in your own words really brings it home."

"The truth finally did come out, several years later, when the starlet got on the wrong side of Guilbert. He and my former wife had married by then, and she would have none of his philandering, so the starlet was fired. In retaliation, the starlet started talking to the entertainment rags."

Neither man spoke for some time as several miles rolled by. Buddy stared straight ahead while Geoff reflected on the other man's revelation. Buddy had shed a little more light on the woman Alex had become. No wonder she wasn't into serious relationships. She'd had a front row seat at the unraveling of her parents' marriage. Without siblings to turn to, she'd had to absorb the hurt and disappointment on her own.

Yet this man seemed like a low-key good guy. Alex got some of that from him.

"Never seen this part of the state before," Buddy said finally, once they returned to I-80, the east-west thoroughfare through the state. "It's not as flat as I said earlier, is it?"

"In spots, but no, a lot of rolling hills."

"You like living here?"

"Don't have much to compare it to. Lived here all my life, although I touched on some of the border states when I was on the road."

"Ever thought of moving west, to the coast?"

Was the man just making conversation, or was there more to the question? "I tried out the idea last summer when Mitch and Aubrey got serious. For a while, it looked like he might follow her back to L.A. I wondered then how I would react if I faced similar circumstances." Why had he said that? He was leaving himself open to more probing.

"Come to any conclusions?"

Yep, there it was. "Realized I wouldn't know until and unless I encountered a similar situation. The Mitch I knew before Aubrey would have dug in and refused to go. In fact, that's what happened when he was engaged prior to Aubrey's arrival. His fiancée wasn't happy practicing law in a small town in Iowa and set her sights on practicing out East. They broke up when they discovered they wanted different things."

"My wife, Iris, was a little bit like that fiancée. She grew up in your town, you know? Married a guy from there. But she wasn't happy. Thought she wanted more for herself and Jenna. Ironic, huh, how not only Jenna but also Aubrey wound up in the very place she so disliked?"

"I hear they've invited her back to see the place after all these years, but so far, she's not been interested."

They'd been on the road a little more than four hours as they approached Iowa City. "I'd like to stop here for lunch, Buddy. If you don't mind the side trip, let's drive through the University of Iowa campus."

Buddy exited the interstate and headed through the small town of Coralville on the west. "A lot of students who don't live on campus live here," Geoff explained. "I used to be one of them." He pointed out his old apartment complex as they went by.

Shortly, they reached the Iowa River, which separated the east campus from the west. Students dotted both shores and flocked across the winding pedestrian overpass on their way to and from class.

"We seem to have hit town at a peak time of day," Buddy said.

"It's Monday. Spring semester is just about over. May even be finals week."

"Where are we?" Alex asked from the backseat.

"My alma mater." The pride coming through in his tone surprised him. Hadn't thought much about his college years in a long time. "Place is blooming. Probably the prettiest time of the year, except for fall." Buddy pointed to an upscale franchise restaurant. "That place okay? There's a gas station across the street, so we can fill up. You hungry, hon?"

"Thirsty. But you guys go ahead."

"Guess I had more appetite than I thought," Alex said later as she devoured half of her dad's burger and stole several onion rings from Geoff.

"Good sign. You're recuperating." Buddy glanced at their waitress, who'd showed up to remove their plates. "Thanks, ma'am. That burger was so good my daughter took part of it."

The waitress grinned. "I'll tell the fry cook. He takes great pride in using only one-hundred-percent Iowa beef." As she started back to the kitchen, she pivoted, squinted at Buddy. "You look familiar, but you're not one of our regulars. Where else would I have seen you?"

Geoff waited to see how Buddy would respond.

Did he milk recognition or shy away?

"I know. You've been on TV. A while back, but I still remember you," the waitress said.

Buddy gave her a moment to say the name of his old show herself, but her memory continued to struggle. "Perhaps it was *Pike's Peeking?*" he asked.

She scrunched up her nose, trying out the title. "Maybe. That show was on, what, well over ten years ago. I was a teenager then, but yes! That was it. My mom loved it. Watched it every week." Her eyes brightened. "You were the dad, weren't you? You were a private eye, and your daughter helped you solve cases when she wasn't busy being a, what, a reporter?"

"Columnist, but otherwise your memory is on point."

"What on earth are you doing in Iowa? Do you have a student at the university?"

Buddy shot a glance at Alex, smiled. "No. We're passing through on our way to Burlington."

"Oh."

Alex's father seemed to be waiting for one more shoe to drop.

And it did. "Would you mind taking a picture with me?" the woman asked.

"I'd love to. Geoff, would you do the honors?"

Geoff hadn't expected to be brought into this fan worship experience, but he accepted the woman's cell phone, which she produced from her apron pocket, and snapped two shots.

Alex appeared to think nothing of the episode and continued to munch away.

"You were so gracious with that woman," Geoff said to Buddy, once back in the car. "Doesn't it ever get old?"

"Sometimes the recognition comes when I least want it, when I'm in the middle of something else, but no, gotta keep that fan base going and growing."

Geoff wasn't sure he could always be "on" and receptive to the demands for photos and autographs like Buddy. The man was growing on him.

Fifteen

Alex slept for shorter periods the rest of the trip.

When she wasn't sleeping or on the cusp of wakefulness, she took in the conversation between her dad and Geoff. He'd never really talked to her about the breakup of his marriage to her mother. What she knew about her dad's losing his job came from stilted references from her mother, who'd apparently omitted her part in the collapse of Buddy's career, or from others in the business a few years later when she'd been a production assistant.

She'd always believed in her dad's innocence. He couldn't possibly have forced himself on that woman, let alone raped her. But she'd also witnessed firsthand how people in the industry turned on him based on mere innuendo. Solid proof wasn't necessary. He hadn't completely dropped out of the Hollywood picture by doing guest shots, but he'd never regained his former standing, although he'd come close when the producers of another sitcom considered him for a supporting role.

That's when Loretta had entered the picture, with her so-called inside knowledge about Buddy's private life. He'd been so excited at the prospect of doing a new show Alex had been willing to do anything to spare him from a second turn on the rumor mill. Including leave nursing school to manage Loretta's infant acting career.

By the time Buddy learned he'd been second choice, she'd left nursing. When she hinted to Loretta she might go back, Loretta had turned the screw, suggesting, no, outright telling her, the stories about Buddy could still see light of day anytime she wanted.

Geoff seemed able to get her dad to talk about things. That wasn't really a surprise, though, was it? She'd told Geoff things about herself she rarely shared with anyone else. She'd even come close to telling him about Loretta's hold over her.

Rather than curtail the discussion up front, she rolled her head over and gave in to sleep.

She awoke when the car stopped but was too groggy to do much more than open an eye. Where were they? The sound of the door opening made her jerk.

"Rise and shine, sleepy lady," Geoff said. "If you can make it up the stairs to your room, I'll bring your things."

She ascended the stairs slower than usual. Someone pulled down the covers on her bed. She climbed in, clothes and all, and immediately went back to sleep.

G EOFF SET her overnight bag on a nearby chair while Buddy tucked her in. Silently, they both left the room, and Geoff led Buddy to the kitchen. "Beer?" he asked as he retrieved one for himself. "I'll show you my apartment downstairs in a little while, but I thought Aubrey, Mitch or Gray might be around so I could introduce you to them."

"I'd like that, although I've met Graham a couple times. And, of course, I know Aubrey."

"Did I hear my name?" Gray asked, coming into the room. He, too, went directly to the fridge. "Needed a break from the schematics I've been studying most of the day." Then he noticed their visitor. "Hi, Buddy. Thanks for driving Alex and Geoff back from Sioux City. You freed Mitch up to work on some brief that's due soon. Don't know whether that was a favor or not." He reached to shake the older man's hand, then flopped into one of the chairs at the kitchen table.

"Glad to do it. I rarely get to spend much time with my daughter, not that I did today with her out cold in the backseat. But Geoff and I had a nice talk."

Gray turned to his brother. "How is she, besides sleeping a lot?"

"Doc said she was doing well enough to travel. She's gonna be laid up in bed a few days, because he doesn't want her up and around much while the concussion settles. She's not gonna like being tied down. She wanted to get back to California soon, but the doc nixed that idea. So we'd better be prepared to keep her occupied."

"I'd be happy to take my turn," Buddy offered, "if you don't mind my sticking around? Don't worry about putting me up. I'll keep her rental car and find a motel."

"What about your wife? Will she be okay staying out there on her own?"

"Iris? She'll hardly miss me, what with all her clubs and activities."

"We've got an extra room at my parents' house," Gray said. "Paige'll need to move all her sports paraphernalia out, but she'll be happy to see her grandpa."

"Jenna won't mind?" Buddy asked.

"She's hardly there these days, what with the piano lessons and playing for the community theater. Paige could use the company. Any day now she'll be tempted to sneak a boy in after school when no one else is there. This'll slow her plans a bit."

Buddy choked on his beer but quickly recovered. "That's a new role for me, chaperoning my granddaughter. But I'd love to take you up on the offer. Until Alex gets back on her feet."

"Hey, I've got an idea. I'm involved with the community playhouse here too. Boning up on theater architecture. Already got a small project out in Middletown. Acting group out there is converting an old barn to a place where they can perform. They'd love to have you come by and talk about your experience."

Buddy blinked. "That's a nice invite, Graham, but I'm a TV man. I've never appeared on stage."

"Then talk about TV and let them compare it to what they know about the stage. I can set up something for tomorrow night, if you're interested?"

"I, uh, well … okay."

Gray wrote down directions to the McKenna house for Buddy, who agreed to show up around five thirty. "See you then, man. For now, I'd better get back to those schematics." He finished his beer, stuck it in the recyclables bin in the cupboard and headed off.

"You okay with me staying at the old homestead a few days?" Buddy asked Geoff.

"Yeah, great idea. I would've suggested it myself, but now that Jenna and Gray are living there, it's not really mine to offer." He finished off his beer. "How about talking to the playhouse group? You okay with that?"

"I love the idea, but I'm not sure what I'll have to say will be of much use to them."

"Just having a celebrity in their midst will be enough."

"What do you think Alex will say when she hears?"

Geoff gathered and disposed of their two empties. "You have to ask? She's really proud of you."

Buddy's eyebrows rose. "Really? I don't see her much, you know? She's had her own place, closer to her mother's, for years. It's only been in the last five years or so that she's paid much attention to me at all. Her mother's doing. Even before our divorce, Deidre badmouthed me whenever she got the chance. I didn't believe her capable of such nasty tactics until some of her friends told me."

"Friends who wanted you for themselves?" Geoff couldn't help asking.

"Wondered the same at the time. But later I overheard more than one conversation between Deidre and Alex. Poor girl, she tried to defend me, but Deidre has a way of cutting off every objection. All in the name of a mother protecting her daughter from her dastardly daddy."

"Was it always like that? Your wife snipping away at you?"

Buddy seemed to think back, consider how his marriage dissolved. "Interesting question. We met in an acting class in L.A. Things heated up fast between us until she got a part in an off-Broadway show. Didn't see her for another three years, but then our relationship reignited. She got pregnant with Alex, which forced her to turn down a huge part back East. We married, and for a while, she was happy being a mother and homemaker, although I suspect deep down she secretly resented this new role."

"And you, for putting her in that position?"

Buddy studied him, his dark brown eyes so much like Alex's, seeming to read Geoff's mind. "You seem to understand resentment well."

"Had a little experience with it, yes." Some days, without seeing it coming, he'd wonder why he was the one to contract MS rather than his brothers. His pity party would last until he'd remember Kyle and their respective situations and hate himself for being so petty. After all, the guys had more than sacrificed for him these past few years.

"I was blithely unaware of my wife's feelings until things were already out of control. Deidre was a good person, but I think having had to give up a career she'd worked so hard for did something to her spirit, her better judgment. In the end, she not only wanted out of the marriage, she wanted to take my beloved daughter away from me too. She did everything she could to turn Alex against me." He lifted his head and gazed directly at Geoff. "But Alex is her own person. She didn't let that happen."

Geoff nodded. In the short time Buddy had been with them, it had been obvious how much father and daughter cared for each other. Gray, Mitch and he had enjoyed a similar bond with their parents, so he got why Buddy had suddenly gone silent. Some feelings ran too deep for a guy to express.

The silence between them wasn't strained. Simply two men sharing a moment.

Sharing a moment. That reminded him of Kyle. "I need to make a phone call, Buddy. Need to check on a sick friend."

JUST OUTSIDE THE DOOR, where they couldn't see her, but she could hear them, Alex leaned against the wall, tears streaming down her cheeks. She'd only guessed how the friction between her parents had developed. Hadn't known she was the reason her mother's acting career had come to a close nor how much she meant to her dad. How could she have been so blind? Her mother was the one off on some new expensive vacation while her dad had flown to Iowa the minute he heard about her injuries.

She backed away so they wouldn't spot her and returned to her room. Her headache had come back, but she didn't want to disturb the two men to ask for help. She'd wait. Hopefully, one or both would check in on her soon. Meanwhile, time to assess her situation. Couldn't very well continue her stint as Geoff's health aide if she couldn't hold a blood pressure cuff or thermometer. They needed an alternate plan to keep Eileen from assuming her duties.

She was going to be stuck here at the firehouse the next few days. Not much chance to work on Jenna, unless Jenna came by. Maybe she could work on Jenna through Aubrey. Or Graham, whenever he was in the building.

There was also her phony cover story about needing Iris's help to keep her dad from going out for parts for which he was no longer suited. She'd have to remind him to be on the alert for any questions Jenna or Aubrey might ask.

None of her clients would accept her injuries as an excuse to postpone their needs. She had no idea how she would deal with this problem. Perhaps it was just the throbbing in her head keeping her from concentrating.

Finally, there was the issue of Geoff. Geoff an issue? Wrong term. But she'd had sex with him. More than once. Great sex. Sex they both wanted, enjoyed and agreed not to take seriously. Now that she would be here longer than she'd planned, how did that affect their agreement? More to the point, she was starting to feel something for him. Couldn't define it, probably because it had been cut short with the storm and her trip to the hospital. But there was something there.

"You look mighty thoughtful there, my dear. Anything you want to share with your old dad?"

She asked for help taking her meds.

While her dad went to get water, Geoff appeared. "How's your head?"

"Could be better. I don't want to overmedicate, but I've got plans to make, and this stupid headache is clogging my thinking."

"Plans, huh? How can I help?" Without asking, he settled on the edge of the bed.

"That's part of the problem. I'm supposed to be helping you with Eileen. Now she'll have an excuse to resume her mothering efforts."

"No problem. I'll tell her I'm still checking in with you daily to report my vitals."

Okay, one problem addressed. "You've been gone a day longer than planned. Won't she be showing up soon to reclaim you?"

"She called already, wanted to know why I prolonged the trip. So I told her about your situation. Told her I felt guilty for your accident because I was off with the guy at the front desk when the lights went off. Don't be surprised if she shows up after work ready to take care of you as her excuse for sticking around."

"Hadn't even considered the possibility. How do we counter?"

"Already taken care of." He told her about her dad remaining a few days and Graham's having asked him to stay with them. "We'll let your dad do the overprotective thing to scare her off, because he'd be doing it anyway. My guilt thing will explain my being in here as much as your dad and you can stand me, as well as why I don't feel I can be off doing anything with her."

"Think that will do it?" She'd observed Eileen in action. The woman had a tough skin and one goal: Geoff. She wouldn't be dissuaded easily.

Geoff pursed his lips, slid a little closer to her. "Uh, no. We have to move to Act Two in our plan. With your dad here, I probably can't climb in bed with you, but there's no reason she can't walk in on our kissing and hand-holding. Your dad's aware of our scheme. He and I talked."

"I heard some of your talk in the car."

"Really? Thought you were asleep most of the ride."

"In and out. Couldn't really hear your words."

"Your dad's a pretty nice guy. Easy to talk to. A lot of great stories."

That he was. And she was glad he was here, although Iris must be having fits. The thought amused her. Now both her daughters and her husband were hanging out in the very place she loathed.

As if he knew he was being discussed, her dad arrived at that moment with water and a vial of pills. "Here you go." He glanced at Geoff. "Has Geoff told you about my sticking around?"

"Yes. Even though I don't think it's necessary, I'm glad you're here. I just hope you won't get too bored."

"Bored? Girl, my to-do list has been fuller since arriving yesterday than it has been in some time. I enjoyed the drive today. Now I'm playing nurse to you. And Graham even invited me to speak to his acting group tomorrow night."

Seemed like a lot had happened. And her dad was already accepting engagements? Interesting. "I'm impressed. You're not letting any grass grow under you. Geoff tells me he's already briefed you on fending off his girlfriend."

"I'm to be a buffer. That's what they call it, right? Be here with you at times she might visit so she can't take over your care?"

"Right. You may walk in on Geoff and me, uh, showing affection to each other. That's aimed at Eileen also, so don't assume anything else."

Her dad studied her, then Geoff. "Uh, okay. So I should dismiss any hanky-panky I might interrupt?" His eyes sparkled as he asked.

"Holding hands, Dad. Or maybe kissing, depending how much is called for. Anything more—"

" … is not in the plans," Geoff finished for her.

"Too bad. You two would make a great couple." He held up a hand. "Just sayin'. I've already decided I like this guy."

"Thanks, Buddy. I like you, too," Geoff returned. "You don't by any chance cook too? None of us, including your daughter, is very good in the kitchen."

"She inherited that from me, I'm afraid. Her mother, too, come to think of it. But I can dial a mean telephone number. Hungry yet for dinner?"

"Getting there, but shouldn't you be on your way to Gray's? Paige should be home by now."

"Ah, yes. Need to go check in so I can be back here in time for La Girlfriend."

Geoff remained behind after Buddy left. "You don't have to keep me company," Alex told him. "I'll be fine up here by myself."

"I know. I've put my number in your speed dial, in case you need me. I have to check my messages, but I'll be back in a little while."

He was gone long enough for her to shut her eyes a bit, grab a little more sleep. She was no longer fighting off slumber, having realized each time she nodded off, she was a little stronger when she awoke.

She was just waking again when Geoff popped in. "We need to talk."

"Does that mean what I think it means? 'It was great fun, but now …'"

"That your take?"

"You're the one who said it."

He swiped his hands down his pants. "Even though I started it, I'm beating around the bush, waiting for you to show your hand. But you're just as cagey. Damn, Alex. I feel like a chemical reaction that got bottled up before the chemist had a chance to see the results."

"Sorry, I don't follow. Why not say what you mean?"

"Okay. I enjoyed our trip, really enjoyed it, up 'til the lights went out. I was just wondering, I, uh, need to find out, what would've happened if there'd been no storm and you didn't run into that planter." He gazed back at her with eyes begging her to give him the right answer.

"Well, I'd say, from my standpoint, we probably would have repeated our performance from the afternoon. Most likely more than once, possibly adding new dimensions to our interaction. We would have returned yesterday, maybe after a stop alongside an off road for yet one more go. When we got back here, we probably would've had a conversation very similar to this, only a day sooner."

"Safe answer. Want to go for broke and tell me where we would've gone from there?"

"That depends. As long as our dalliance has been for show, your timeline for dealing with Eileen has been fine with me. But if we decide this is for real, even if only for whatever time I'm still here, you can no longer lead her on."

"You want me to initiate the breakup?"

"I know you wanted to leave it to her, even though you've been pushing her. But that was before we, uh—"

" ...went beyond pretend?"

He was calling the question. Why couldn't he be the one to say it? "Is that what you're saying?" Why was she so hesitant to declare herself?

"We both seem to be dancing around the question. I like you, Alex. Even with all the bad stuff that happened this past weekend, it was one of the best times I've had in ages. But you'll be leaving soon. It doesn't do either of us any good to hope for anything beyond that."

How could the man paint their relationship so positively and still sound so bleak? "No, I suppose not. So you want to cut it off here?"

He reached for her good hand, squeezed it. "No! I'm probably setting myself up for a hard fall, but if you're okay with it, I want to take advantage of every minute you're still here."

"But still keep it casual."

He slid closer, his eyes bored into hers. "If you mean no ties, yes. But I don't intend to walk away from the great sex."

"Even with one hand and arm laid up?"

His eyes twinkled. "Oh, lady, what you can do with rest of your body would put a hooker to shame."

"Good to know. I should've asked the doctor about mixing sex with a concussion."

"You have to stop if you feel the least bit nauseous or dizzy. Otherwise, you're good to go."

"And you know this how?"

He grinned. "You don't think I let us get away without asking? Give me some credit. I have big plans for you while you're still here."

Sixteen

"Knock, knock. Coming through." Eileen's voice actually trilled her entrance.

Geoff still held Alex's hand but quickly removed it as soon as he was sure Eileen had seen. "What's all this?"

Eileen directed her gaze at Alex. "Heard you had some kind of accident this weekend. Thought these might brighten your day." She held out a vase of spring flowers, then sought a place to put them.

"Uh, yes. A ceramic vase and I collided in the dark after the power went off in my motel. Thanks for the flowers."

"I stopped by yesterday, and Aubrey updated me about your accident. Then I called Geoff earlier to see if you'd returned yet." Her tone was that of Geoff's confidante.

"How'd you know we were back?" Geoff asked.

"I wanted to know Alex's condition, so I called the hospital and asked to be put through to her room. When they were unable to transfer my call, I assumed she'd been released."

Good grief! Did the woman have no sense of propriety?

Before he had a chance to react, Eileen switched her attention back to Alex. "How ironic. Here you've been so kind to do a daily check on

Geoff's health, and suddenly you're the one who needs your own care provider."

"Not real—"

"So here I am. Heaven knows Geoff and Graham aren't up to the task with all they've got to do these days. And Aubrey, bless her heart, just isn't the hands-on type."

As a third-party observer, Geoff saw his soon-to-be ex-girlfriend in a different light. He'd only glimpsed some of this side of her personality in the past, especially recent days. She was not only bold and pushy, she wasn't one to give up easily. Good thing they'd anticipated this move. But he'd let Alex handle that part.

"That is so sweet of you, Eileen. Especially since we didn't get off to a very good start."

Eileen made a sweeping motion with her hands. "Old history. You're a guest of the McKennas and I'm a friend of the family. So why shouldn't I take care of you?"

Geoff waited. Alex could stick up for herself. She was also used to the tug and pull of entertainment negotiations. This was going to be fun to watch.

"Actually, there isn't much involved with my so-called care, other than providing a second hand sometimes. It's asking too much for you to come over a couple times a day from work and your home, especially when Geoff, Aubrey, Graham or at least one of them is usually around."

"But now that you can't check on Geoff's health daily—"

"Oh, but I can. We'll just do it here, instead of in his apartment, at least for the next few days while I'm supposed to have bed rest."

Though she continued to smile, visible lines radiated from Eileen's mouth as she fought to maintain her friendly demeanor. "But—"

"Hey, kiddo, I'm back," Buddy announced from the door. He glanced at Eileen. "Oh. Hello?"

"This is Eileen Summers," Geoff said. "A friend of the family."

Buddy did his thing, shook Eileen's hand, presented his most impressive self.

"You're Buddy Appleby, Alex's father, right?"

Someone had been searching the internet to vet Alex. No surprise there.

"That's me," Buddy answered, apparently unfazed by Eileen's knowledge. "Flew back here to see for myself how my little girl is doing."

"How nice." An icy edge slipped into Eileen's tone.

Buddy came over to Alex, felt her forehead. "How you doing? You don't feel warm."

She smiled up at him. "I'm fine, Dad. Other than getting a little tired again."

"Then why don't we all leave you alone? I brought Paige back with me. She'd like to stop in, too, but not until after you've rested. Ah, I see you've got flowers. That was very thoughtful, Ms. Summers. Thanks for dropping by."

Buddy was even better than his daughter at thwarting Eileen's interference. He put a hand on her back, opened the door and ushered her through it.

Geoff winked at Alex and followed. "Be back later."

BUDDY WENT off to the living room, where the sounds of a video game blared. Geoff went downstairs to his office.

Eileen followed in Geoff's wake. "It seems I'm out of a job before I even started. But since that frees me up, why don't we go out for dinner? I'll pay."

"I, uh, can't. I need to deal with the calls and other details that have piled up since Saturday." He caught himself before suggesting they do it another time. He really should follow through on Alex's suggestion to make a clean break, but he needed time to plan how he was going to tell her. No, that was bull. He was a coward.

"You've only been gone from work a day," she reminded him. "Surely, you could catch up later?"

"I need to stick around for Alex."

"But her father is here."

"For a while. But he's staying at Gray's, and he's got Paige with him. She'll be wanting to leave before long."

"I thought her dad was here to take care of Alex, not Paige."

"Hey, she's his granddaughter who he hasn't seen in some time. Can't blame him for taking advantage of this trip."

They'd reached the door to his office, where he deliberately landed instead of the door to his apartment. He smiled dismissively. "See you again soon." *Please take the hint before I have to tell you to leave.*

"How 'bout I get us some sandwiches and bring them back?"

"Thanks for the offer, but no." He didn't suggest a reason. That would only initiate another move on her part. Their relationship had become a giant chess board.

To underline his point, he opened the door, almost closed it behind him. "Bye."

He stood behind the closed door, ready to stop her if she came through after him. A minute later, when the door remained closed, he decided he was safe and ambled over to his desk. Not that much work had piled up during his absence. What business-related calls, emails, and texts he'd received, and there weren't many, he'd taken care of as they arose.

He and Alex hadn't finished discussing his approach to gaining new clients. She hadn't appeared very impressed when he'd gone through his efforts. He'd wanted her to expound on her opinion, but she'd been hesitant, and then time had gotten away from them. Speaking of which, there was something else, besides sex, they hadn't gotten back to, but it was still in the car. The rental car Buddy now claimed.

He made a quick trip to the kitchen, where he found both Buddy and Paige along with Aubrey and Mitch.

"Buddy ordered in dinner," Aubrey called. "Roast beef and ham sandwiches."

"Just met this guy, and he's already impressing me with his culinary skills," Mitch added.

Buddy placed a comradely hand on Mitch's shoulder. "As long as you're okay with takeout, I'm your man, although it's my granddaughter here who suggested this deli. Got potato salad and kosher dills too."

"Hi, Geoff. Isn't it cool that Grandpa Buddy came to visit?"

Geoff sent Buddy an amiable nod. "Sure is. Did you get him settled in yet?"

"We're gonna move my things out when we get back."

"Go ahead, Paige. Tell him the same thing you told Aubrey and Mitch," her grandfather said.

The girl rolled her eyes. "I'm sorry I blew up when I was here last week. Mom and I have issues, but you all shouldn't have to listen to us quarrel."

Obviously repeating what her mother had told her to say, but a good sign. "Apology accepted, if that's what it was?"

The teenager nodded.

"Did you and your mom work it out?" Geoff asked.

She hung her head. "Not exactly. But she isn't going on tour for a while. For now, guess that's as much as I can ask."

"Have you apologized to Alex yet?" Not that the apology was so important, but it might give Alex an in with Paige. He owed her that much.

"She will before we leave tonight," Buddy said for the girl. "In fact, maybe Alex is awake now." Before he escorted Paige to Alex's room, though, he held up a bag for Geoff. "Found this in the car. Thought you might be missing it?"

Geoff accepted the package. "That's what I was coming to inquire about. Thanks. You saved me a trip to the car."

"Souvenir?" Buddy arched a knowing brow.

"Yeah. I introduced Alex to our Dutch settlement on the way north."

"I don't remember going through there."

"No, we took a different route coming back. A little faster."

Alex was just waking up when they peeked in. "Back already, Dad?"

"Brought you dinner and"—he pushed Paige into the room—"my granddaughter."

"Hi, Paige."

"That's some cast you've got." Paige came closer to admire Alex's arm wear. "Can I write my name on it?"

"You can try. They're made of a different material than they used to be."

Buddy handed her a ballpoint pen, and Paige promptly drew on the cast. "You got a sling too?" she asked as she noted the dark blue fabric hanging on the backboard.

"The works. My arm got banged up pretty well."

Paige finished her writing and backed away. "Uh, when I was here last week for dinner?"

"Yes?"

"I, uh, shouldn'ta gotten so angry at the table. Involved all of you in my fight with Mom."

Just when she was starting to think she'd never get the lease from Jenna, this beautiful child was offering her one more chance. Had to play this cool. Opportunity might not smile on her again. "Thanks. That took a lot of courage to tell a relative stranger."

"Courage? Mom made me."

"Ah, moms can be like that. It's been years since I was a teen, but you never forget."

"You did stuff like that, too?"

"Not quite, but I had my own ways of getting back at my mom." She tried not to check the expression on her dad's face. She hoped he understood what she was doing. "I once showed up at one of her garden parties in Goth garb."

"Really? What'd she do?"

"Told them I'd gotten a small part in a movie and was in costume."

"Fast thinking."

"That's my mom, when it comes to saving face. The next party she gave, she got concert tickets for me and three friends and had our chauffeur take us."

"You had a chauffeur?"

Her dad cringed. "That was before I put Alex's mother on a restricted budget," he stuck in.

This could be the opening she needed. "Did you and your mom resolve your problems with her tour?"

Paige settled a hip on the bed. "Sorta. She promised she wouldn't do anything this year. Maybe next summer. I'll be sixteen then and maybe old enough to tag along."

Yes, yes, yes! That left next fall, when Loretta wanted the coach, open. One major obstacle removed. "That's great news for you. Does that mean your mother will continue leasing the coach to others?" She held her breath. Didn't want to appear too interested.

"Beats me. All I cared about was her not using it."

"Oh, sure. But the money she'd receive in return would go a long way toward paying your college tuition."

"True, but Mom says she's got that covered with a trust fund my other granddad left her."

Lucky kid. "How about a house?"

"For now, the McKenna place is fine."

This was becoming much more difficult than she'd anticipated. One more try. "Then I guess finances aren't such a big deal. Unless you were hoping for your own car once you turn sixteen?"

A large smile seized Paige's face. "Now that's an idea!"

"Are you allowed to drive to school?"

"If you live far enough away, which we do."

Alex shrugged, forgetting her arm. But the sharp pain was worth it. This should be incentive enough for Paige to talk her mother into further leasing. "Well, there you go."

"We should get you back home, young lady. If I recall, you still have homework to do," Buddy told Paige.

"Okay." Was that reluctance in her tone? "You ever do that Goth stuff with your makeup anymore," she asked Alex.

Oh-oh. Dangerous ground. "That something you're interested in?"

"Maybe. Goth stuff has sorta faded out. But it would be cool to show my girlfriends."

"I can't use two hands to apply the makeup right now, but if your mom approves, and only if she approves, sure, we could play with it."

Paige actually clapped. "Terrif! Tomorrow?"

"Have your mom call me first." No, scrap that. She didn't want Jenna thinking she was behind Paige promoting the lease. "Rather, have her talk to your grandfather and he can let me know the next time he's here."

"Pretty smooth move. Getting Paige on your side, suggesting she might get a car from continued leasing of the coach," Geoff said once Paige and Buddy left. He bent over to kiss her. "You can thank me now or later, after the lovebirds have gone to bed."

"Thanks, but why?"

"Your dad had no idea you were at dinner that night Paige went ballistic. After she apologized to me, I suggested she needed to do the same for you. Ta-da! Now kiss me or lay on as much praise as you think my grand action deserves."

"You've pretty much delivered on your side of our bargain. How about my part? Did you talk to Eileen when the two of you left my room earlier?"

"No, I didn't call things off with her. Yet. I was almost there, the way she kept pushing to go out, even after I told her I had work to do."

"What stopped you? She gave you the perfect entrée."

"It didn't seem like the right time."

"Oh, well, wouldn't want to put you off your schedule."

"Figured you'd be about this thrilled. I could make it up to you with a roast beef sandwich?"

"That my dad brought?"

"You know about that? Let me think of another way."

"Tell me how I'm going to survive the next few days in this bed."

He went to the vase of flowers Eileen had brought, took a whiff. Returning, he pulled a chair up to the bed and settled onto it. "Survive. Keep that word in mind, because that's what you did. You survived that storm and what might have even been a worse accident."

"I get that. And if Jenna agrees, which I doubt, I'll have about an hour playing aesthetician and transforming a beautiful teenager into a Goth. But I can't do much work."

"Why not? You've only lost the use of one hand and one arm temporarily. Headache or not, which should have subsided by now, you can still think. And you've got your phone. What else do you need?"

"Ideas. Got any to spare?"

"I've got ideas, all right, but probably not what you're talking about. Tell me more."

"This trip is costing me progress for my clients. Don't get me wrong, I love being here. But I've got to start making things happen for them."

"You want to discuss them? Or is that all confidential?"

"You and I are beyond that point, don't you think? But I also don't want to keep you from your work more than I have. You've got your own clients to find."

His eyes widened. "You've given me an idea. How 'bout we make another deal? I help you with your clients and you help me find mine?"

Seventeen

Why hadn't this occurred to him before? They came from two different worlds, but in many ways they thought alike.

"Trade places with each other?" Alex asked.

"More like trade ideas, feed off each other's energy."

"I suppose we could try. Beats lying around all day feeling sorry for myself with nothing to do."

"What's holding you back? You reacted the same when we were on the road Saturday. We got to talking about my approach to finding clients, and you clammed up, rather, changed the topic."

She played with the edges of her blanket, rolling it through her fingers, letting go, then repeating the process. "The truth? I saw some real flaws in your approach, but I didn't want to talk about them then because I didn't want to spoil the trip."

"No trip now. If you hurt my feelings, I'll tell you. And I'll argue any points I don't agree with."

"You want to start tonight?"

"Why not? I'm pumped to get going."

"Got pen and paper or your tablet handy?"

Great. He'd piqued her interest. "Right here." Good thing he'd thought to bring his tablet. "Okay, shoot."

She wasted no time responding. "Your client sourcing approach is too passive. Once you've picked your targets, you leave everything up to them. Sure, you may follow up with phone calls, but that still keeps them in the driver's seat, so to speak." She chuckled at her pun. "They need more incentive. Ninety-seven percent have proven they're unlikely to take your bait."

"Where'd you get your stats?"

"Didn't you say only three showed up for a tour out of a hundred brochures sent?"

"Right. Data like that's usually Gray's bailiwick. I'm the people person, remember?"

"You need to start ingesting that data and spew it out to potential clients as appropriate."

Maybe this exchange of ideas wasn't such a great idea after all. "How do I zero in for the important stuff? Too many numbers in my head could be injurious to my health."

"Ask your brothers. Graham knows the accounting side, right? As well as your best product features? And as a litigator, Mitch should be aware of the kinds of data that have the most impact and when to use them."

Geoff checked his watch. "How long have we been at this? Ten minutes? In that time you've told me I'm too passive in my approach, to find better incentives and use more statistics. You're a dynamo."

A contented smile slipped across her face. "Thanks. Feels good to use that part of my brain for once."

"Got anything left? Like how I take a more active role finding clients?"

"Let them come to you."

"Sounds great, but how do I lure them in?"

"The key here is to separate the wheat from the chaff. You need some way to determine who can actually afford your coaches and who's just curious. Consider how exclusive clubs and high-end residential outfits do their winnowing."

Alex was wasting her talents in her current job. She could easily pull in six figures as a business consultant. "Hold up. My head's spinning. I get the concept, but how to do I put it in play?"

She changed position, scooted down. "Honestly, I have no idea. You'll need to pursue that one yourself. Like make yourself a potential client at one of the town's social organizations. See how they go about vetting you."

"Got you. Guess I could also check into the new high-rise condos out west."

Alex yawned. They'd maxed out for the night. "Get some sleep," he told her. Tomorrow we do you."

"Okay." Her eyes had already closed.

SHE AWOKE the next morning feeling much more like herself. Her head felt better, and her body seemed to have grown more accustomed to the ache in her arm. Even the sight of Eileen's bouquet across the room didn't faze her. No, today was going to be a productive one. She'd do Geoff the courtesy of hearing out his suggestions for handling her clients, since he'd been so insistent on the mutual exchange, and then she'd do whatever needed doing.

She'd just finished dressing after a clumsy shower when there was a brief knock on the door and her dad bounded through with a tray.

"Good morning." His enthusiasm bubbled over. "Got Paige off to school, so I stopped at a bakery I saw on the way here last night. You still like sticky buns, I hope?" He parked the tray on the chest where the flowers resided.

"Dad, you're terrific. I haven't had one of these things since I revamped my appearance."

"You revamped your appearance? Tell me more," Geoff said, entering the room behind her dad.

"Onscreen talent aren't the only ones who have to look good in L.A. When Loretta's career took off, she started making noises about getting a manager who understood fashion and makeup. So I lost twenty pounds, started working out, hired my own wardrobe consultant and went to one of the swankiest salons in Beverly Hills for a makeover. This goddess you see before you is really a fake."

"How can you say that, kiddo? You've always been a showstopper. But I like the few touches you made."

"Spoken like a proud dad. But let me add my approval as well," Geoff said.

"You two. I may be I injured, but you don't need to make me feel better with compliments,"—she grinned—"although I appreciate the effort."

"Brought you coffee, too, Geoff, if you're interested?"

Geoff thanked him and offered the chair he'd occupied the night before. "I'll go get another chair for myself."

"Hey, I'm not interrupting something? Just thought you wanted me here in case that Eileen person stopped by."

"Good plan, although we may have nipped that one in the bud. She's regrouped and is now finding new reasons to check in on me. Tried to get me to go out to dinner with her last night. I begged off by telling her I had work to catch up on."

Geoff left briefly to snag a chair from another room. While he was gone, Alex said, "I encouraged him to break things off with her instead of waiting for her to do the deed. He says he came close when she showed up, but lost his nerve. My words, not his."

"Like I've already said, Geoff's a nice guy. Probably doesn't want to hurt her."

"I know. Nor step on her pride."

"Any particular reason you're pushing him to cut things off?"

"Besides allowing them both to move on with their lives?"

"Thought maybe you now have a stake in the moving on you want him to do."

As an actor, her dad was too used to reading others' words and body language. "I've barely known Geoff a week. I like him, sure, but don't rush things."

"Just the opposite. I'm stretching out this visit as long as I can, because I'm having a great time."

"Good, we're happy to have you here." Geoff returned to the room, kitchen chair in hand. "Want to stick around a bit? Alex and I were about to toss ideas at each other on client management."

Buddy lifted the hand that wasn't holding his coffee cup. "Not sure how much I could help. I've always been on the other side as the client. But I'll give it a shot."

"It's Alex's turn to run her client issues past me for my input, but before we go there, I'd like to follow up on one of her great thoughts last night."

"Which one? There were so many." She smiled.

"I've been too passive in the way I've gone after new clients. You suggested I needed to have them come to me through some kind of incentive. It's the last part that's kept me waking up throughout the night."

Buddy stretched out in his chair, folded his hands behind his neck. "Incentive, huh? What's the goal, get folks to come here to the firehouse to view your work or attend some special show?"

"Special show?" Geoff repeated. "Like an exhibition?"

"Whatever your industry does to showcase new products," Buddy said

"Great idea, Dad, but not an industry show. You'd get mostly looky-loos there. We need to come up with some big get-together where the rich and powerful gather. Like a fair for millionaires."

Geoff considered. "Interesting concept, except the McKennas don't swim in those waters. Still ..." He keyed in a few strokes on his tablet. "Hey! Such things actually exist. Oh. In Dubai, Monte Carlo, Istanbul." He let the names of those locales hang in the air. "Yeah, well, like I said, out of our league."

"So refine our definition a bit. What do you call gatherings where people come to see the newest models?"

"Motor coach rallies?" Geoff offered. "But those are where several different dealers show off their products. We want to be the only show in town."

Buddy pursed his lips. "Got it. How many buses, uh, motor coaches, do you have here at any given time?"

"Two. Three at the most," Geoff answered. Buddy shook his head. "Not enough. You need at least five."

"Where'd you get that number, Dad?"

"Out of the air. Based it on the smallest home shows Iris and I have attended. She loves the things. Swears she gets the best redecorating ideas from them. As if we haven't torn that house apart a half dozen times already."

"We've only customized twice that many coaches in our four years of operation, period, Buddy."

Alex had been following this discussion with one part of her brain focused on the exchange between the two men and the other part already thinking ahead to her own client problems. But now she was interested, in spite of her desire to move on to her items. "That's it, Geoff. Gather together some of your former clients. In the classiest place in town. Preferably to coincide with some other big event."

"Steamboat Days is coming up next month. Could we put something together that fast?"

Alex mentally listed every step. The hardest part would be to find a time when they could get at least five McKenna Custom Coach owners together in town at once. "Depends on your former clients. How often are you in touch with them?"

"Whenever they call with questions or complaints."

"Don't you follow up, check in with them?"

"Sure. Usually the first few months after they take them on the road."

"After that?"

He shook his head. "I see where you're going with this. I'm making a note to start calling them more frequently."

Buddy slid forward in his seat. "They're like your critics, Geoff. They're the ones who spread the word promoting or badmouthing your business."

"I hear you, Buddy. I'll get on the line with them as soon as we're done. Can't set a specific date until we get a feel who'd be willing to come and when. But I love the idea."

"Check with your dealers too," Alex advised. "Surely, they do at least an annual trade show. Get them to invite you to participate."

"I'm impressed, you two," Buddy said. "Especially with you, Alex. Those are great ideas."

"You sure it's okay for me to stick around while Geoff helps you? You don't usually like to talk about your clients."

"If we can keep their identities out of it, we should be okay."

As if on cue, Eileen swept in after a brief knock. "Geoff, I need your help." Her face was flushed, and she was breathing heavily.

Though he rose, Geoff didn't approach her.

"What's up?"

"It's my mother. She's refusing to get out of bed."

Geoff raised a brow. "Is she sick?"

"Depressed. She won't talk to me, and my brother, Tommy's, at school. She'll only talk to you." At this, her eyes went wide, pleading. "Since Alex's father is here for her right now, surely you could spare the time to talk to my mother?"

Geoff scrunched up his nose, apparently caught off guard by Eileen's news. He shot a look at Alex. "Guess I'd better go. We can pick up on this when I return."

"Sure. I hope you can help."

As soon as Geoff and Eileen had taken off, Buddy glanced Alex's way. "What was that about? Isn't the woman in question Iris's cousin?"

"That's her. Both Jenna and Aubrey told me she'd welcomed them warmly when they arrived. I haven't heard a thing about her being despondent or prone to depression."

GEOFF DROVE the few miles to the Summers' house wondering what on earth was going on with Eileen's mother. Depressed? He'd never known the woman to be anything but positive and encouraging. When he and Eileen had first started seeing each other, Peggy had invited him to dinner often, probably guessing he hadn't enjoyed home-cooked meals in years, since his own mother's death. But even the most stable person could break down on occasion. Still, why had she asked for him? What could he do to help her?

Eileen tried to get him to go with her, drive her car. But once he'd decided she wasn't freaking, he begged off. Didn't want to get stuck at their house for hours, unless something was really wrong.

Eileen led him to her mother's bedroom but asked him to remain outside the door until she checked first. She returned within a minute. "You're to go in, and I'm to wait out here."

Weird. What was it Peggy didn't want to discuss in front of Eileen?

He edged into the room. Didn't want to alarm the woman. "Peggy? Eileen said you wanted to see me?"

"Oh, Geoff," Peggy said in a tone he didn't recognize. Subdued, sad. "Please, have a seat. Bring one of the chairs along the window closer to the bed."

He did as she asked, studying her face for clues to her current problem. "Are you ill?"

"I'm sick at heart, dear."

Uh-oh. This didn't bode well.

"Eileen has been keeping me apprised of your, uh, relationship. I've been so pleased to see the two of you together over the past months. I've begun to think of you as my own son. Anticipate the day you and Eileen made things official."

Surely, the woman hadn't brought him here to chastise him for the deterioration of things between him and her daughter? This wasn't like Peggy. She was a strong woman. She didn't let personal matters get to her. How in hell should he respond? "And I've grown fond of you as well, Peggy."

"Eileen has been very upset lately. Rather than moving toward a permanent commitment, she says you've been steadily cutting your ties with her. You weren't even here to celebrate her birthday. Instead, you were off on some kind of fling with your houseguest."

Geoff couldn't believe the woman was attempting to manipulate him, make him feel guilty for the way things were evolving with Eileen. Nor could he believe Eileen would stoop to using her mother to repair things between them. His heart rate increased at the same time his palms began to itch. He had to stop this now, even if it meant showing disrespect for Peggy. He rose. "I'm sorry you're taking this so personally. I certainly don't want you to be ill. But this is between Eileen and me. It isn't like you to interfere."

He charged to the door.

"Wait, Geoff. I have more to say."

"Not to me," he called over his shoulder.

Eileen dashed over to him as he crashed through the bedroom door. "Is everything okay?"

He pulled up. "How could you do that to me? You knew your mother wanted to call me on the carpet. Our relationship is none of her business."

She grabbed his arm. "Then stay and talk this out with me. Things have gotten bad between us, and I have no idea how to fix them."

He gave a vigorous shake to his head. "Not now. I'm so angry I can't think straight."

He didn't give her time to say more or hold him up further. Instead, he slammed through the front door and out to his car.

Alex was right. He should've ended things last night. His hesitation had caused Eileen to call in her big gun. His anger continued to mount. If Peggy truly was ill over their impending breakup, he was sorry. But that didn't mean he had to prolong something that was no longer viable. If he'd been able to speak without shouting, he would've stayed. But he needed to calm down first.

He considered driving around until his heart rate subsided, but he feared his frustration would only escalate.

BUDDY WAS STILL in Alex's room when Geoff got back to the firehouse.

"Is Eileen's mother okay?" Alex asked immediately.

"No, but she's not really sick." Alex cocked her head.

"She's depressed. Because she sees things going downhill between me and Eileen. I know, you warned me to take care of this, but I had no idea Eileen would pit her mother against me." He kept pacing near the foot of the bed, one fist pounding the other. He couldn't land.

"We parents sometimes don't know when to take a step back," Buddy said.

Geoff stopped pacing. "I blame Eileen more than her mother, although I had no idea Peggy would turn to emotional blackmail."

"Didn't I see a basketball hoop out back?" Alex asked. "Why not round up one or both of your brothers and play off some energy?"

Geoff appeared to consider. "Doubt if Mitch has any time, but I'll check on Gray." At the door, he turned. "Thanks."

Eighteen

"That's one agitated guy," Buddy said after Geoff was gone.

"Can't say I blame him. Have I ever used you to send a boyfriend a message?"

"I sent my own messages when you first started dating, like, 'Don't hurt my daughter,' but no, you've pretty much kept your dating life to yourself. Or maybe that type of assignment went to your mother?"

Alex was always on the alert for questions one parent might ask about the other, which would only result in more dissention between them. "Mother couldn't keep up when I was serial dating a few years back, and since there hasn't really been anyone in the picture for a while, she no longer asks."

Her dad was about to respond when the door burst open. "Where is he?" Eileen shouted. Her face was still flushed, but now her tone was shrill and her face contorted.

"If you mean Geoff, I don't know. He left here not long ago, but I don't know where he went." Alex kept her voice calm but controlled. Shouldn't be surprised that Eileen had followed him, but really, how tacky could she get? Eileen was one desperate lady.

"Since you and Daddy didn't ask about my mother, I assume Geoff was here long enough to tell you how rude he was to an ailing woman."

"That's between you and Geoff."

"Oh, really? Ever since you showed up, you seem to know every-thing that's been going on between the two of us and more."

Eileen stalked to the bed, leaned forward so far Alex thought she would yank her out. As wired as Eileen appeared to be, she'd probably have no trouble hauling Alex across the room by her bad arm.

"Like I said, this is between you—"

"And Geoff. Yes, I heard you. Now that Geoff and I are having some communication problems, you go 'no comment,' although that hasn't seemed to stop you from sharing your opinion of our relationship before now. Things were going fine between us until you showed up. What did you do, invite him to your bed while you were on the road? Surely, you had time to get it on in your motel room before that storm hit?"

Alex wanted so much to share a few details of her time with Geoff in the motel just to shut her up but held her tongue. Even if Alex had begun to respond, her father placed a light touch on her injured arm.

"Would you like some tea, Miss Summers? Why don't we go to the kitchen?" he asked.

Eileen swiveled to face Buddy. "I don't want tea," she screamed. "I don't want to calm down. I want Geoff to explain why he's been treating me so poorly."

Geoff shouldn't have to deal with this woman's outburst a second time in one day. Sure, he'd brought it on himself by not ending things with her sooner, but with both Geoff and Eileen as keyed up as they were at the moment, this wasn't the time. How was Alex going to get rid of her?

"Why don't you try to contact Geoff later? Sounds like your mother needs you more at the moment," she said.

Eileen opened her mouth to retort but stopped. Apparently, she realized if she claimed her mother didn't need her, she would be admitting her mother's depression was a scam. She sputtered, then bounded from the room, slamming the door behind her.

Alex glanced at her father, who simply shrugged. "More drama around here today than on some sound stages I've been on."

"I'm glad you were here, Dad. Who knows what I would have said to that, that, you know, if your gentle restraint hadn't been in the room."

He rose and went to the window, which faced the back. "Looks like Geoff took your suggestion. Got Graham to go out there with him."

"Hope Eileen left the building and headed home."

"Not to be. She just stormed up to Geoff."

Alex released a long sigh. "So she isn't giving up. Doesn't she see—"

Her dad waved a shushing hand behind him. "Does this window open? This scene is too good to miss."

"Dad!"

DOWN ON THE IMPROVISED COURT, Geoff twisted around from a lay-up and nearly rammed into Eileen, who'd planted herself right behind him, hands on hips, tapping the toe of one foot.

"You can't stick around to placate my mother, but you can shoot baskets?"

"Blowing off steam."

"And I'm not allowed to blow off my steam?"

"Not now, Eileen."

"Yes, now. You've been refusing to face this ... whatever ... between us for days. I'm calling the question."

Gray stuck a hand between them. "Game over. I, uh, have some work back at my office." As soon as the words were spoken, he trotted off.

"Out here, in the open? That what you want?" Geoff challenged.

"We need to get back on course. In fact, we need to take the next step. Commit to each other."

Geoff heard her statement but couldn't believe she was under the delusion they were still a couple. His stomach felt like first-day flu.

The kind where you know you'll feel better only if you make yourself feel worse first by vomiting. Damn! This wasn't the place, but it was definitely the time to cut the strings. His brain kept shouting, "Do it! Do it now and get it over with."

He attempted a calming breath before he said his piece. "I've put this off as long as I could, hoping you'd be the one to take the lead. I wanted to save your pride and not hurt you, but you've left me no choice. As of now, we're done." To emphasize his point, he picked up the basketball and headed for the building.

"Don't you dare say things like that and just walk away." She grasped his arm.

"There's nothing more to say." He replied in a monotone but kept walking, pulling his arm out of her grasp as gently as he could.

"It's that Hollywood hussy, isn't it? I wasn't good enough for you in bed, but apparently with her tight pants and expensive haircut, she is."

He blew out a breath. "Leave Alex out of this. You and I were going different directions long before she arrived." He almost said "She just helped me realize it," but clammed up before he made things worse. Eileen wanted to blame Alex. Ironic. That had been his original plan, but the idea was to force Eileen to end things, not to go for broke. He'd had no idea this could get so out of proportion. Nor did he care to hear Alex's name impugned.

Above, he could see Buddy standing at the window, taking in this whole episode. Alex would know the state of things within the minute, if she didn't already.

"Please don't do this, Geoff." Eileen bent, clutched her stomach with one hand and swiped tears with the other.

He pivoted. "I didn't want it to go down like this, but you haven't left me much choice. Don't follow me into the building."

"You'll regret this, Geoffrey McKenna!" Her voice had grown cold, malevolent. But she remained behind.

He didn't turn back. Instead, he closed the building door behind him and headed to his apartment. Once inside, he locked the door, unable and unwilling to speak to anyone else.

BUDDY TURNED AWAY from the window, searched Alex's eyes. "That is some hurt boy. Think you should go to him?"

She considered. "Not yet. Graham witnessed the incident. He'll check on Geoff. I'm more worried about what Eileen will do next."

"She didn't follow Geoff into the building. I'd say she's gone off to lick her wounds."

What would she do if a guy she was desperate to marry called things off? Especially if she thought there was another woman behind the breakup, maybe even calling the shots? She'd be tempted to get revenge. But, no, she had her pride. Most likely she'd pick up the pieces, regroup and move on. But would Eileen react the same way? "I don't know. Wounded animals are difficult to predict. Maybe humans operate along the same lines."

"Then I'm glad I'm here, in case she comes back."

Though it was reassuring to have her dad around, she had no idea what to expect from Geoff's former girlfriend. "I'm glad you're here, too, Dad."

"This town kinda grows on you. I like being able to get from one place to another without having to add a half hour or more onto the trip because of traffic. I like finding parking available at grocery stores and bakeries. And these boys. Not used to having guys around me. Love you and Iris very much, kiddo, but the testosterone around here is addictive."

"And I like having sisters, well, stepsisters, even though I haven't been able to spend much time with them."

Her dad approached her. "What's happening between you and Geoff?"

"Damned if I know. I'm attracted to him, no doubt. I like him. But there hasn't been time for more to happen, and I won't be around much longer to find out what could have been."

He settled into the chair he'd occupied earlier. Moved it even closer to her. "Really? What's pulling you back to the coast? Not me. I'm here."

She laughed. "True. It's been great hanging out with you." She reached for his hand with her bad arm. A bit awkward. "This has been nice. But you'll be leaving in a day or two, won't you?"

"Yes. No. Hard to say. I don't want to leave you here to face the aftermath of what just went down. With that bum arm, you're vulnerable if that woman were to get physical."

Would Eileen get physical? Didn't think so, but who would've guessed the woman would so totally deny things were over between her and Geoff? "The problem is, she knows this place and the players so well. During the day, other than our bedrooms upstairs and the office downstairs, she has ready access to the rest of the building, as we've witnessed more than once the last two days."

"I'll talk to Geoff. See if we can figure out some way to keep her away."

"Enough Eileen. I've got to get back to my clients and their needs, but Geoff's heart probably isn't in our joint consultation at the moment."

"Can I help?"

"Oh, Dad, I'd love your insights, but one situation is so far flung from your experience, and the other, uh, may be too close to home."

Buddy coughed, as if something had gone down the wrong pipe. "Want to explain that last one?"

Damn. Should've lumped the two in the first category. How they could get into this and not touch on some of her dad's own history? "I, uh, can't use names, remember." She waited for him to nod understanding. "This is an aging supporting actor on a television show who's trying to convince his producers to give him more story line." She went on to outline what Gaylord St. John was after and why he probably couldn't get it.

Her dad didn't respond at first. He got up, paced back and forth in front of the dresser. "Why did you say this might be too close to home?" he asked at length.

Didn't escape that one. What did she expect? Her dad was no fool. She owed him the truth. "Relations with younger women have plagued your career too. I was just a teenager when you and Mom divorced, but I was old enough to understand the rumors about you and a younger actress on your show."

Her dad's eyes didn't leave hers. "Vicious rumors, Alex. Untrue rumors. I hope you know that."

"I know you, Dad. You're a good man. You'd never hurt a woman."

He continued to stare at her, but his expression softened. "You don't know how much that means to me."

"Even though the rumors were later proven unfounded, once planted, they've continued to follow you. So you know what an uphill battle my client is facing. Especially because, unlike you, he's not so innocent."

He rubbed the back of his neck. "How 'bout we chat more over lunch? Come to the kitchen and watch me make sandwiches. You could use a break from this room."

He helped her out of bed, then accompanied her to the kitchen.

After he'd assembled two sandwiches, poured two glasses of water and scavenged a cold fruit salad from the fridge, he settled into a chair across the table from her. "For starters, this guy is damned lucky to still have his job. Hope you've told him as much."

"I will. I'll work it into whatever counsel I give him."

"Why does he think increased visibility will get him a bigger story line?"

"He's counting on viewers to lobby to see him more."

Her dad asked about the client's history with the show. Was he once a lead? Briefly. Was he involved in any main story lines? Tangentially. And those took place years ago. Only longtime fans would remember them. Had he ever been linked romantically in a story with a current actress? Years ago, but she left, and the part was retired.

Buddy rooted through one of the cabinets. "Think they'll mind if I open these chips? Iris frowns on having such things in the house."

"Be my guest. I went grocery shopping with Aubrey last week and paid for several items in their larder."

He rejoined her at the table but went into a brief feeding frenzy before getting back to their discussion. "Find out what kind of relationship he has with the executive producer and the writers, especially the head writer," he said finally, brushing away potato chip crumbs. "Don't believe whatever he says, but his side of the story will give you a clue about his view of reality. If he says they get along just fine, they don't. If he says they hate him, they probably do."

She settled into her chair and listened, fascinated, to a part of her father she'd never heard before. This guy was a font of knowledge. "We chatted a bit about those things when he first signed with me, but I didn't pursue his answers like you suggest. What else?"

"Check with his agent also. Get their slant. See if they've pitched a bigger story for your guy to the show's producers. My bet is they have, probably more than once, and the show's execs have said no, repeatedly, which is why your client is now grasping at straws like talk shows."

"So appearances on several talk shows won't do much to boost his popularity?"

"Don't get me wrong. Exposure on talk shows can give an actor credibility, like, you know, the entertainment world has given them their blessing, so the audience should too. But it's the fans who get listened to by the producers. Many fans, not just a few vocal ones. I'd say your job is not so much to get him on a talk show, at least not for now, as to grow him a larger fan base. One that likes to express itself."

Her mind had been lost in the overgrown jungle of Gaylord's career for so long, relief overcame her. For the first time in days, as if her dad had cut through the confusion with a machete, she could see a clear path ahead. "What else do you want to eat, Dad? Your brain is on hyperdrive."

"Can you use any of my thoughts?"

The guy was a marvel. "Even if they don't work, they've gotten me out of the rut concerning this client. I've been focusing too much on the end result and not the problem."

Her dad leaned back in his chair, folded his hands behind his neck. "What do you know? My experience may actually pay off."

A GENTLE RAPPING drew Geoff from slumber. He sat up on the sofa, rubbed his eyes and drew a hand through his hair.

"Geoff? Door's locked. Can I come in?" Gray asked from outside.

He rarely locked the door, but he'd needed alone time after sending Eileen on her way. But now, sure, he could use the company.

"Figured you wanted some time to yourself, but it's going on five. Buddy and I are leaving. Aubrey had to pick up some items from a supplier and Mitch isn't home yet. Buddy didn't want to leave Alex here on her own."

Alone? She'd probably welcome the privacy. Then it hit. Eileen. "Good thought. Even though we could lock the front door, as presumptuous as Eileen has become lately, she might have had her own key made."

"No telling what she might do, bro. She was pretty hot when she confronted you out back."

"Even more upset when she left. I broke up with her."

Gray took a step back, studied him. "Thought you were pushing her to do the dirty deed."

"All my *pushing* did was convince her it was time to commit, presumably with a marriage proposal. I didn't have a choice."

"You're okay with your decision?"

"Yeah."

"And Alex? Where does she fit in all this?"

"The minute Alex showed up in town, Eileen assumed the worst between Alex and me, so I used Alex to take advantage of Eileen's jealousy."

"Yeah, you told me about that screwy plan, but from what I've observed, you may have succeeded more than you intended. You seem taken with the woman."

Geoff studied his shoes. He needed a new pair of sneakers. Ever since their stay at the motel, things between him and Alex had changed. Not just the great sex they enjoyed, but something else had been growing between them. He'd put off thinking about it, especially after she'd been injured. His guilt over leaving her alone at the motel and worry about her condition had taken over. "You're right. I like her. A lot."

"What're you gonna do about it?"

Geoff blinked several times. "Do? Enjoy it, her, while I can. She'll be leaving soon."

"Ah, yes. That old adage. Mitch said as much about Aubrey when he first realized he had feelings for her. I got Jenna safely back to California, thinking I wouldn't see her again, and yet here she is now, living in our parents' house. Who's to say Alex wouldn't do the same, especially since her stepsisters are here. You never know until you ask."

He and Alex weren't there yet, but he sure wished she'd stay longer. "Her job's back there, Gray."

"It's amazing how much one can do long distance these days."

Geoff wasn't ready to discuss Alex further, but now that he'd ended things with Eileen, perhaps he could at least consider the possibility that something was happening between them.

No. He shouldn't, couldn't, go there. He had MS, a disease where his condition could deteriorate any time. Maybe not immediately, but sometime in the years ahead. He couldn't do that to Alex, or any woman. Until now, he hadn't confronted the personal limitation he'd placed on himself when he'd first learned of his condition, that marriage was not in the cards, because he didn't think it mattered. He hadn't been in love with Eileen. Until recently, he'd been under the impression she was okay with a casual relationship. When she'd begun pushing for marriage, he knew he had to end things. But that was because he realized he didn't love her, not because of the marriage thing.

Pursuing whatever he was feeling with Alex was different. It wouldn't be right.

Gray turned for the door, then twisted around. "One other thing. All this talk lately about commitment has gotten me thinking. It's time for Jenna and me to take the next step. How'd you like to have a sister?"

"That's terrific, bro." Weird. Interesting timing. Almost like he'd said the word "marriage" out loud. He hadn't, had he?

"I haven't said anything to anyone else yet. Probably need to have a chat with Paige next, but I think that'll go fine."

For the briefest of moments, Geoff experienced the same old bitterness he felt when he was first diagnosed.

Why him and not his brothers? In this case, why could Gray, and soon probably Mitch, marry and have families and not him? He had to get over these feelings. What was done was done. He was relieved they hadn't had to deal with this demon. He swallowed, took a deep breath, embraced his brother. As he stepped away, a new thought hit him. "Been holding off until I settled things with Eileen?"

"Probably would've gone ahead if you and Eileen kept things dangling much longer, but this works better."

Better? Maybe for Gray, Jenna and Paige. Who knew how Mitch and Aubrey would react to the news, since they'd been together longer. But for him? Last thing he needed to hear about right now was marriage. It would be difficult enough to keep his distance from Alex the way it was. Once Gray and Jenna made their announcement, wedding fever would sweep the firehouse.

The only good thing? Eileen was no longer part of the equation.

Nineteen

After Buddy departed for Gray and Jenna's place, Alex moved to the living room to follow up on her dad's suggestions, starting with the call to her client's agent.

"Gaylord's producers offered to expand his role just last year?" She repeated the information she'd just gleaned from the agent, Vicky Lessing.

"Yes. He was to be diagnosed with some kind of major illness or condition with a story arc spanning six months," Vicky said. "More than ample time to build a new image. But he wouldn't consider it. Said it was their backdoor way of getting rid of him down the road by letting the illness kill him."

Besides being a dirty old man, her client was a fool. Great combination. "They were willing to keep him even though he turned down the story line?"

"They drag him out once a month or so for parties and other events. He gets just enough lines and air time to comply with his contract."

Alex asked if the writers could bring back old flames or family members in the life of Gaylord's character. There'd been two great loves for his character; one actress had passed away, and the other was suffering from dementia. A couple of family members were still part of the cast, but they were now secondary characters like him.

"Is there much chance of expanding his role in the near future?"

"One never knows with these people," Vicky said. "They go off on tangents I rarely understand. But realistically, no. Our mutual client is too self-assured— translated, egotistical—to realize his acting abilities are mediocre at best. He's lucky they've continued to keep him around all these years, although I'll deny ever telling you this."

Alex chuckled. Why hadn't she thought sooner to contact this woman? Because she'd focused on the talk show aspect. But her dad had been smart enough to expand the questions to focus on Gaylord himself and his show. Now that she had, maybe she and Vicky could work a deal for Gaylord that would appease him.

Swearing the agent to secrecy, Alex told her about the charge Gaylord had given her. "What do you think about finding him some-place to appear other than that talk show, like a game show or a streamer?"

"I'm all for it," Vicky replied. "He'll probably claim these vehicles are beneath him, but if you can convince him these are as good as it gets, I'll pitch him."

"What I wanted to hear. I'll get back to you." She didn't mention the numerous calls she figured it would take to make even something like these appearances happen. Vicky already knew. But this was a start. More progress than Alex had made in weeks.

"How's it going?"

She turned around to find Geoff leaning against the door frame. He looked remarkably refreshed. Much better than the last time she'd seen him. "My dad gave me some great advice about one of my clients. Should've thought of it myself, but I've been so intent on going directly through the obstacle course that I forgot I could maybe go around."

"I didn't listen in, but your conversation with whoever it was sounded pretty upbeat."

"It was. Still a long way to go though. Speaking of upbeat, I could say the same for you."

He dropped onto the sofa, next to her, his body not quite touching hers, but close enough she could breathe in the heady smell of his aftershave.

"I made some calls myself this afternoon. Started tracking down and checking in with old clients. Your dad's not the only one with a knack for giving good advice. That was one great idea you gave me."

"Yeah?" She'd forgotten about their earlier session. "What did you learn?"

"First off, the guys and I did one hell of a job on their coaches. For the most part, our clients are happy as clams, especially with all the built-in creature comforts."

"Terrific. Any possibility they could make a fast trip to Iowa?"

"I couldn't believe my luck. Two were already planning to check out Steamboat Days. One for the art fair, and the other is pals with one of the featured musical acts and is coming to see him. The third is currently in Florida but welcomed the opportunity to come north to escape the heat. Needs to check his schedule and make a few calls, then will get back to me."

"Wow. I'm impressed. You got a lot accomplished, especially considering ..."

"... what happened with my former girlfriend earlier? Actually, once I'd dealt with Eileen and survived an hour or so of self-loathing, I took a nap, and then I got motivated."

Good. Stress took a lot out of a person. He could use the rest.

He leaned in, fiddled with a strand of her hair. "Thought you could use some company."

"In other words, you're here to protect me from anything Eileen might attempt in retaliation."

"Something like that. Although I also just wanted to see you. Eileen refused to see how we'd grown apart, how we were so mismatched. Instead, she blamed you for horning in."

"Only after you strong-armed me into going along with your crazy scheme to make her so jealous she'd call it quits."

"After you told me you needed my help with your stepsister. Which I provided."

"So we're even." Although she hated to think their partnership had come to an end. "I don't have my lease yet, but I'm headed there. Especially with help from Paige."

"How about my brother?"

"Graham?"

He leaned in even closer. "We need to keep this just between us for a few days. Promise?"

He had her interest. "Of course. What's up?"

"Gray's going to ask Jenna to marry him."

"No! That's wonderful. She'll say yes, won't she? Otherwise, why would she have moved here?"

"She may no longer believe in the institution, because her last marriage ended so poorly," Geoff answered. "But I'm betting she'll say yes." He took her good hand in his, rubbed his thumb over the back side. "You get what that means, don't you? More than likely, Jenna's not going on tour for some time. The coach should become available soon."

"That's right." Her brain started considering how to use this latest news to her advantage. Of course, she'd have to wait until the couple actually became engaged, but then she needed a catalyst, or more than one, to trip the trigger.

"You're already working out a plan in your head. I can almost see the circuits light up."

"Guilty."

"Can't blame you. Despite my incredible allure, that's why you're here." He pulled her hand to his lips, delivered a gentle kiss. "But first, how 'bout a break? We've both had a busy day."

"Dinner?"

He returned a leer that could only mean one thing.

"Well, yeah. That, too."

"Have you forgotten I'm physically impaired?"

"I've been fantasizing since the other day about you lying in bed, your bad arm out to the side, and me ravaging the rest of your body. Like that scenario?"

"Hmm. Somewhat kinky and something I've never tried. Shouldn't pass up the opportunity."

"I locked the doors downstairs. Mitch and Aubrey have keys. We can also lock the door to your room. Don't know how much time we have to ourselves."

"Then why have we been sitting here?" She jumped up, yanked him up with her good hand, and they slipped off to her room.

"Just lift up my top. Getting it on and off is too big a production." One-handed, she pulled down her yoga pants with the elasticized waistband to reveal a navy blue thong.

"Leave that," Geoff said. "My job."

She lay prone on the bed, her bad arm out to the side and cushioned by a pillow. "Job?" She said it as a challenge.

He climbed over her. "My pleasure, then." He made short work of unbuttoning her shirt, opened it. He halted, his eyes drinking her in. "God, Alex, you're beautiful."

"Even with all my injuries?"

"Temporary inconveniences."

"Not the scar I'll have on my forehead."

"You're already unique. A scar will only add to your beauty. You're even more gorgeous now than you were Saturday."

"Been feeling deprived?"

"You bet I have." He reached behind her back, groped for the closure.

"It's up here," she said, indicating the front of her bra.

"Ah. How efficient."

"Thank Aubrey. Her idea."

He undid the clasp and ogled her. "You are gorgeous, woman."

She liked how he took his time while his gaze appreciated her. But he couldn't hold back very long. He bent, ran his tongue over the outside curve of one breast.

Involuntarily, her hips rose. She seemed to float above the bed, watching his tongue do its work. Her voyeurism inflamed her, made her crazy for more.

But Geoff was busy claiming her body inch by inch. His fingers joined the examination, trailing over one ridge, skimming down a valley, probing the flesh of the underside.

Then his hands took over.

Beneath him, Alex squirmed, ached for him to drive himself into her.

Her mood went from titillation to intense pleasure to frenzy as her body responded to his ministrations. "Oh, Geoff." She panted as her one hand snaked around his neck and grabbed the hair at the nape.

He lifted his head slightly, studied her. "You okay?"

"Umm. More than. That approach should come with a warning. 'Beware of high voltage.'"

His eyes flickered, as if surprised by her response. "That's how much you turn me on, Alex. You don't know how much I want you."

"If it's anything like what I'm feeling, I have an inkling."

"That thong is a killer, but all it makes me want to do is this." He grabbed one side of the front and drew it down her legs. "Just keeps getting better."

"Really? What else have you got planned?" Her question was a hoarse croak.

"How about …" He placed his mouth on parts south, way south, and nibbled as his hands parted her legs. Heat rushed through her limbs, and she felt herself go wet. While his lips worked wonders, his fingers traced feather trails down the inside of her legs.

As much as she appreciated his take-charge attitude, she wasn't content to simply lie there. She lifted one foot and draped it over his shoulder and repeated the same with the other. Good thing her legs hadn't been affected by her accident.

Geoff moaned, then moaned again as she opened herself to him. His mouth slid forward, his tongue flicking back and forth. Her hips rose, heightening the sensation.

Eyes closed, she gripped the bedspread for balance as her brain sailed through swirling electric lights. A blinding rush swept through her. She released a heavy sigh, then struggled to catch her breath. Good lord, that was incredible.

She wanted to scream with delight, tell him how much she enjoyed what he was doing. But she couldn't talk. Couldn't make a sound, except for "ah."

Had they really said they'd keep this whatever it was casual? What he was doing to her, for her, now, was not casual. This was intense. Insane. Indescribable. And she didn't want it to end, as she knew one of these days it must. But for the moment, this was all she wanted. He was who she craved.

She was still somewhere beyond the stars when he sheathed himself and entered her. As he moved back and forth, her universe burst open. Each thrust was beyond fantastic. All she could do was grab hold, figuratively, to the sensations his lovemaking generated, and literally, to the side of the bed with her one good arm as he rode her.

Finished, he dropped to her side and caught his breath. That… was…unbelievable."

"Believe. Because both of us were there."

Sometime later, as he helped her replace her clothing, her phone rang.

"Hello?"

"I hear the reason you don't have a signed lease yet is because you're screwing yourself silly with one of those bus salesmen." How had Loretta known? Alex quickly eyed the room for a hidden camera. Eileen! Eileen had contacted her. It would have been easy for Eileen to check the internet to find a picture of Alex with Loretta. How Eileen had gotten through to Loretta, Alex didn't know, but that explained why they hadn't heard from Eileen since she'd charged out of the firehouse.

Alex wasn't about to reply directly to Loretta's speculation. "I've been out of commission the last two days due to a broken arm and concussion sustained during a tornado," she said instead. Not quite the case, but she laid it on thick to get her client to back off.

"No denial. Meaning I'm right."

"No, that's not the case." Technically, that was correct. There was no lease because Alex hadn't pitched the offer to Jenna yet.

"This is your last chance, Alex." Threat delivered, Loretta hung up.

"What was that about?" Geoff asked. "The way your smile died, I thought it might be Eileen calling to threaten you, until you explained about your arm and concussion."

"No. It was my client checking on the lease again. This is supposedly my last chance."

"Then what?'

"Didn't say. She likes to keep her threats open-ended." Would Loretta really follow through and fire her? If she did, would that be so bad? It always came down to this question, and thus far, the answer hadn't changed, despite recent talks with her dad. Even if he never went out for another part, Loretta's insinuations about his infidelity and sexuality could sully the good name he'd worked hard to reestablish.

AUBREY AND MITCH were already at breakfast the next morning when Geoff joined them. He wasn't sure if they'd heard him leave Alex's room sometime after midnight. No point bringing it to their attention if they hadn't.

"Morning, bro. You're looking mighty, uh, well, can't say *rested*, but certainly *relaxed*."

"As a matter of fact, I am. Sorry to involve all of you in yesterday's drama with Eileen, but that's over now."

Aubrey finished pouring a glass of orange juice. "I heard about your run-in with her. Did she really convince her mother to guilt you into proposing? I can't believe Peggy would put the screws to you like that."

"Didn't ring true for Eileen, either," Geoff replied. "I had no idea until recently how much she wanted to get serious."

Aubrey set down her glass, stared at him. "Get real, Geoff. Every time the six of us have been together in the last months, she's seen Mitch and me and Jenna and Graham together. Why wouldn't she want something similar?"

Geoff flopped in a chair, cereal and toast momentarily forgotten.

"We never talked about the future, so I assumed it didn't matter. We were having fun in the present."

Neither Aubrey nor Mitch spoke. Geoff's words seemed to crystalize in the air. What was with that? Didn't they believe him?

Mitch rose to pour himself another cup of coffee. "Doesn't matter any longer. It's over."

"Just so she doesn't feel it necessary to strike back," Geoff replied.

"You think that's a possibility?" Aubrey asked. "Eileen has a solid head on her shoulders."

"That's what I thought once. But lately, she's been out of control, like a runaway train."

"You think she could do something to harm you?" Mitch asked.

Geoff shook his head. "No. But she blames Alex. The firehouse is unlocked during business hours. I want to make sure Eileen can't get into either my apartment or Alex's room. I'm changing the locks."

Mitch returned to his seat with his coffee. "Think that'll stop her? All she'd have to do is wander into the kitchen or the living room and wait for Alex."

"Buddy plans to stick around during business hours. At least for a few more days. After that, hopefully Eileen will have cooled down. Realized there's no chance I'll change my mind."

"How can we help?" Aubrey asked.

Geoff couldn't hide his surprise. "You'd do that?"

"She's my stepsister, Geoff. Buddy can't be expected to hang around here all day. I'll check with Jenna and see if she can help too."

"Thanks. Alex has been wanting to spend more time with both of you." His cell rang. He checked the number. "I, uh, need to take this."

The readout showed Pam Sutton's number. He took the call in the living room, where there would be more privacy. "Hi, Pam. How's our boy doing today?"

There wasn't a response at first. "Kyle passed away an hour ago, Geoff," she finally managed to get out. "There, uh, wasn't time to call you." Her voice was strained.

Geoff collapsed onto the sofa. His body reeled, as if he'd collided with a five-hundred-pound punching bag. What with getting Alex back to town and then Eileen's fireworks, he hadn't made it to the hospice since Kyle had been taken there. Deep sorrow cut through him. He should have found time to visit Kyle, even in the midst of all the drama surrounding him. Should have known the final minutes in Kyle's life were ticking away.

Hell, all the regrets in the world couldn't give him one last chance to talk to his friend.

He struggled to find the right words for Pam. He wanted to make this easier for her, relieve her grief, but nothing profound occurred to him. "Oh, Pam. I'm so sorry." Sorry for her and Kyle's parents, but also sorry for himself, full of remorse he'd allowed his personal life to rob him of one last chance to see Kyle while he was still alive.

"His passing wasn't a surprise. It's just so final."

"How can I help? I'll come right over to the hospice and help with arrangements," Geoff asked as some other part of his brain took over.

"Not necessary. Kyle and I put those in place months ago. They've already taken him to the funeral home."

Damn. He should've known. He and the guys had been through a similar procedure with their dad and mom. "Surely, there's something I can do to help?"

"I hope you'll come to the funeral. It will be a simple affair. That's how Kyle wanted it. If you feel up to it, maybe you could say a few words." The service would be the next day. Kyle wasn't one for big productions. Just a few relatives and friends. And Geoff.

Geoff closed his eyes, said a silent prayer he'd have the strength to go through one more of these trials. He'd barely healed from the loss of his parents. Hell, he had to for Pam's sake. Somehow he'd manage.

Before he hung up, he promised Pam he'd be there the next day and would say something.

Mitch picked up on Geoff's mood change as soon as he returned to the kitchen. "What's up, bro?"

"My friend. Kyle Sutton. He's gone. MS."

Mitch and Aubrey immediately shoved away from the table and came to him. Aubrey hugged him, Mitch placed a sympathetic hand on

Geoff's shoulder. "Sorry, guy. You and Kyle were close. This has to be hard."

Geoff tried to speak. His mouth felt like it was filled with marbles. "Yeah. I'm, uh, gonna hole up in my apartment for a while," he finally said. "Could you look in on Alex?"

"Of course, we will." Aubrey broke away from her hug. "You take care of you."

"Yeah, bro. One or both of us will stay up here with her when Buddy isn't around."

Geoff nodded his thanks, since talking was still difficult, and fled to his apartment.

Away from the sympathetic eyes and ears of his brother and Aubrey, he shut himself away and let the tears flow. Kyle was gone. He didn't care if crying was deemed unmanly. At the moment, it was all he could do. He crashed onto his sofa, buried his face in his hands and wept for some time.

When he could sit no longer, he made his way to his shower where, with the water running full out, he banged his fists on the walls, shouted whatever epithet came to mind.

Having expended his energy cursing the gods in Kyle's name, his skin pruning, he toweled off and got down to work. The rest of the morning, he attempted to put his thoughts about Kyle down on paper. Never should've agreed to speak at the funeral, but it was the one thing Pam had asked of him. Couldn't refuse. He really wanted to tell the assemblage about Kyle being his barometer, his measure of how bad this condition that plagued him could really get. How at some point he might himself deteriorate and someday die. But this speech had to be positive, upbeat for Pam and Kyle's parents' sake.

He kept the door to his apartment locked, just in case Eileen got word of Kyle's death and came to "comfort" him.

His gut felt over full, and his head throbbed. He wanted to plow under his blankets and let sleep make all this pain go away. Knew better. This was real, as Pam Sutton would experience every day the rest of her life when she awoke to an empty side of the bed.

Light knocking at the door. Geez, he thought Mitch and Aubrey respected his privacy.

"Geoff? It's Alex. I'll leave, if you want, but could I just come in for a minute?"

He paused. Debated whether he'd gotten the worst part out of his system. He went to the door. "You heard?"

"Yes. I'll leave as soon as I know you're okay."

"Come in." He locked the door behind her. "I'm okay. Physically. Well, not even that. My gut is killing me. But emotionally, it's like the congestion you get just before a bad cold."

"Do you want to talk about it?"

"No," he answered a little too fast. "Yes. I don't know. I'm all over the board on this."

She settled on the sofa, while he continued to stand. "Take your time. Tell me what you feel comfortable sharing."

He slammed one fist into his other palm. "I'm furious. Kyle was a great guy. Bad enough he got the X-rated version of MS and dealt with excruciating pain every day, but the damned thing killed him, long before his life was over."

"I wish I'd gotten to meet him."

"Maybe not. He had a way of cutting to the chase. Might have gotten you to tell him why you're an indentured servant to that witch of a country singer."

Her dark brown eyes flickered. "What did he get you to talk about?"

Did he really want to get into this with her? It was difficult enough dealing with Kyle's death. Revealing his feelings on the subject would make him all the more vulnerable.

"Kyle helped me accept my condition. Funny, huh? His symptoms were so much worse than mine, yet I was more scared about the future than he. Until it struck, I'd lived a really active life. I thought that life defined me. When I saw it potentially coming to an end soon, I freaked. I was ready to quit my job, leave town and live out the rest of my life as a beach bum."

"But you didn't. Was that Kyle's doing?"

"Gray and Mitch were there for me too. Started this company so I could make a living and come off the road. But I balked. One part of me didn't want to see them sacrificing their old lives to strike off this direction. But another part..." Should he go on? He rarely shared what he'd been about to admit. "The other part resented their help. Why had I been afflicted with this thing and not them?"

She continued to watch him, as if expecting him to say more.

"Didn't you hear me? I hated it that I was the sick one and not them. That they were the ones coming to my rescue and not the other way around. Horrible thoughts, but I was looking at the end of my life. At least the way I knew it."

"How did Kyle help you?"

"Let me rant. So I did. One night when his wife had to work late, I took him dinner and proceeded to use my status as guest to dump on him. He let me go on and on until there was nothing left to say. At that point, I thought he was going to lecture me about appreciating what I had. Or get me drunk. But he didn't. When I asked him why not, he led me over to a hall mirror and told me that guy had the answers. I had to listen to him."

She rose and took his hand, guided him back to the sofa with her. "And did you?"

"I accepted the guys' help and launched this business. But every time they start acting like mother hens, it makes me crazy. I understand their concern, but it triggers that ugly old resentment, which I've tried so hard to repress. Now that Kyle can no longer talk me down from these periods, I don't know what I'll do."

She touched his cheek. "Do your brothers have any idea you feel this way?"

You'd think she'd known Kyle. "Kyle asked the same question."

"And?"

"If I understood why their concern makes me crazy, I'd do something about it. But it makes no sense. They care for me. But every time they start to hover, it's like they're reminding me they're still healthy and I'm not."

"It's doesn't have to make sense if it bothers you so much and is preventing you from taking advantage of your brothers' help. Maybe you should also tell them to stop dumping all their unwanted tasks on you at the same time."

"Let's drop it for now. Okay?"

She studied him a moment. "I don't think so. You're at a crossroads, Geoff. It's time for you to come clean with them."

"I said no!" The intensity of his response surprised them both.

"But ..."

"Didn't you learn from my experience with Eileen? She thought she knew what was best for me too."

"I just ... we've shared ... I thought we were friends."

"I thought so too. But friends give each other space. They don't hassle each other."

"If you'd just listen to me."

He broke away from her, stumbled from the couch. "Get out of here, Alex. Before I say something we both regret."

"You have already." She rushed from the apartment and stormed up the stairs.

AUBREY WAS WAITING for her in the kitchen. "How's he doing?"

"Sad. Angry. Confused. Scared, though he won't admit it. Kyle seemed to be Geoff's way of measuring the status of his own health. Like he thinks if MS could defeat his friend, maybe it will get him too."

"But from what Mitch has told me about Geoff's case, his condition has manifested much differently than his friend's."

"That's true, but with his friend's death so recent, he can't or won't let himself see beyond today. I called a doctor friend of mine to ask what you all could do to help him. I checked with her before, when Geoff first hatched this plot of me being his health-care provider. She said you should make sure he continues with his treatment plan and just be there for him if he wants to talk. She said he might retreat into himself, and if that happens, you'll have to walk a fine line between staying involved and respecting his privacy."

Aubrey raised a hand. "Hold up. You didn't include yourself in that plan."

"He's upset with me. I pushed too hard. Assumed too much about our relationship. Damn! I've really grown to like the guy. And this town too. But given this blow-up, it's time for me to return to California."

Aubrey pulled two cans of pop from the fridge, offered one to Alex. "This may not be the best timing, but with Geoff's mind and spirit elsewhere at the moment and the threat of retaliation from Eileen still possible, Jenna and I thought it was time for the Appleby clan to circle the wagons. Even if you do feel you have to leave, how about for tonight we do a girls-only thing. Are you up for it?"

Last thing in the world she wanted, to put on a happy face and make nice with Jenna, Aubrey and Paige while her heart was breaking from Geoff's rejection. But the opportunity was too good to resist. She took a deep breath, swallowed. "Girls only? What do you have in mind?"

"Jenna says you invited Paige over for a makeover session. Why don't all four of us do it? Mitch and Gray are going to take your dad out for pizza and bowling, so it'll be just us girls in the apartment. We can make popcorn and watch a couple chick flicks while we do each other's hair and makeup."

Was this for real? Her stepsisters had never made such an overture before. On the other hand, they'd never been together in the same place this long. Geoff certainly didn't want to spend any time with her at the moment, possibly from now on, so it wasn't as if she had something else to do this evening.

"Uh, sure. I have a few phone calls to make, but after that, bring on the movies and popcorn."

NO SOONER HAD Geoff thrown Alex out of his apartment than second thoughts plagued him. He was tempted to go after her, apologize and seek her comfort to get him through his grief. But he held back. She'd only been trying to help. She had no idea what he was going through, but that shouldn't have mattered. She cared. She wanted to ease his burden. And he'd turned on her.

If she'd kept it up much longer, he would have caved. That's what scared the hell out of him most. It would be unfair to involve her further, because she'd see it as tacit acknowledgement their relationship was getting serious. He couldn't allow that to happen.

Say good-bye to what might've been. All he had to do was observe Pam tomorrow to see firsthand what he had to avoid at all costs—leaving behind a grieving widow.

He couldn't go to either Gray or Mitch for help either. With Alex pushing him, he'd come that close to telling his brothers how their concern sometimes affected him. As he should. But he couldn't. To do so meant coming clean with the guys, making himself even more vulnerable than he was with this damned MS. Asking for their help. He owed them too much to ask for more.

He'd tackle his speech for tomorrow on his own.

He generally composed from his notebook computer, but for this task, he grabbed an actual notebook to jot down his thoughts. He'd just go for it, let himself remember his relationship with Kyle and see what happened. A half hour later, he'd come up with five whole lines. Not bad stuff, but hardly enough to do the job properly.

He placed his elbows on his desk and sank his face in his hands. Why had he agreed to speak? He was no good at this. How did you tell others about the deceased's ability to keep you from thinking about death? *Deceased.* God, he'd already moved on and placed Kyle in that category.

He felt hung over, and he'd hardly had anything to drink in days. Too preoccupied taking care of Alex. Until he'd barked at her today. A beer or stronger wasn't going to get him through this. Just had to tough it out.

"Geoff?" Mitch called from the other side of the door.

Geoff opened the door to find not only Mitch but also Gray and Buddy. "What's up? You all here to check on me?"

"Figured you might be tired of your own company by now," Gray said. "We're going out for dinner and then bowling. Come with us. We need a fourth."

"Hope you didn't invent this outing for my sake. I've got this eulogy-type thing to write before tomorrow morning. Kyle's wife asked me to say a few words at the funeral."

"Ah, well, you've saved me from certain embarrassment," Buddy said. "Haven't bowled in years. Even though the three of us agree it would be a good idea for you to get out for a bit, we're really escaping the hen party upstairs."

Since none of the trio moved inside, Geoff leaned against the door frame. "Hen party?" First he'd heard about this.

"The women are having a combination chick flick, pizza and makeover night," Mitch informed him. "Their way of protecting Alex, should Eileen return."

"Guess we'll skip bowling," Gray said. "Haven't decided where we're eating, but if you change your mind and decide to join us, just call."

Under other circumstances, it would've been fun to go along. Get to know Buddy better. Damn. Why was he even contemplating a night out with the boys? His friend was lying in a casket across town, ready to be buried tomorrow. No more boys' nights out for Kyle.

Geoff picked up his pen and notebook. The least he could do was send Kyle off with a fitting good-bye speech. Even if he was up all night composing, editing, tearing up one draft after another, by God, he was going to do this right.

Twenty

Alex and Aubrey threw themselves into makeover and movie night preparations. Aubrey gathered large bowls, bags of microwave popcorn, a couple of different toppings, and napkins. Both retrieved hair things and makeup and set up their mini-salon in the living room, then searched Aubrey's computer and decided which films to view.

"Hey, you two, this looks great," Jenna said when she and Paige arrived.

"Do I get to try all that stuff?" Paige rooted through the assortment of goodies Aubrey and Alex had arranged on the coffee table.

"Only if we have plenty of makeup remover and tissues," Jenna replied. "You have school tomorrow." She turned to Alex. "Paige and I have compromised about the makeup. No Goth stuff this time, but she'll get the full treatment with the makeover."

Alex placed a hand on Paige's shoulder. "I told her it was up to you. Won't disappoint me a bit to skip the Goth thing tonight. I wasn't even sure I'd remember, so this works for me."

"We've got the popcorn and movies," Aubrey added. "What did you two bring?"

"Pizza and soda," Jenna answered. "As well as chocolate to go with the popcorn."

"You eat chocolate with your popcorn?" Alex had never tried the combination.

Jenna raised a brow. "Sure. Don't you?"

"Uh, no, but it sounds like a great way to get a sugar high."

Aubrey listed the films they'd picked, Jenna weeded out two she felt were too mature for Paige, and they voted. Before they settled down to watch, they popped the corn and passed around pizza and soda.

By the time the film ended, they'd knocked off all but two pieces of the second pizza and gone through three bags of popcorn. Paige settled back on the couch, holding her stomach.

Jenna checked her watch. "Wow. Eight thirty already. I don't think there'll be time for the second showing, Paige. You still haven't had your makeup lesson."

"Ah, Mom. You're such a killjoy."

"Don't you have homework?"

"Only my Spanish. I can knock that out in twenty minutes."

Alex picked up a bottle of foundation. "C'mon, Paige. We'll start with the basics. Have you ever applied this stuff with a sponge?"

Paige took the bottle from Alex, removed the lid and sniffed. "I've never used this stuff period."

Paige settled in an easy chair, and Alex wrapped a towel around her shoulders. Then she set to work doing her magic.

"Wow!" Paige said when Alex finally let her check the mirror. "I look great!"

Jenna scrutinized her daughter's appearance. "You really do look terrific, hon. And Alex didn't have to use a ton of cosmetics."

"Now do me," Aubrey said.

Jenna took Paige's seat. "No, me first, so Paige and I can get going."

"I don't know what more I can do to enhance your looks, Jenna. You're no stranger to wielding a makeup brush. Plus, you're a natural beauty."

"Could you lay on the flattery a little thicker, Alex?" Aubrey said. "I don't think Jenna's ego has swollen enough yet. You must really want her to sign that lease."

Alex's hand froze midair. "What did you say?" She could barely breathe.

Aubrey glanced from Alex to Jenna and back again. "Don't look so surprised. It's not like we haven't guessed why you're here."

Aubrey's statement had been so matter of fact. Her tone neither snide nor defiant. More like how Alex had always imagined a sister's candor.

"I'm not … I'm, uh … I told you, I need your help convincing my dad not to go out for leading men parts. Plus, I'm here to interview a potential client."

Aubrey picked up empty soda cans. "We've both been talking to Buddy. He admitted he'd been going out for leading men roles. But only after we reminded him."

Jenna crushed an empty pizza box and stuck it in a garbage bag. "You interviewed that girl near Sioux City a couple days ago, and nothing's come of it."

"Yet you're still here," Aubrey said.

How had everything changed in the course of a minute with one statement? Alex realigned the makeup containers. "I'm sorry if I've overstayed my welcome. I moved in here to help Geoff, and now that he's broken things off with Eileen, I should be taking off, except for this arm."

Aubrey held up a hand. "Whoa. Don't get so worked up. We were giving you a rough time, like sisters do. I thought you got that. This evening has been Jenna's and my way of extending an olive branch. Why shouldn't the three of us become a trio, like the McKennas?"

"We all have Buddy in common," Jenna added.

After all these years, Aubrey and Jenna wanted to bond? Before Alex had a chance to reply, Paige went to her mother. "What's this about a lease? Is she going to rent your motor coach, Mom?"

"Not Alex. Her client," Jenna replied. She turned her gaze to her stepsister. "Isn't that right, Alex?"

Foiled. Might as well confess. "Yes. The more you put me off, the more my client pressured me to get it. I thought if I came here and put it directly to you, maybe you'd realize what a good deal this is for you."

"When were you planning to 'put it directly to me'?" Jenna asked.

Foiled again. "I was hoping something like tonight might happen if I stuck around town. I told you both that day at the tearoom that I wanted to get to know you better."

"So you could do business with Jenna?" Aubrey asked.

"That's how it started, even though I wouldn't have proceeded unless I got you a good deal."

Paige wouldn't be appeased. "If it means more money for us, Mom, why aren't you interested? Don't you trust Alex?"

Jenna flinched. "Paige! That's uncalled for," Aubrey said.

Alex placed a hand on the girl's shoulder. "No, that's okay, Paige. I see how it looks, Jenna. I should've said something about the deal sooner, but I thought you needed to get to know me first. So you'd realize you could trust me. I've accomplished just the opposite."

"Mom!" Paige was practically howling. "Why haven't you signed? You said you were putting your concert tour on hold."

Jenna didn't reply at once. She probably didn't like her daughter putting her on the spot. "I've decided I'm not going on tour, Paige. Not this year or next or probably ever. I'm happy with my life here with you and Gray. And ..." She didn't finish.

Paige smothered her mother with hugs and kisses. "That's great. So why not rent the coach again?"

Once again, Jenna turned to Alex. "I've put you off because I've also been thinking about selling the coach. Maybe your client would like to buy it?"

The suggestion hit Alex like a bucket of ice water thrown in her face. "Oh, no, Loretta would never consider a deal like that." She gulped, realizing too late what she'd revealed. Great. She'd told Aubrey and Mitch that Loretta was her client and suspected that

Aubrey had probably shared the information with Jenna, but this was the first time Alex had revealed Loretta was the client wanting to lease the coach. She hadn't even told Geoff that part, although she suspected he knew.

"Loretta? As in Loretta Kinsolver?" Jenna asked.

"Forget the name. Your suggestion threw me, and I forgot myself. I shouldn't have told you who wanted to lease the coach."

Jenna sank onto the couch and indicated for Alex to do the same in the nearby chair. "Last year, there was a big mix-up with the costumes I ordered for my tour. Loretta Kinsolver received them in error."

Aubrey dumped the few remaining popcorn kernels in the garbage bag and joined her sister on the sofa. "Alex was involved in the other end of that fiasco, trying to get both sets of costumes sent to their rightful owners. I didn't know about her part in that disaster until recently, when she told me Loretta Kinsolver was one of her clients."

As if on cue, Alex's phone rang. "Speak of the devil. I'd better take this."

She pivoted to leave the room. "No. Stay. Put it on speaker," Jenna called.

Alex considered the implications of breaking client confidentiality. But this was her sister, and they were making such great progress toward leasing the motor coach to Loretta. "No one say anything."

"Well? Have you been successful?" Loretta demanded.

"I, uh, I'm working on it, Loretta."

"That's all you ever say. Either you've convinced that second-rate pianist to rent me her coach, or you haven't."

"Look, Loretta …"

"Don't give me that. I want that lease. If you can't or won't get it for me, I'll find someone else who can. But not before I make sure the entertainment community learns about the secrets you've been hiding about your father."

Both Jenna's and Aubrey's eyes went wide. Before they spoke, Alex held up a hand. "No, Loretta, please. Give me a couple hours. I'll get back to you." She rang off before Loretta said anything else.

Jenna sprang from the couch. "Second-rate pianist?"

Aubrey cut her off. "Forget the insult for now, Jenna. There's more going on here. She's blackmailing Alex with something she's got on Buddy."

Alex considered her options. She never should've put her call on speaker. This was her problem alone. Not her sisters'. "She does that. Throws her weight around with unsubstantiated implications."

"Is that why you've been representing her all these years?" Buddy stood in the doorway, Mitch and Graham behind him.

Alex clutched her stomach in a vain effort to calm the eruptions inside. Things were moving too fast, closing in on her. "Dad. I thought you went bowling." Inane attempt to change the subject.

"Couldn't find a fourth to bowl with us when Geoff begged off, so we got dinner and then came back to join you ladies. Sounds like we arrived just in time. So, daughter, answer my question."

He wasn't going to let her off the hook. Nor could she think of any way to defer this discussion. "Let's go to my room. We'll talk there."

"No. Since so much of this involves me, I want to hear the answer as well," Jenna said.

"Jenna, I don't think you should all hear this." Alex nodded toward Paige.

"Mom?"

"She's fifteen, Alex. I'll let her stay." Paige raised a brow but didn't say anything.

The men moved into the room. The three women and Paige sat. Alex tried without much success to collect her thoughts. She related how she'd come to represent Loretta.

"That was before her singing career took off?" Buddy asked.

"Right. She was into acting then. When she actually got the part, she insisted I represent her. I refused, because I didn't want to get involved in the industry again, but she wouldn't drop it. I later learned she'd been turned down by every agent she'd tried to hire. I was her last hope."

"What made you change your mind?" Jenna asked.

Alex didn't want to answer the question. It would embarrass and hurt her dad.

He must have read her mind. "Go ahead, kiddo." His voice remained steady, encouraging.

If she went further into this, it would change things forever. But at this point, she didn't have much choice. "Even though you were cleared of that starlet's claims of rape, Dad, suspicions continued to linger. Loretta told me there was another victim of your supposed sexual overtures. He was the brother of some unnamed friend on your show and hadn't come forward when he witnessed the furor over the starlet. I wasn't sure your career could withstand another rumor of impropriety, even though I was certain it, too, was totally bogus. This time, it involved an underage boy, and who knew what kind of havoc it would provoke if it came out."

The room went so still the clink of ice dropping into the refrigerator's ice maker was audible.

Buddy's eyes narrowed. "That was years ago."

"I knew you were innocent, but that doesn't mean much in Hollywood sometimes, especially if someone else has already chipped away at a person's credibility. You'd suffered enough because of my mother. I assumed some of her guilt, because I hadn't stopped her lies and innuendoes. I didn't want you to face any more bad press."

Buddy hung his head. Was he upset with her? Embarrassed?

"And Loretta has held that threat over your head ever since?" Aubrey asked.

"Once I said I'd represent her, she didn't mention it again for some time. I actually enjoyed the first year or two. Getting her started. Helping her make the switch to music. She is a talented singer, and that bonded us for a few more years. Then fame went to her head, and the job was no longer fun for me. I wanted out. That's when she brought out the so-called dirty laundry from years before and threatened to go to the press."

"My God, Alex. You've been dealing with this woman on your own all this time? Why didn't you come to me?" her dad asked.

"You'd put your career back together. I didn't want to risk ruining things for you."

"Oh, Alex." Buddy swiped an eye with his palm and stumbled from the room.

She'd hurt him. The one thing she'd tried so hard to avoid. A pain so real it could have come from an actual knife ripped through her heart.

Alex rose to go after him, but Jenna grabbed her arm. "Give him a few minutes."

Unwanted tears streamed down Alex's face. She had to make sure her dad was okay. "I've tried so hard to shield him."

Mitch came over to her, touched her shoulder. "He's absorbing that idea right now."

Jenna took her hand. "As a parent, I get what's troubling him. He sees the shielding part as his responsibility, not yours. It must be tearing him apart that you've been carrying this burden for him all these years and gave up your nursing career for him."

"The very reason I didn't want to tell him."

Aubrey gave her a sisterly hug. "You shouldn't have had to deal with this on your own."

"I didn't have any confidants. Certainly not my mother."

"We should have been there for you," Jenna put in.

"If Mitch thinks it's okay, I'll sign the damned lease."

"Oh, Jenna." Alex sighed.

"Once you tell her it's a done deal, you can resign and get her out of your life."

Alex squeezed her sister's hand. "You don't have to do that. She won't drop her threat once she gets her lease. Blackmailers never do."

Aubrey, the fixer, pushed her forward. "Go see your dad. The rest of us will figure out what to do with that shark."

Alex found her dad in the kitchen, downing a glass of water. "Needed something to drink."

"What you didn't need was for me to dump this whole mess in your lap."

"Alex, sweetie, for such a bright woman, you should have done exactly that the first time that woman suggested she could hurt my career."

"I told you, Dad, you'd been through enough. I wanted to spare you."

Buddy set down his glass and clasped her shoulders. He gazed directly into her eyes. "I'm not a child, Alex. My innocence prevailed with that starlet, and it would have with that boy also."

"I never doubted you, Dad. You've got to believe that."

He bit a lip, but tears came to his eyes anyhow. "I do, sweetheart." His voice hoarse, he pulled her into a bear hug. She clung to him and relished the safe harbor of his arms. He held her close for several beats. Though this bonding moment helped them get past the revelation of Loretta's threats, she suspected he was also prolonging the embrace to gather himself.

When they eventually broke apart, he led her over to the table. They each took a seat. The tears were gone as he offered her a tentative smile. "I've been doing some hard thinking since I've come to town. One of the best vacations I've ever had. Anyway, there's no question, you need to terminate your association with Ms. Kinsolver. But not until Jenna has extracted the most iron-clad, demanding and expensive arrangement possible. No need for her to turn her back on all that money."

"Agreed. But how do we deal with Loretta's threats?"

"I don't have to act anymore. Got a tidy cushion stashed away. Just been doing it to get out of the house and keep the old brain occupied."

Was he saying that to make her feel better?

"We need to find you something else to do. Something Loretta can't harm," he said.

She allowed herself a moment to dream about life without her difficult client. Or maybe difficult *clients*? "Dad? How would you like to take on my other two clients? The ones we discussed? You'd be a natural. You thought of checking with my aging soap star's agent within an hour of hearing his story. I'd never even considered the idea."

He inclined his head, the idea apparently intriguing him. "That part was fun. But coming up with ideas and follow through don't always go together."

"I'd be there as your partner for the detail work, if you wanted."

"You'd stay in the business?"

"Maybe. Maybe not. The more I've thought about it, the challenge of guiding Allison Corley's career, the girl I visited the other day, makes my heart beat faster."

He rose and stuck his empty glass in the dishwasher, his way of pondering her idea. "What about nursing?"

"I've been thinking about that too. Even though I was a pretend caregiver for all of about five minutes for Geoff, it reminded me of what I'd given up. Later, in the hospital, I found myself observing the new kinds of equipment around me and asking my nurse several questions. Do you think I could juggle both jobs?"

"You can do anything you set your mind to." He paused, as if debating whether to say something more. "Gonna stay here in Iowa since your potential client lives here? I'm sure there's good nursing schools here. As well as the man of your heart."

She jerked in her seat. "What?"

"You heard me."

Man of her heart? She hardly knew Geoffrey McKenna. Love him? She'd never been in love. Would she know it when it came knocking? Why was she even questioning herself? Geoff had thrown her out his apartment when she got too personal. "I don't think that's in the cards. Geoff and I had words earlier today."

"About his friend's death?"

"About his reaction. Even if we got past this, I hardly know him."

"Too bad. Thought he was great son-in-law material."

"Son-in-law? You're getting carried away. We had a good thing going the last several days, but that ended when he told me to mind my own business."

"Give him time. His friend's death hit him pretty hard."

She'd never dealt with the loss of a loved one or friend, and yet she'd thought she could advise Geoff. Stupid. Insensitive. Perhaps she'd been premature telling Aubrey it was time to leave. "I can't go anywhere with this arm for a few days. We'll see."

"Good, because I'm gonna need his PR skills to help me deflect whatever Loretta throws at me as well as announce our new partnership. Whatever happened between you, fix it. Don't let this man get away."

Twenty-One

lex and Buddy returned to the living room, arm in good arm. "Sorry for all the drama, folks," Buddy said. "Alex and I had some issues to work through." Paige hugged him and made him sit next to her. The rest of the room's occupants returned anxious looks.

"Everything okay?" Jenna wanted to know.

"Between us, yes." Alex said. "As for dealing with Loretta, we could use some input." She and her dad shared their plans to partner up managing her remaining clients, once she got rid of the country singer.

"Does that mean you're gonna stay here in Iowa with us, Buddy?" Paige asked.

He smiled, patted her hand. "Not sure your grandmother would ever consider a move back to her hometown. But if you, your mom and your aunt remain here, you can plan on my visiting every so often. Your grandmother might just give in and accompany me."

"Speaking of which," Graham said, "I hope to speak for both you and your mom, Paige, and assure Buddy you'll be here." He rose, went down on one knee if front of Jenna. "Lady, I've been in love with you since the day you showed up to claim your runaway daughter. We traveled west and back together. How 'bout traveling with me the rest of our lives. Will you marry me?"

The moment his knee hit the floor, Jenna's hand shot to her mouth, and she closed her eyes. Now she jumped up and pulled him with her. "Oh, Gray. Of course, I'll marry you." She turned to Paige. "What do you say, hon?"

Paige raced over to both of them, nearly knocking them over with her exuberance. "I say it's about time!" She stopped in her tracks. "Wait. Are you going to take his name? That'll be so cool. Jenna McKenna!"

Jenna chuckled. "I, I never thought of that."

Graham said, "Well, I did. Hoped it wouldn't influence your decision."

"I rather like it. Not that I'll be using it anytime soon on the road." She looked to her new fiancé. "Uh, is this a good time to share our other news?"

"You don't want to tell Paige first?" His voice was a stage whisper.

"Tell me what?" Paige asked.

"I'm pregnant." Jenna's expression was positively beatific.

After a minisecond of silence, Aubrey reacted first. "That's wonderful!" Her eyes sought out Mitch.

"I'm going to be a sister?" Paige hugged her mother again. "Oh, will I hurt the baby if I hug you like this?"

"Not in the least. That's why I'm putting my concert career on hold indefinitely and why I held off answering you about the lease, Alex. I wasn't sure of my condition until a few days ago."

"Oh," was all Alex could reply with so much happening so fast.

"Get the lease from Loretta," Jenna continued. "Mitch can oversee the wording to protect my, our, interests."

"How 'bout we let you two lovebirds celebrate the rest of the evening and we reconvene tomorrow morning to consider our moves?" Buddy suggested.

"Good plan. Ready for bed, Aubrey?" Mitch said.

At nine thirty? Something told Alex they wouldn't be sleeping for some time yet. And that didn't necessarily mean sex either. She'd caught the look the two had exchanged when Jenna accepted Graham's proposal. Too bad Geoff hadn't been present to witness the scene.

GEOFF FINISHED DRAFTING his comments about Kyle around two the next morning but still rose early. Couldn't sleep. Though Gray stopped by with the good news about his engagement to Jenna and the new addition to the family, all Geoff could offer were perfunctory congratulations. The last thing he needed right now was to be around happy people. He'd get excited later, once Kyle's funeral was over.

He left an hour earlier than necessary. Time on his hands, he drove around a bit, finally wound up parked in the same spot overlooking the river he'd shown Alex days before. Although it had overflowed its banks and sandbagging had nearly broken him, he loved this river. Maybe some of its power and majesty could infiltrate his spirit and get him through this day and the rest of his life, however much time he had.

When he arrived at the funeral home, Pam was closeted with Kyle's parents, so he didn't get to talk to her. He did run into Dr. Roettger, though. They shook hands solemnly, both well aware of the common bond they shared.

"How are you doing, Geoff?"

"Got over that rundown feeling shortly after I saw you that day, Doc. Just needed rest. Like you said."

Roettger pulled a sort of frown. "Good to know, although I meant how are you doing in regard to this day?"

Even his physician sensed his unease. "Getting through it, best I can. Kyle and I got to be good friends."

"He told me."

"I'm going to miss him." Understatement.

"We've got people at the hospital you can talk to, if you want."

Yeah, yeah, yeah. Counselors. Psychologists. Shrinks. If he couldn't take Alex's comments, how could he deal with professionals? "Uh, thanks. I'll keep that in mind."

They parted, more ill at ease than when they'd greeted each other.

He checked in with the funeral director, who placed him in the second row, behind the family.

Most of the service went by without sinking in. Like a sleepwalker, he made his way to the podium. He withdrew his notecards and began to read. He'd gone through maybe three sentences before he stopped. "I wrote out my words, because I wasn't sure I could think straight when I got up here. But now that I've started, there's more I want to say."

He gazed out on the few faces who were privileged to be part of this service, finding comfort in their eyes. "Kyle was a rarity. A once-in-a-lifetime friend. We met in the midst of incredible personal sadness and disillusionment and helped each other deal. Well, he helped me deal. Can't say as much for my impact on him, although I hope he got at least a fraction of the comfort and hope from me that I received from him.

"Kyle lived with adversity every day of the last four years. He went from difficult physical limitations to overwhelming pain almost every minute of his remaining days. Yet he was a man in control of his destiny. He knew this illness was going to take him sooner or later, but he didn't let it defeat him. He lived out the remainder of his days with honor, dignity and decency. None of us can aspire to any greater way to live our lives."

Though his mouth moved, his heart spoke. He didn't realize he'd returned to his seat until the person next to him leaned over and touched his arm.

After the service, he paid his condolences to Pam and to Kyle's parents.

"Thank you so much for speaking today, Geoff," Pam said. "It couldn't have been easy, as close as you were to Kyle, but your words were heartfelt and much appreciated." She glanced at the next person in line, who seemed anxious to speak to the widow. "See me at the reception. I have something for you."

Great. He'd hoped to slip away as soon as the casket was lowered into the grave. That would be difficult enough to witness. He didn't feel up to attending the reception and making chit-chat. Yet Pam was getting through it, and she'd lost much more than he.

At the reception, he skipped the food line but accepted a cup of coffee, which he placed on a nearby tray after a couple sips. His stomach churned every so often. He wasn't sick or nauseous. Just ill at ease.

At length, Pam appeared. "Thanks for coming to this reception. I could tell by your pained reaction when we talked earlier you hadn't planned on being here. I didn't want this to wait any longer. I thought it might help you get through your grief." She opened her purse, pulled out a tiny object and handed it to him.

"Binoculars?" slipped out before he had time to say something less incredulous.

She offered a tiny smile. "Opera glasses, actually. He inherited them from his grandmother."

Geoff examined the device, burgundy with gold trim. What on earth? Kyle had never mentioned the opera or this pair of glasses.

"He made me promise I'd get these to you as soon as possible after his ... after he passed. There's a note too." She rooted through her purse and brought it out as well. "The night before he died, we talked for hours. Claimed he didn't need rest where he was going." She stopped and chuckled.

"We'd settled all the details about his estate and his wishes regarding his funeral months ago. We quietly recounted memories of good times. But Kyle was worried about you. In some ways, you were like his child, even though he was younger than you. He knew he wasn't going to make it, but he believed you would. He wanted the best for you, but he feared you'd give up hope when he was gone, even though your cases are so different."

Geoff tried to speak, but he choked.

"It's okay," she replied. "I've been living with the reality of our situation longer than you. Though it wasn't as long as I would've liked, I cherished every minute with Kyle. Our life together was a blessing. Take these glasses and read the note when you get a private moment. I hope they'll prove to be your own blessing."

He gulped his thanks and took off, headed straight to his car. Back at the firehouse, he slipped into his apartment unnoticed. Wasn't ready to see any of the family or Alex yet. Needed privacy. He stared at the note several beats before he opened it. Kyle had left him a message of some kind. Did he really want to know what it said? Once opened and read, there was no going back; Kyle's passing would be real, unlike the surreal nature of today's events. On the other hand, maybe the note explained the weird gift he'd received. Hell, nothing ventured … It read:

Hey, guy.

If you're reading this, then I'm dead. Sorry, maybe too blunt, but I'm making myself say and write that word several times to get used to the idea. I've known for some time that I wasn't going to see forty and have come to terms with it. Awareness that you're going to die soon clears your vision about what's important and what's not. You're important to me. When the health cards were doled out, you got the better hand. At times, you've marveled at how I could accept my fate and not resent you for yours. Truth is, I did. At times. Human, I guess. But I soon realized that wasn't going to change my last chapter. Instead, I put my faith in you to grasp the gift you've been given of a longer life and do something with it.

I wanted to leave you something to remind you every day of that gift. Finally decided on my grandmother's opera glasses. They're more sentimental than valuable.

They symbolize how you should always look ahead, focus on your future. Because it could be great.

Yeah, you got the raw deal compared to your brothers' health, but they aren't you. I'll bet if you ever got down off your high horse long enough to tell them how you feel, they'd tell you at times they resent you for your people skills. Even Mitch, if he was honest with himself.

I'm no longer physically present to jump-start your mood. From now on, you're on your own. But I'll be around. Just look through these glasses and I'll be there.

Kyle

Geoff finished reading and read the note again. Then again. Finally, he raised teary eyes and simply stared across the room, his thoughts disjointed. He picked up the opera glasses. Funny, he'd never known Kyle to be one for symbols. The guy had always been a "what you see is what you get" kind of guy. Yet the baby binoculars and note had gone right to the heart of things. Geoff had been afraid of his future, because he didn't know how much of a future awaited him.

Kyle's message said that didn't matter. Even if all you had was one more minute, it was still the future. Precious, not to be wasted.

Geoff rested his head against the back of the sofa. Closed his eyes. If only he could open them again and discover this had all gone away. But that wasn't to be. He knew it as soon as he blinked open his eyes.

Though she hadn't handed him a pair of opera glasses, Alex's words paralleled Kyle's. He'd turned on her for trying to help him. Wasn't her fault. Over the past several days, they'd shared many personal trials.

Why shouldn't she think it was okay to push him?

Time to stop running from his future.

THE MORNING FOLLOWING the infamous call from Loretta Kinsolver, Alex entered the living room to discover the chairs had been arranged in a semicircle in front of the davenport. Several pads of paper, markers, pens and a laptop were lined up on the coffee table in the middle. "Wow, if I didn't know better, I'd think I was in a war room planning our next battle against the enemy."

"Might as well be, since your pal Loretta has shown herself to be no friend," Aubrey said. "We have to figure out how to counter that woman's threats."

Buddy appeared with a box of pastries.

"Appreciate you all taking time away from your jobs to help Alex and me. Least I could do was provide breakfast goodies."

"Uh, before we start," Mitch said, helping himself to a doughnut, "Aubrey and I have something to tell you."

Aubrey stuck out her left hand, which until now she'd kept behind her back, and showed off a sparkling diamond ring. "Mitch asked me to marry him last week, but we kept it quiet until he could put this on my finger. He had it with him last night, but once Graham popped his question, we decided to hold off. Since we're discussing other changes in our family situation, we wanted you all to know today."

Alex joined the rest of the family in wishing the couple well. "I'm so glad I was here to share in your good news." She glanced from Aubrey to Jenna. "That's one good thing Loretta instigated, my being here when both my sisters got engaged."

"I'll tell Geoff as soon as he returns from the funeral," Mitch said. "Hope all our good news will help him get through his sorrow."

Buddy turned to her. "Anything you want to announce, sweetheart?"

"Me? Oh, you mean Geoff and me? He has to speak to me first. So, no. Two brothers getting hitched plus a new baby is more than enough for even the McKennas right now."

"But not inconceivable," Graham added. "We've seen how he looks at you. He's been quite protective since your accident."

She imagined finally being brought into the circle by her stepsisters and then reinforcing it by hooking up with Geoff. How often did three brothers marry three "sisters"? Not unheard of, but not the everyday family circle either. She shook herself mentally. *Get over it, Alex.* "Maybe so. But that was before his friend passed away. When I attempted to comfort him, he blew up. In fact, had all this with Loretta Kinsolver not happened, I probably would have headed back to California today."

Aubrey put her arms around her. "Surely, you've reconsidered? We've got weddings to plan and a baby to anticipate. Plus, first order of business, we've got a wicked witch to knock off her broom."

"Give our brother another chance," Mitch said. "He gets antsy about sharing his feelings when it comes to his MS. God knows, Gray and I have tried more times than we can remember to get him to talk."

She gave a sigh. "He told me. But from what I've been able to observe, he still appreciates the gesture. He just can't cope with it."

"So," Jenna put in, "Geoff aside, what about la Kinsolver?"

"As I see it," Mitch replied, "we have to deal with her on two fronts, getting the best deal from her with the lease and counteracting any dirt she tries to spread about Buddy. I'll work with Jenna on the lease language. Aubrey, you, Gray and Buddy should formulate a plan for offsetting any negative publicity the woman might generate. Alex, we need you in both places."

Graham retrieved a pad of paper from a nearby desk. "Wish Geoff was in the right frame of mind to help with the media thing. He's the expert there. Maybe by tomorrow he can join us."

"We rarely get walk-in traffic downstairs," Mitch said, "but just in case, Jenna and I will set up shop in Geoff's office. He'll be taking off soon, if he hasn't already."

Alex remained with the others gathered in the living room to strategize long-term plans for dealing with Loretta.

Aubrey settled into the sofa. "Buddy, tell us what happened the last time rumors circulated about you. Jenna and I didn't know you then, so we're not very familiar with the havoc that caused."

"Not my favorite topic," Buddy said. Nonetheless, he recalled how he'd been called into the office of the show's executive producer and told of the charges made by someone in the production company. He wasn't told who. Supposedly, the party didn't want to go to the police. She had no physical proof, only her word against his, plus a couple of others in the company who had purportedly seen them together and witnessed Buddy forcing himself on her.

"I denied it up one side and down the other, but the two corroborating witnesses tipped the scale. We were coming to the end of the season, so instead of firing me outright, which might have given me grounds to sue, they wrote me out of the story for the next season."

Aubrey was incredulous. "You had no opportunity to face your accuser?"

"Not how it works in my business. It could have ended there, except word leaked to a reporter, who ran with the story, pretty much pulling details out of the air. But once that one person reported it, others piled on, using the first story, unsupported though it was, as their launching point. Not surprisingly, their stories and speculations just happened to show up around the same time my divorce proceedings got underway."

"That's all it takes to ruin someone's reputation?" Graham asked.

"The media is constantly searching for compelling stories. Those sell newspapers and magazines and generate viewers for entertainment-news shows. Not everyone is unprincipled in their reporting, but all it takes is for one unfounded story to pique the public's interest and everyone jumps on board."

"Interesting," Aubrey said.

"What are you getting at?" Alex asked her.

Aubrey cocked her head, as if considering something. "Loretta was just starting out in the business when she blackmailed you into representing her. At the time, you said Buddy was making a comeback, and you feared more negative publicity would derail things. But the tide has turned since then. Loretta is the big star now. She has a lot more to lose than Buddy."

"Good thought," Graham said.

"You're right, Aubrey. I never considered it in those terms," Alex answered. "Guess I was too close to it and too concerned about protecting my dad."

"Appreciated but not necessary," Buddy said. "What could Loretta lose, as Aubrey suggests?"

Alex considered. Despite Loretta's lack of scruples, as her representative, Alex herself couldn't divulge confidential information about her client. But not everything was confidential. For instance, how she was persuaded to represent Loretta in the first place. "What if we make the lease contingent on her continued silence?"

Buddy swiped his chin. "Great idea, but how do you know she'll keep her word? It's too easy to plant stories and never be held accountable."

"Which is exactly how we'll keep her in line. If anything comes out about you, the media will learn how she's been blackmailing me. If she can plant stories about you without a trace, we can do the same with her. The big difference? Our story will be true."

"Could we get away with that?" Aubrey asked.

"To tell the truth, I don't know," Alex told her. "But she doesn't know, either. She's close to signing a couple of big deals she won't want to jeopardize."

Buddy put an arm around Alex. "Let's get Mitch, then, and strategize negotiations."

By early afternoon, the lease language had been drafted, and Mitch and Jenna rejoined the others. "Besides the outrageous fee she's demanding," Mitch reported, "Jenna has also added inspection-at-will, damage and depreciation charges for every mile over the designated allowed mileage, and a stipulation that all drivers must be reviewed by her representatives. Plus several other goodies I came up with. In addition, Jenna will refuse to even consider negotiations unless Loretta first agrees to the 'no discussion of Buddy Appleby' clause."

"That pretty much covers it," Alex said.

Mitch beamed back at her. Clapped his hands together. "Good. Ready for me to call this woman?"

Alex screwed up her face, shot a glance toward the door. "Could we wait for Geoff? He may not feel up to it after the funeral, but he's been the one pushing me to reconsider representing Loretta. I'd like him to be in on this part." No need to mention he'd been helping her in her mission to get the lease.

"Speaking of Geoff, he should be back by now," Mitch said. "Haven't heard anything next door in his apartment, but I'll check."

Twenty-Two

Geoff brought the small pair of opera glasses to his eyes. The first item to come into view was a picture on the wall of the three McKenna brothers taken several years earlier. They'd been on a fishing trip in Minnesota and stood proudly holding their catches. Ironic. Kyle's words said the binoculars would help him focus on the future, yet here he was, zeroing in on days gone by, days when he was still in good health.

So much for Kyle's advice.

No, wait. Maybe there was something to this. He wasn't supposed to see three brothers celebrating in times past. That was simply the catalyst. The essence of the photo was the idea of family. No matter what had happened in the intervening years, they were united. Maybe no longer working together, and one of them soon to marry with a baby on the way and a teenager already in the picture, but that only meant they were expanding their nucleus.

A gentle rapping on the door broke through his thoughts. "Geoff? You back yet?" Mitch.

Was he ready for this? As soon as Mitch entered the room, the next phase of Geoff's life would begin. The phase that anticipated the future. He shot another glance at the photo of the three McKenna boys and took a deep breath. No better time than the present. "Yeah." He unlocked the door and invited his brother to join him.

Geoff described the funeral, committal and reception in a few sentences and then showed Mitch the opera glasses, summarizing the story behind them.

"He really cared about you, about how you're going to live the rest of your life."

"Yeah, about that …"

"Yeah?"

"I went to that funeral today dreading the whole affair. Thought everyone would dwell on this devastating disease. But it turned out to be a celebration of the life of an incredible guy, positive, optimistic."

"Good to hear. You've been pretty much in shock since you got the news."

"Kyle anticipated my reaction. That's why the opera glasses. And the note, which reminded me no matter how much time I have left, not to squander it but live my life to the fullest."

"So? You're in a better mood?"

What was Mitch getting at? "Guess I've been a real downer for everyone. But, yeah, I'm feeling much more positive about things."

Mitch had him sit while he continued to stand. "Gray told me he stopped by earlier to tell you about him and Jenna. And the baby."

"We're gonna be uncles. The McKenna clan is growing."

"Definitely good news." He paused. "How 'bout doubling it?"

Geoff mulled the statement for a second before he realized what Mitch had said. "You and Aubrey, too?"

Mitch beamed back at him. "Pretty crazy, huh? Gray and I didn't plan it that way. In fact, neither of us knew the other was about to pop the question until he did it in front of everyone last night. Wish you'd been there."

He hadn't planned to broach this topic so soon, but Mitch had provided the perfect entrée. "Wish I had, too. In fact, where's Gray now? Let's get him in here for a little brotherly celebration."

Gray arrived two minutes after Mitch called him, his forehead screwed up in apprehension. "What's up?"

Geoff traded places with Mitch and asked Gray to sit as well. "Mitch just shared his and Aubrey's news with me. Thought the three of us should take a moment to celebrate both my brothers tying the knot. Quite the occasion."

"You're okay with this, right?" Gray asked.

"I'm happy for you both, and I already love your women as sisters. Until today, though, deep down, buried inside my heart so you wouldn't see it, I would've resented the fact you two could live normal lives and look ahead to married life and families."

Both Gray and Mitch furrowed their brows, then exchanged looks. Mitch, always the attorney, picked up on the key word first. "Resented?"

"Ever since we learned of my MS, you guys have been my saviors. You left your job in Minneapolis, Gray, and you put the bar exam on hold, Mitch, so we could start this business. Your support overwhelmed me, but at the same time, I hated being the recipient of all that sacrifice, to the point of resenting you both for being the healthy ones."

Neither brother spoke at first, although both studied him, as if waiting for him to say more. "Finally!" Gray said after a few seconds.

"Yeah, at last," Mitch added.

Geoff took a step back. "You knew?"

"Suspected," Gray said. "When you were first diagnosed, as family members, we received counseling too. They suggested at times you might be bitter about the challenge life had dealt you and not those close to you, especially if those people had no idea how painful your disease could be."

"They also warned us you might attempt to hide those feelings," Mitch said. "We weren't supposed to push you to admit them. You'd either come around and tell us or you wouldn't."

"You've been there for me every step of the way. How could I tell you that wasn't enough?"

"We hear you, bro," Gray said. "You're only human. If either of us had this disorder, who knows how well we'd handle it. Most of the time, you've been a real trouper."

Mitch rose and came to him. "The important thing is that you opened up. Major milestone."

"Yeah, well, that was thanks to Kyle and his advice. And Alex. She urged me to tell you how I felt, and I threw her out."

Yet again, Mitch and Gray seemed to share some private thought. "Ah, yes," Mitch said. "Alex."

"You know, you don't have to be the odd man out here. All three of us can go down together," Gray said.

"Go down together? You mean? Nah, not gonna happen. I hardly know the woman."

"But you didn't say marriage, to Alex or anyone, is out of the question because you have MS," Mitch said.

"Good cross-examination, counselor. No, I'm finally not ruling out marriage and a family. Again, thanks to Kyle. But at the moment, Alex and I aren't speaking. Even if we were, she'll be heading back to California soon."

Gray and Mitch looked at each other again. What was with this? Did they have some kind of comedy routine going?

"Maybe not," Gray said.

"A lot's happened in the last twenty-four hours. If you're up to it, you need to go check in upstairs," Mitch told him.

Now what? "More than you two proposing to your women?"

"And having a baby." Gray was beaming again.

"Yeah," Mitch replied. "We'd fill you in, but you need to hear it from Alex and Buddy."

Gray announced their arrival to the group gathered in the living room upstairs. "Guess who's back."

Aubrey, Jenna and Buddy, who'd been in heavy discussion, stopped talking and turned inquiring faces toward the three brothers. Alex stared at her hands.

"Geoff, how did everything go?" Aubrey said.

"I'm fine. It was a heartfelt funeral. Sad but meaningful."

"I'm so glad you're back," Jenna added. "We need you for a little PR work."

"Yeah? Does this PR assignment have anything to do with the

news I hear I've missed?"

Everyone twisted around to face Alex, waited for her to explain.

Though she knew Geoff would return sooner or later, Alex still struggled to describe the changes her life had undergone overnight. "As you've probably guessed already, Loretta Kinsolver is the client who wants to lease Jenna's motor coach. Jenna's open to an agreement, provided she gets the deal we've been working on all day."

"Tell him about that woman's call," Jenna urged.

Alex went on to explain the threat to "expose" Buddy that Loretta had held over her for years.

Geoff came straight to her. "That bitch!"

Alex opened her mouth, but Buddy replied for her.

"Alex thought she had to protect her old dad's name."

"God, Alex, I wish you'd told me."

"What would you have done? Advised me to tell my dad? I wouldn't have, even though I would've known you were right, just like you didn't want me pushing you to talk to your brothers." Damn. The part about Graham and Mitch had just slipped out. Now he'd be furious with her again.

Instead, Geoff took her hand in his. "That's what the three of us have been discussing. I've come clean with them. And you were right. It was long overdue."

She glanced toward his brothers, who nodded. Looked like more than just her situation with Loretta had been getting resolved.

"Go on," Geoff said.

"Had Jenna and Aubrey not been here when I received Loretta's latest demand and made me put her on speaker, none of you would be the wiser."

"I'm trying to absorb all this, but what I still don't get is why that harridan wants Jenna's motor coach in the first place."

Alex took a deep breath before plunging ahead. "Okay, I'll tell you, now that you all know who my mysterious client is. But this may not make sense. You're all rational beings. Loretta's not. At one time maybe she was, but from the beginning of my association with her, she's been so driven to make a name for herself she was willing to threaten, bully and blackmail to get ahead."

She paused long enough to gather her thoughts about the next part. "That gives you background about the woman's mental state. She's not unbalanced, but she has her own unique perspective about how the world operates. In her mind, the world revolves around her. Maybe she's had to develop that outlook to stomach the sacrifices and actions sometimes required to achieve fame."

"You described her to me once as a narcissist," Geoff cut in.

"I was being kind. She's also amoral. Once she gained a certain amount of celebrity, her lack of morals coupled with her self-absorption got out of control. Her obsession with the motor coach is the most recent example. About the same time her costumes were sent in error to Jenna, she was slated to appear on national television. She had planned to wear one of her new costumes. When it didn't show up in time, she went over the edge."

"But didn't she have other things she could've worn?" Aubrey asked.

"Her wardrobe bulged with numerous never-worn items. But the fact she was unable to appear in what she'd planned freaked her. Her performance was fine, but she didn't think so, especially a week later when the nominations for this huge industry award were announced and her name was missing. It didn't matter that there were five other great women on the list. She'd been ignored. And in her mind, it was because her recent TV performance had been off. For that, she blamed you, Jenna."

"Me?" Jenna replied. "I didn't get my things either."

"I told you, she has a warped sense of logic. In her mind, you kept her from receiving the award she felt only she deserved. month or so later, when she learned about your coach, the idea of taking it from you, albeit legally through a lease arrangement, took over her thoughts. Consumed her enough to constantly pressure me to get the lease or risk Buddy's good name."

Alex stopped, eyed the rest of them. "That's my best attempt to explain the seemingly unexplainable."

Jenna came to her, put a sisterly arm around her shoulder. "I love that coach. It brought Gray and me together, but I'm still willing to lease it to that bitch."

Aubrey joined the two of them. "I love the coach too. I would never have met and fallen in love with Mitch if Jenna hadn't sent me here to finish the interior. But I vote to lease it to that woman too."

Though tears streamed down her face—all three of their faces, actually—Alex had what she'd wanted more than the lease. Sisters.

Buddy couldn't stay away from his girls, as he attempted to embrace all three of them at once.

When the family hug finally dispersed, Geoff pulled her toward him. "Could we talk?" He drew her back to her room for more privacy. "I'm sorry for blowing up at you," he said once they were alone. "You were only trying to help. I just couldn't handle your getting so close."

"I'm sorry, too. I didn't mean to make things more difficult for you. Just the opposite."

"We've been calling whatever it is between us casual, but that's not how it feels anymore. I really care for you, Alex, and I've been afraid to let you know because I've felt my future was so unclear."

His words sent a wave of relief through her. "I really care for you too."

"My friend, Kyle, left a message for me. Told me I'd better start looking ahead and living my life while I still had this wonderful life to live."

Her heart ached for him. He'd discovered what had been obvious to her. She squeezed his hand. "I'm glad. Your friend left you a wonderful legacy."

"What about you? If Jenna signs this lease, will you be leaving soon?"

How much should she reveal about the plans she and her dad were discussing? She didn't want Geoff to feel obligated. "As soon as Jenna gets the terms she wants, I'm going to rescind my contract with Loretta. I'm taking Dad on as my partner. He'll handle my other two clients, and if Allison Corley reconsiders, I'll represent her."

"All this happened in the last day while I've been reeling from

Kyle's death?"

"There's more. I've also decided to go back to nursing school. Ever since my hospital stay, I've been playing with the idea, but I didn't believe I could end things with Loretta without her striking back at my father."

He blinked, still taking this all in. "That's great. The nursing school part, anyhow. But what's changed with your client to make you believe she won't retaliate?"

She told him how they planned to give Loretta a taste of her own medicine if she threatened them further. "Loretta is so close to reaching the next level of her career, I don't think she'll want to tempt fate."

"Back up. I get the part about her, but you also said you're going back to nursing school?"

"Yeah. How 'bout that?"

"And your dad is going to pick up your L.A.-based clients?"

"That's the plan." She held her breath. Would he realize the significance?

"Then? You could stay here in the Midwest. Go to school here?"

She released her breath. "I'm considering it. I've got two weddings to help plan and a new baby to look forward to." She studied him. "Would that make you uncomfortable? I know how you reacted when Eileen assumed too much too soon."

"I didn't love Eileen."

That got her attention. "Uh, did I hear you right?"

He tilted her chin up. "Crazy, huh? Happened much too fast, but there you are. My new philosophy is to enjoy life while you have it."

Did she dare believe his declaration, or was this just the high his friend's message had provoked? Whatever. Standing up to Loretta had freed up her brain and heart to see and feel things more clearly. "Guess we're both crazy, then, because I love you too."

"Yeah? Not just because I …"

"No! I probably wouldn't have told you yet, because I'm just now admitting it to myself. But I couldn't let you go out on that limb alone. From here on, we're a pair."

He took her in his arms and kissed her like she'd never been kissed. "There's something hard in your pocket," she said when he pulled away.

He returned a leer. "Of course, there is. I get that way whenever you walk into a room."

She shook her head. "No. Well, maybe that, too, but this is in your breast pocket."

"Oh." He reached inside his jacket and brought out a tiny pair of binoculars. "My bequest from Kyle. To remind me to stop looking back at what could've been and instead focus on what's ahead."

"What a thoughtful gift."

He snapped his fingers. "Gift. Right. Wait here." He took off for his bedroom. When he returned, he held a small package. "Got this when we stopped in Pella. With everything going on with your injuries and Kyle's death, it slipped my mind. Here. This is for you."

Her heart couldn't get past the idea that he'd bought her a gift days ago. The man who'd only days before that sent her to buy a gift for Eileen. She opened the package and took out a small blue and white object. A windmill. "It's beautiful."

"It's real Delft. The windmill's to remind you what we saw that day. But I also wanted you to take a part of Iowa back to California with you. Not forget me. That was the first day we made love. We called it sex at the time, but it was too good for just that label."

"It was good. Has been every time since."

"And will continue into the future."

They kissed again, Alex keeping her new windmill close to her.

"We'd better go help the others," Geoff said when they finally pulled apart. "Tell them we're a couple."

She held up. "It's still so new. Let's keep it to ourselves another day or two."

He considered. "You're right. We've got the rest of our lives to share our good news."

Dear Reader

Looking for more contemporary romance? Check out *And He Cooks Too*. Read on for an excerpt.

Thank you for reading this book. If you liked it, won't you please take a minute to leave a review?

To learn more about the eleven contemporary romances and two novellas I've written, sign up for my newsletter at https://www.subscribepage.com/BBContempRom.

I've also written two cozy mystery series, the Mah Jongg Mysteries and Nailed It Home Reno Mysteries. You can learn more about them on my website, www.barbarabarrettbooks.com.

Follow me on Facebook: http://bit.ly/2aXZvG9
Follow me on Twitter: https://twitter.com/bbarrettbooks

Sneak Peek

AND HE COOKS TOO

Here's an excerpt from the contemporary romance
And He Cooks Too.

Boy, did life slam its ironies in your face. Why couldn't he stand up to Leonie the way that dazzling dynamo had with her boss? Louis Whatever-His-Name was a fool. If Reese, the runaway chef, had prepared the few bites of pasta he'd been able to get down, she was a keeper. He'd figured that out even before she released that gleaming cascade of dark hair. The city was full of good-looking women, but this one was extraordinary. Those wide-set, coffee-brown eyes, pale neck and full, red lips could easily heat up any guy's kitchen.

Wait a sec. Real chef. Great food. Beaten out of her job by someone with two minutes of television experience. She could be his ticket off the show! Either his replacement or the inducement Leonie needed to take over as host. The timing of her exit couldn't have worked better.

Who was he to turn down his nose at Opportunity?

Couldn't let her get away. He threw several bills at the cash register and sprinted for the door. There she was, near the curb, engaged in a futile attempt to flag down a cab. Even a looker like that couldn't stop traffic at this busy hour.

He called out to her heaving back. "Miss? You probably don't want company, but if I didn't catch you now, I'd have to hire a private investigator to hunt you down."

That got her attention. She pivoted to face him, taking one last swipe at the tiny river of mascara running down her cheek. "Excuse me?"

God, she was gorgeous, even with a tear-stained face. "Back there in the restaurant, I overheard you. You're a chef, right?"

"Yes. At least I used to be."

"And they're letting you go because you don't have television experience?"

She blinked. Damn! He'd gone too far.

Her expression turned guarded. "Do you make a habit of eavesdropping on others' conversations?"

"Sorry. I didn't have much choice. Couldn't get past you and your pal."

She glanced back at the street. "Whoever you are, this isn't a good time. I just want to get out of here, go home and fall apart."

"Looks like you've already started that last part."

"Cut the counseling act. I don't want anything from anyone right now." She resumed her attempt to snare a cab. "Unless you're here to offer me another job?" she added, almost as an afterthought.

"Although I sense sarcasm, as a matter of fact, that's why I followed you." He extended a hand as she jerked her head around to stare at him. "I'm Nick Coltrane. I host a cooking show called *And He Cooks*

Too—the executive producer's title, not mine. Ever heard of us?"

She studied him a moment. "I don't watch much television."

He moved a little closer. "Even if you did, you'd be hard-pressed to find us. We're on a local channel." *Geez, Nick, can you make it sound any less enticing?* "But we've built up a respectable following."

She didn't respond. But she didn't dismiss him either as she kept scanning the street.

He kept talking while she was still there. "Can't offer you anything in front of the camera." Couldn't offer her anything period, since only Leonie and Jasper, their supervising producer slash director, did the hiring. But that was beside the point at the moment. "We do need a production assistant, though. Probably doesn't pay as much as the job you just left, but it would add television experience to your resume. Sounds like you're going to need that to stay competitive."

"How do I know you're for real?" she asked, her eyes narrowed. "You could have invented that story just to pick me up."

He waggled an eyebrow, attempting to lighten the situation. Like he could. The woman had just quit her job, and her former boss had threatened retaliation. "Any guy in his right mind would consider that possibility, but the offer's legit." He pulled a card from his tailored black Hugo Boss jacket. "Here, take this. Watch the show. This gives the time and channel."

She took the card. "This doesn't mean I'm interested. I'm being polite, which is about all the civility I have left." "Got it," he replied, stifling an amused grin.

"Like you overheard back there, I expect people to mean what they say. This had better not be a scam."

He did the thing with his eyebrow again, attempting to reassure her. "Don't worry. I'm bona fide." He stepped into the street and stuck his arm in the air. Least he could do for a lady in distress. An approaching cab screeched to a stop in front of them. The female driver behind the wheel smiled seductively at him.

"My friend here will give you the address." He turned back to the unemployed chef. "Hey, wait. I need your name and number."

She stared at him a moment. "Reese. Reese Dunbar." She let down her guard enough to give him her cell phone number as well.

Learn more at BarbaraBarrettBooks.com.

Acknowledgments

Thanks to The Wild Rose Press, who first published this book. I learned so much about the publishing world from them.

In order for this book to take on new life after I received my rights back for it, it needed a brand-new, snappy cover suggesting the loving relationship that develops between Alex and Geoff. My grateful thanks to my cover artist, Chris Kridler of Sky Diary Productions, for taking the few snippets of ideas I fed her about this story and bringing them together in this lovely cover. I also have her to thank for the formatting.

Thank you, Harriet Sawyer, for proofing the reedited version of this manuscript. Although many pairs of eyes have reviewed the book over its lifetime, the updates required one more look.

Thanks always to my husband, Veryl, for his continuing support of my writing career. He has seen me through more typewriters, tabletop computers and laptops than I can recall.

Books by Barbara Barrett

Cozy Mysteries

The Mah Jongg Mystery Series

Craks in a Marriage

Bamboozled

Connect the Dots

Beware the East Wind

Flower Power

Jokers Wild

The Charleston Challenge

The Dragon Lady Gets Her Due

Courtesy Call

also available in paperback

Nailed It Home Reno Mysteries

Measure Twice, Murder Once

Loose Screw

Death by Drywall

Homicide by Hammer

Nuts and Bolts

Snared by the Snake

A LITTLE ABOUT
BARBARA BARRETT

Barbara Barrett skipped a midlife crisis by writing romance novels at night when she wasn't at her day job as human resources analyst for Iowa State Government. The first took longer to complete than she likes to admit and remains unpublished. But after that, the words flowed, especially after she joined the local chapter of Romance Writers of America.

Her first book was published in 2012. She has now published eleven full-length contemporary romance novels and two novellas. More recently, she has published nine cozy mysteries in her Mah Jongg Mystery series and six in her Nailed It Home Reno Mysteries series. This is the final book in "The Matchmaking Motor Coach" trilogy, which she wrote as a love letter to her hometown of Burlington, Iowa. The motor coach in this book is the linchpin of this series as it unites three sisters with the McKenna brothers.

Barbara is married to the man she met her senior year at college. They have two grown children, eight grandchildren and two great grandchildren.

Now retired, she spends her time in Florida, Iowa and Minnesota. She earned her B.A. degree in history from the University of Iowa and her master's degree in history from Drake University.

When not in front of her laptop creating her next story, she plays Mah Jongg, is learning to paint with acrylics and enjoys lunches with friends.